THE HEARTS WE SOLD

♥

THE HEARTS WE SOLD

EMILY LLOYD-JONES

LITTLE, BROWN AND COMPANY

New York Boston

Little, Brown and Company
Hachette Book Group
1290 Avenue of the Americas, New York, NY 10104
Visit us at LBYR.com

Originally published in hardcover and ebook by
Little, Brown and Company in August 2017
First Trade Paperback Edition: July 2019

Little, Brown and Company is a division of Hachette Book Group, Inc. The Little, Brown name and logo are trademarks of Hachette Book Group, Inc.

The publisher is not responsible for websites (or their content) that are not owned by the publisher.

The Library of Congress has cataloged the hardcover edition as follows:
Names: Lloyd-Jones, Emily, author.
Title: The hearts we sold / Emily Lloyd-Jones.
Description: New York ; Boston : Little, Brown and Company, 2017. | Summary: After Dee Moreno, seventeen, makes a deal with a demon, trading her heart for the chance of a good education, she becomes part of a group "heartless" teens engaged in fighting a paranormal war.
Identifiers: LCCN 2016022401| ISBN 9780316314596 (hardcover) | ISBN 9780316314633 (ebook) | ISBN 9780316314565 (library edition ebook)
Subjects: | CYAC: Demonology—Fiction. | Supernatural—Fiction. | Boarding schools—Fiction. | Schools—Fiction. | Love—Fiction. | Family problems—Fiction.
Classification: LCC PZ7.L77877 Hed 2017 | DDC [Fic]—dc23
LC record available at https://lccn.loc.gov/2016022401

ISBNs: 978-0-316-31455-8 (pbk.), 978-0-316-31463-3 (ebook)

Printed in the United States of America

LSC-C

10 9 8 7 6 5 4 3 2 1

To all the Dees out there

What if I told you I'm incapable of
tolerating my own heart?

—Virginia Woolf, *Night and Day*

ONE

A demon was knitting outside the hospital.

Dee Moreno froze. The smokers' area was where she always took her lunch break; she didn't smoke, but it made for a good place to eat—at least, when it wasn't already occupied.

If she returned indoors, she would have to eat her lunch with the other high school volunteers, and that thought made her stomach shrivel up. It was the kind of afternoon one could only find in Oregon—grass still doused with last night's rain, lit up by what sunlight managed to escape the cloud cover. Dee considered her options.

Demons weren't supposed to be dangerous, or only as dangerous as your average used car salesman. This demon sat on one of the benches. Red yarn trailed around its fingers as it knit, and the sight made Dee feel brave.

Still, she sat on the farthest bench.

"It's a bit low," she said quietly.

"What?" the demon said. In a silky voice, because of course that's the only kind of voice a demon would have. The demon didn't look at her; it kept knitting, its fingers deftly sliding a stitch from one needle to the other.

"Lurking outside a hospital," said Dee. "Kind of going for the low-hanging fruit, aren't you?"

The demon's mouth twitched. "How do you know I'm working?" It finally looked at her. The look wasn't a once-over, or at least not the kind Dee was used to. The demon wasn't tallying up her bra size or even leering at her. It was simply staring, and Dee took a moment to do the same.

The demon had dark hair cut evenly down its neck. It wore a suit with more grace than most humans could manage, the light gray material untouched by wrinkles or dirt. Despite the sunny weather, an umbrella rested against its leg. The demon was beautiful, but something in its face was subtly off, the way ancient portraits or statues never looked quite true to life. The demon also looked decidedly male, although Dee couldn't let herself think of it as a *him*. It was altogether too alien.

The demon's attention sharpened. "You're a little young to be working here."

"I'm a volunteer," said Dee. She'd learned from a young age to answer adults quickly and succinctly. It didn't matter if this thing wasn't human; her old reactions still snapped into place. "It's required for all Brannigan students to do community service."

"And is it customary for such students to seek out demons on their lunch break?"

"I didn't," said Dee. "I came here to eat a sandwich."

Said sandwich was mangled from hours spent shoved in her backpack, but Dee fished it out. They sat in silence for a long minute or two, until the demon heaved a sigh.

It said, "All right. What do you want?"

Dee kept her attention on her sandwich. "I don't want anything."

The demon went back to its knitting; it frowned and unraveled a stitch. "You must want something."

Dee tried to change the subject. "Are you really knitting?"

The demon's eyes never left its work. "Actually, I'm purling at the moment."

This startled a laugh out of Dee.

The demon looked taken aback. "I said something funny?"

"It's just..." said Dee. "I had a mental image of demons getting together for knitting parties. I mean, is this a normal thing? Do demons pass the centuries doing arts and crafts? Do you go yarn shopping?"

The demon echoed Dee's smile. Or at least it tried to.

It was like watching an archer draw back a bowstring—the thing armed itself with its perfect white teeth and charming face.

"I got this yarn the way I get everything I want," the demon said, very softly. "I make deals."

Looking into the demon's eyes, Dee remembered all those stories she used to read as a kid—tales of ill-advised deal making where people gave teeth to fairies, queens trading firstborn children in exchange for gold-spun straw. Stories filled with magic and ambition, with dead stepmothers, wicked smiles, and cursed monkey paws. Dee found herself meeting the demon's eyes, her defiance flaring to life.

Dee didn't believe in magic.

"What do you want?" repeated the demon.

Dee refused to look away. "I don't want anything."

The demon's smile widened. "Now, I know that's not true."

A loud clanging made her jump. She whirled around, grabbing at the back of the bench. One of the hospital doors had been slammed open, and two nurses walked out, talking animatedly. Heart still pounding, she turned back to face the demon. It watched the two nurses with a tolerant smile; they barely gave Dee and the demon a glance before rounding a corner. They hadn't recognized the demon. If they'd known what it was, they'd have reacted. Looked excited or afraid or—something. But their gazes had slid over the creature and moved on.

It leaned closer to Dee, its voice lowering to an intimate tone. "You see, my dear, only a human that wants to make a deal can see a demon for what they are."

Dee discovered she was shaking when the crust of her sandwich dropped into the damp grass.

The demon was still smiling at her. A cool, almost smug smile. Again, Dee felt that little flare of defiance. "I don't want to make a deal with you," she said firmly.

The demon returned its attention to the knitting, to the bloodred yarn trailing through its fingers.

"Well, if you do," said the demon, "you know where to find me."

TWO

Dee was once an avid reader of fairy tales.

Some of her earliest memories were of her grandmother's house, of a place that smelled like cinnamon and old books. The house felt like a secret waiting to be discovered, as if she might open a cupboard door and find a whole new world. It was quiet and just a little too small—but in a way that felt cozy, rather than stifling. At night, Grandma would read aloud from one of the many old books—and Dee always picked a tome of Grimm's fairy tales. She listened to tales of frog kings and magicians, of glass slippers and brave girls in red cloaks.

But as she grew older, as her awareness of the world changed, so did the stories.

She listened to tales of a man who murdered his brother and left the bones to sing to passersby, of talking dogs that were abandoned by their owners, and sorcerers who abducted unwary young women. Her own world had become a more frightening place, and the stories reflected that.

And when her grandmother died, when the house was sold and the books were dumped into a dollar bin at her estate sale, Dee's belief in magic waned. Her own world became a place of broken promises and whispered apologies.

She learned to believe in tangible things instead: in kind words and filled seats at parent-teacher meetings. Magic was just another fantasy. It was something she created to comfort herself. There were no true fairy tales, no knights in shining armor. Just herself and her own wits. As the years went on, Dee learned how to microwave her own meals, to make excuses, to lie to everyone around her. She became her own knight; she collected those broken promises and whispered apologies and fashioned them into armor.

By the time she was ten, Dee had put away her fairy-tale books and decided she only believed in real things.

Then the demons declared themselves not two months later.

〰〰〰〰〰

The demons first appeared in Los Angeles.

There were rumors of strange occurrences—an actress

getting up and walking off a three-story fall; an explosion in a college campus in Burbank; a sighting of a strange, glowing being that conspiracy theorists swore was an alien.

Pictures flitted across the Internet. Dee hadn't given them any attention; it was like sightings of Bigfoot or alien-abduction stories. It was human nature—people blew things out of proportion. There were people on street corners shouting about the end of days while others bought holy water in bulk. On the whole, it reminded Dee of stories she'd heard about Y2K—a great deal of fuss over some imagined threat.

To stave off worldwide panic, the so-called demons organized a press conference.

We exist, they said. And we have a proposition for you.

A person could trade away a piece of themselves for a wish come true.

At ten years old, Dee accepted the demons the way she accepted everything else—she hadn't. When she looked at pictures of supposed demons, all she saw were *people*. Very beautiful people, but people.

Demons weren't real, she said. This had to be an elaborate hoax. Like those doctored fairy pictures. Future generations were going to laugh at them for their stupidity. You couldn't buy luck with a finger. You couldn't trade a foot for beauty. Just like you couldn't trade a whole arm for a life.

Her father had agreed.

"Aren't demons supposed to go in for souls, anyway?" he

complained. He sat on their old love seat, the yellow fabric stained so often that it appeared brown. "What would they want with body parts?"

Mrs. Moreno was fumbling in her pocket, pretending to look for her cell phone, but Dee knew she was looking for a lighter. "Maybe body parts are more useful?"

Dee surprised herself by speaking up. "How is a foot more useful than a soul?" she asked, wondering if perhaps this was something an adult would know.

"Maybe hell has an overpopulation problem," said Mr. Moreno, his voice heavy with finality.

Dee knew better than to push her parents for answers. So she went to the place she always did when she needed to know something—the Internet. After all, it had taught her how to get wine stains out of the carpet, how to fix a clogged sink, and exactly what a period was. It seemed only natural to investigate the demons on her own, too.

She went searching for info—and of course, she found plenty of that. In fact, the demons seemed to dominate the Internet very quickly. In a matter of months, some demons had fan clubs. Not quite cults, but close. There were whole blogs dedicated to tracking their movements, candid photos snapped by daring paparazzi, lists trying to determine which body part what celebrity had sold for their success, even theories about which political leaders were consulting demonic entities.

There were also a great many articles trying to either prove or debunk the demons' existence. Half of the writers were convinced, saying they just *knew* the demons weren't human. The other half said that these were simply people who were using stage magic to trick the world. For every believer, there was someone trying to prove them wrong. And then there were those who believed but disapproved.

These were the people who tried to ward off the demons with signs and shouted words. Websites sold supposed relics and holy water. Some people took up swords and guns, and went hunting. There were literal crusades going on until the US government declared such endeavors illegal. Rumors about Homeland Security setting up their own occult branch flew across the Internet, made all the more plausible by the fact that the feds didn't comment on it.

Dee found the footage of the original press conference on a blog. She hadn't watched it when it first aired; her father told her that watching too much television was a sure way to end up a loser—and while she wasn't sure she believed him, she also didn't want to risk his annoyance by turning it on.

Dee glanced about the computer room—empty and safe—before she hit the play button on the video.

"We don't hire out to criminals or governments," said a woman with cool gray eyes and a polished smile. "We won't even work for minor officials." She turned that smile on the conference host, and he withered beneath it. "We don't get involved in politics. And above all, we do not harm humans."

"Why not?" the man managed to say.

"Because we live here, too," said the woman. "And you humans have a frightening tendency to wreck things when you get scared. We will not involve ourselves in your wars, in your petty conflicts. You have nothing to fear from us. We only offer covenants to individuals. Also," she added, turning her eyes on the camera, "we don't work for corporations, either."

"How do we know you're real?" said one audience member, echoing Dee's own thoughts.

The woman smiled, gesturing off camera. "I don't expect you to believe me. So I'll direct that question to one of my colleagues."

The screen flickered, and then changed to the scene of a hospital room. The conference host's voice boomed out, saying that they were now broadcasting a live feed of a nearby hospital.

A beautiful man stood next to a bed. The camera slowly panned over the image of a child—unconscious, breathing through a tube, and utterly still.

The man gave the camera a steady look. "Doctor?"

A doctor stepped into the spotlight; his face shone with sweat. "This girl was in a car accident a week ago. She's on life support—"

"Her mother," said the man, interrupting, "has agreed to a covenant."

The camera spun around, came to focus on a middle-aged woman. She was sitting in a chair and looked oddly lopsided. It had taken Dee a second to realize it was because the woman's left sleeve was hollow.

"Now," said the man, and touched a hand to the girl's chest.

Later, people would claim it was bad special effects or the camera guy panicking. Because the screen went fuzzy, jerking away, and seconds later, when the scene was finally visible again, there was a ten-year-old girl choking on a tube and doctors rushing around her, and the desperate, horribly relieved sobbing of the mother.

Everyone had wondered at the demon who had made such a miracle happen. But the thing Dee fixated on was that empty sleeve, the arm traded away. On the person who would do that for another.

To her, that was the most unbelievable thing.

THREE

Dee always showered after her community service. She hated how the smell of antiseptic and plastic clung to her skin, so when she walked into her dormitory she made a sharp left and strode into the girls' restroom. And today, of all days, she looked forward to the sensation of newness that accompanied her after every shower.

Five in the afternoon wasn't exactly prime bathroom time; the room's only other occupants were two seniors. One was bent over a sink, a box of hair dye in her friend's hand. Dee skirted past and ducked into the showers.

She washed off the remnants of the hospital, scrubbing away the sensation of dusty rubber gloves and the scent of bleach. Finished, she bundled her mass of hair into a towel, slipped into her robe, and hurried out of the bathroom.

The hallway was painted a cheerful yellow, with rough, industrial-strength carpet. Pictures adorned the walls—previous deans, news articles about the school's alumni, and a large corkboard crammed full of papers and thumbtacks. She paused there for a moment, her gaze roaming over the hall.

That was the best part about boarding school. It wasn't the fancy meal hall or the teachers or the new computers. It was the fact that when she came home, it was to a tiny room with beds shoved in opposite corners. It was often cluttered with books and dirty clothes, and it smelled like old carpet and burned popcorn.

Dee loved it.

Her roommate, Gremma, sat on her bed wearing boxer shorts and a T-shirt with the periodic table on it. Several stuffed bears were scattered over her desk—all of which had been vivisected and sewn up again.

Gremma had been Dee's roommate since the second semester of freshman year, after Gremma's first roommate had complained to the dean. Dee hadn't understood why any-one would go to such lengths. With her bright red hair and brighter lipstick, Gremma looked like one of those quirky, dimply girls one might see in a romantic comedy.

But Gremma's first words to Dee had been, "Let's get three things out of the way. First, you make fun of my name and I make your life miserable—my father wanted a boy named Greg and my mom wanted a ballerina named Emma. So they compromised. Second, I like girls. Third, I have an antique set of surgical scalpels hidden under my mattress. If you have a problem with any one of those facts, you should say something now."

Dee, taken aback, hadn't thought before speaking. "Are you planning on murdering your way to a single room?"

Gremma blinked. "No."

"Do you snore?"

"Not to my knowledge."

"Then we'll get along just fine," said Dee.

And they had. Gremma had the personality of a grumpy house cat, one that liked to lounge in patches of sunlight and occasionally devour mice whole. Dee could see how that might be off-putting, but Gremma was refreshingly free of pretense. Also, she wasn't stingy with her snacks and fiercely defended their dorm from would-be pranksters.

Dee regarded her roommate with a mixture of fondness and envy. But it wasn't a desire for her designer clothes or high-end laptop or even her careless beauty. It was the way Gremma held herself, shoulders thrown back and head held high as if to say, *I don't give a shit.* Because Gremma honestly didn't.

That was what Dee envied.

Sometimes she wished she could be like that. *Fearless.* Dee couldn't remember a time when she hadn't been afraid— and not even of the big things like death or pain. She was frightened of stupid things, of getting in the wrong line at the cafeteria, of people who spoke too loudly, of forgetting her bus pass, of traffic, of oversleeping.

Today, Gremma was scribbling away in a chemistry workbook. "Chemicals," she was muttering. "We're all just chemicals."

"You know chemistry riles you up," said Dee, tossing a damp towel across her bedpost. She rummaged through her dresser, found a clean pair of jeans and a bra, and began to pull them on under her robe. "It's like coffee—you're not supposed to do it after five in the afternoon."

Gremma made a growling sound. "It's due on Tuesday."

"Which means you've still got two days. Work on history instead." Dee shucked out of her robe and hung it on the hook they'd attached to the door.

Gremma shut her textbook with an audible *whump*. "Oh. Um. Forgot to tell you, but there was one of those official-looking envelopes in our mailbox this morning. I put it on your desk."

Dee's stomach twisted with unease. She reached down, traced the edge of the envelope with her fingertip. The return address said simply, *Registrar's Office*.

Brannigan Preparatory Academy was Oregon's answer to the old-money boarding schools on the East Coast. *If they can have fancy schools, so can we*, went the school's unofficial motto. Or at least, that's what Gremma always said.

Brannigan was as pompous as a school could get in the Pacific Northwest. It was a thoroughly modern crisscross of concrete and tinted glass, built by an up-and-coming architect ten years ago. The main building was the only nod to the school's locale, with its columns of pine and oak. Classes were filled with children of wealthy entrepreneurs, the kids of faculty, and the lucky few who managed to snag a scholarship.

Dee was among the latter. Or at least, she had been.

The waiting room outside the registrar's office was the only room that held an air of dilapidation. The chairs' polish had faded, the carpet looked slightly wilted. Maybe this building was waiting for repair, or maybe no one cared about it. Dee stepped up to the office door, braced herself, then rapped twice. She hoped there would be someone here, despite the early-morning hour. Coming here before classes was a risk, but Dee couldn't stand another moment of solitude; all last night she'd tossed and turned until her hair looked as though she'd shoved her pen in an electrical socket.

"Come in," called a woman's voice, and Dee drew herself together. She opened the door, slipped inside. It was a typical office—large desk, file cabinets, a steaming cup of coffee resting next to the keyboard. MRS. GARRETT, read her metal name plaque.

"Sit down," said the woman, smiling. Tentatively, Dee

went to one of the wooden chairs and perched on the very edge. She kept her face blank, but her fingers were locked together. It took only a moment to introduce herself, to explain the nature of her visit. Mrs. Garrett found a file and placed it on her desk, flipped it open.

"Normally we'd call your parents to talk about something like this," Mrs. Garrett said. "We tried, but they haven't returned our messages."

She was one of the older faculty, probably only a year or two from retirement. Her rusty brown hair was cut at chin length, and it was tinged gray at the roots. She probably had kids, Dee thought. She spoke with a familiar gentleness, like one used to bandaging scraped knees or elbows. But rather than soothe her, that gentle tone made Dee's hands clench. This woman didn't care about her; her calm demeanor was probably the reason she'd been tapped to be this particular messenger.

"Are there any other numbers we can try your parents at?" Mrs. Garrett asked.

The word came out flat and too quickly. "No."

Mrs. Garrett's expression froze. Dee felt her mouth move, the words coming in automatic little jerks. "They work late. Sometimes forget to check their messages." She forced herself to smile so brightly she nearly believed the lie herself. "They always used to say they'd forget their heads if I wasn't around."

A nod. Mrs. Garrett accepted this explanation. "We're trying to find alternate funding right now," she said, "but the school is being forced to cut several of the merit scholarships." Her mouth drew tight. "I apologize."

"Not your fault." Those words also came easily to Dee; she always spoke to adults with the same quiet surrender. "I understand."

"You should talk to your parents. You have until the end of the school year." Mrs. Garrett slid Dee's file back into place. "We'd hate to lose a promising student."

"Yeah," said Dee numbly. "Me too."

FOUR

Dee enjoyed midterms.

In the days following her visit to the registrar's office, she listened to several freshmen quizzing themselves in the library, murmuring to one another in French; two boys Dee barely knew yelled algebra equations at each other until the dorm monitor told them off; a girl's sobbing could be heard through a thin wall; a gaggle of haughty seniors flaunted their disinterest in exams by stripping down to bikinis and boxers and stretching out on the lawn, taking in the weak sunlight. Some of them read textbooks, but most had the latest gossip rags. Dee saw a picture of an actress with a prosthetic leg, decorated in tiny diamonds to match her dress. THE SECRET BEHIND HER OSCAR? went the headline.

Most of the freshmen, sophomores, and juniors looked at the seniors with resentful envy, then went back to desperate studying. When anxiety hung heavy in the air, people were their most honest—and terrified—selves. Dee enjoyed it because it was the one time she didn't have to monitor her every word; with everyone on edge, no one noticed if she slipped up. Her own worry seemed natural when people could blame it on academic pressure rather than the constant thrum of nerves that seemed to never leave her. Her shoulders were drawn tight and her jaw ached from clenching it in her sleep. Old fear beat within her, as solid and familiar as her pulse, and for once she could blame it on the stress of tests, of papers, of final projects.

"What are you doing for spring break?" asked Gremma once Dee got back to the dorm. She slouched on a large green beanbag—a joint purchase of theirs—and a chemistry workbook sat open across her lap. "Got any hot parties planned?" She grinned. In contrast to her designer jeans and high-end computer, there was a slight overlap in Gremma's bottom teeth. It's not like she couldn't have afforded to fix them. Dee wondered if Gremma had refused braces out of sheer stubbornness. It would be a very Gremma thing to do.

Dee set her backpack down and settled on her bed. "What are you planning?"

Gremma snorted. She sat up, the beanbag's foam beads crunching beneath her. "Spend a week at my parents' vacation house in Newport, hooking up with the girlfriends of the boys my parents try to set me up with. Probably drink lots of tequila, dance around bonfires, and run naked down the beach. Want to come?"

It was the first time Gremma had ever offered, and Dee considered it. Escape, if only for a week. She imagined some ritzy beach house, complete with cocktail glasses and mini umbrellas—but she would be somewhere unknown, at the mercy of strangers, and without an escape route. Her stomach twisted at the thought. "Doesn't seem like my kind of scene," she said truthfully.

"The house is nice," said Gremma. "Plenty of room." She paused, then added, "But, yeah, I can't really see you running naked or getting drunk."

Dee's smile went brittle. "Not my thing. You have fun, though."

"Oh, I will. So what *will* you be doing?"

Dee's smile dropped entirely. A familiar hollow ache opened up inside her rib cage. "Maybe hang out with some friends," she said. "Do some cooking with my mom." The lies came easily, as they always did.

"So you're going home, then?" asked Gremma absent-mindedly.

"Yeah."

Some part of Dee yearned for home. For the familiar smells, for the old furniture, for the overgrown yard and the television that only worked if you adjusted the coat-hanger antenna just right.

And maybe—just maybe—things would go well. Hope bloomed within her. Perhaps, when she went back, they would see how well she was doing. Her parents had to recognize she'd made a good life for herself. She'd come armed with a 3.65 GPA and the most responsible of requests. She would ask her parents if they could help out with her tuition. That's what parents were for—in theory. To help their children be more. Other teenagers asked their parents for money for piercings or cars—and Dee had never asked for anything frivolous. At least not since she'd been ten and begged her parents for an Easy-Bake Oven, only to have her father snap that they had a perfectly working oven in their kitchen.

Gremma let out a sigh, as if she couldn't imagine doing something so mundane as going home for spring break. "Well, you have fun with that."

Home looked the same as ever.

It was a pale green, and in the dim evening light she almost didn't notice the peeling paint. Two stories high, with an obligatory attempt at a garden. Dee knew the backyard made no such effort—behind the tall fences and trees was a tangle of overgrown blackberry brambles and a graveyard of abandoned home improvement projects. She'd played in it as a kid, taking plastic dinosaurs through the overgrown grass.

Gremma's shiny black Camaro couldn't have been more out of place. "You sure you don't need help with your bags?" she asked. She'd already dressed for spring break—in high-waisted shorts, a crop top, with her hair twisted into some elaborate knot. She looked effortlessly confident and Dee both loved and resented her for it.

"I'll be fine," said Dee. Her insides clenched at the thought of Gremma following her.

"See ya in a week," said Gremma brightly. Dee pulled together a smile and waved.

"Don't break too many hearts," she said, and Gremma laughed, revving the engine. The high beams swept away, and for a moment Dee stood in complete darkness. Her fingers gripped the worn nylon handle of her duffel bag, stuffed full with dirty laundry. She hesitated, rummaging around in her pocket for the worn house key. Should she knock? Or just walk in? But before she could make the decision, she heard footsteps on linoleum and the door was being pulled open and she found herself being swept up in a hug.

Mrs. Moreno looked nothing like her daughter. Blond and wiry-thin, with worn edges around her lips. Dee always thought they looked ridiculous in pictures together—even their smiles looked nothing alike, with Dee's tight-lipped little mouth and Mrs. Moreno's exuberant grin.

"Deirdre," said Mrs. Moreno, arms tight around Dee. Dee didn't bother to correct her. "How are you? Was that your friend driving away? You should've told her to stay—we have plenty for dinner."

That was something, at least. There'd be fresh food in the house.

"She's meeting her own parents," Dee lied quickly. Her heartbeat quickened and a sweat broke out along her back. The sweet scent of her mother's rose-and-amber perfume barely covered the dry smell of ashes. When Mrs. Moreno released her, Dee felt a moment of both relief and yearning. That small, young part of her longed to step back into her mother's embrace, to take refuge there.

"Your father is just putting on a roast," said Mrs. Moreno, guiding Dee into the house. As if she didn't know how to walk inside. As if she hadn't lived here since she'd been born. "He'll be so glad to see you. How's school?"

Stepping over the threshold took effort. Dee resisted the urge to scratch at her neck. She did that when she was nervous. She'd spent most of the seventh grade wearing scarves to cover the marks.

Old habits, she thought, and forced her hands into her pockets.

"School's fine," she said. "I think I did well on my midterms." Already, she could feel herself falling into her role—trying to be the best possible version of herself, as if she could keep anything bad from happening by simply being cheerful. "Mind if I drop this stuff off in my room?"

She'd learned this dance long ago; the steps were polite and careful. Smiles and nods. Take luggage to room. Spend five minutes in room staring at one's self in the mirror and trying to perfect a realistic smile. Go downstairs. More hugs. More pleasantries. Dinner. Maybe a movie. Spend entire movie staring at the screen instead of the other people in the living room. Claim early bedtime.

Dee knew her role—be quiet but not too quiet, smile until her cheeks hurt, gently steer the conversation to casual, light things. She would spend the next few days working on the house; her parents would expect it. Well, actually, her mother would tell her to stop fussing with the fridge and tell her all about the boys in her classes and had Dee met anyone nice? And how was that roommate of hers, the one with the red hair and all those adorable teddy bears? Her father, on the other hand, would probably hand her a scrub brush and say something about finding mold in the bathroom.

She dropped her bags onto her bed. The air was stale, still, as if no one had opened the door since she'd left after Christmas break. The room held all the trappings of her childhood—toys crammed in an old chest, clothes hanging in the closet, ticket stubs from movies she'd thought she might put in a scrap-book. But she had never ended up making that scrapbook, so instead the papers cluttered together on the edge of her desk. There was a daddy longlegs perched on a cobweb in the corner.

Dee gazed up at the spider for a long moment, then decided to face the inevitable. She drifted down the stairs, feeling aimless and uncertain.

Her mother was nowhere to be found, but her father was in the kitchen.

People always said that Deirdre must be a daddy's girl because she looked so much like her father—light brown skin, dark hair, a tendency toward stockiness. But Dee couldn't see it herself. She was all those things, yes. But she had none of her father's hard-earned strength, the scars on his hands from years of handling lawn mowers and shovels. He had begun his own landscaping business when he was in his twenties and worked his way into a decently comfortable life. Now he had employees (whom he constantly complained about), an office, and better health insurance just in case a weed-whacker tried to take a finger.

He always put her in mind of one of those bulls from the rodeo—thick through the shoulders and waist, all corded muscle and huffing breaths.

Mr. Moreno stood by the stove, hovering over a steaming pot. "Broccoli?" asked Dee.

"Potatoes," said Mr. Moreno. He glanced up. "It's been a while."

He hugged her. This time the hug smelled like sweat and cut grass. At the scent, that knot in her chest twisted a little tighter. Mr. Moreno released her and took a step back, surveying his daughter with a keen eye. Dee held herself rigidly— shoulders back and chin high. Her best self, she thought. Strong and smart, still wearing her Brannigan shirt with the logo on it. A good student. A successful daughter. Someone a parent could be proud of.

"You've gained weight," he said. "You aren't taking a PE class this semester?"

Suddenly, she felt heavier—and she couldn't be sure if it was because she had gotten fatter or if it was disappointment weighing her down.

Dee looked at the linoleum floor. "No time in my schedule."

"You should make the time," said Mr. Moreno, and Dee didn't argue. She opened the cupboard and withdrew three plates, carrying them to the dining room.

Dinner was its usual affair of sitting around a dented wooden table. The roast was well seasoned and Dee cut into it with the care and intensity Gremma used while vivisecting her teddy bears.

"Are you still taking that advanced history class?" asked Mr. Moreno. Dee's heart leaped.

"Yes," she said quickly. "I—I think I'm getting an A in it."

Mr. Moreno bit into a large mouthful of roast, chewed,

then swallowed. "It's a waste of time. You should be taking classes that'll be useful once you graduate. Something that would help the business—accounting or mechanics."

Never mind the fact that Dee hadn't ever shown the slightest inclination toward accounting and had once managed to break a miniature helicopter at school.

Dee's gaze went back to her plate. "I like history," she said, very quietly.

"You like sitting in class listening to someone tell you stories rather than learning how to fix things? How to be useful?" There was no mistaking the edge of scorn in his voice. "Of course you would."

"Are you thinking about next year's classes?" Mrs. Moreno chirped.

Dee's fork froze in midair. She forced herself to eat the bite of roast; it gave her a moment to gather her thoughts.

Might as well tell them. It would be like pulling off a Band-Aid, she rationalized. Best to get it over quickly. She set her fork down and placed her hands in her lap so no one could see her fidget.

"They're revoking my scholarship," she said.

Mr. Moreno's fingers went tight around his beer bottle. "What did you do?"

A shiver of adrenaline passed through her. "Nothing," she said, too sharply. "It was something to do with budget cuts. It was the scholarship students or the art program."

"Like they need a fucking art program," muttered Mr. Moreno.

Mrs. Moreno's hands shook slightly as she pressed a napkin to her mouth. "Well, it's not the most horrible thing that could happen," she said, offering up a smile. "We'd be glad to see you more often."

As if there was nothing to be done—as if Dee coming home was a certain thing. Her stomach turned over. She had thought if she told them tonight, they might spend the rest of the break trying to figure something out. Perhaps see what kind of money they had in savings, research if they could take out a small loan. It was what parents were supposed to do.

"We'd be glad to see you at all," Mr. Moreno said under his breath.

Dee's fork slid through her potatoes with a little too much force. It dinged against her plate. *Because passive-aggressive comments make me want to spend more time here*, she almost said, but managed to hold the words in her mouth through the rest of the meal.

"I'll do the dishes," she said once she was done eating. She pushed away from the table and her father made no comment.

Carry plates to sink. Fill sink. Add soap. Scrub plates. There was almost a meditative rhythm to it. There were no dishes to wash at the dorms. The most cleanup she did there was keeping her side of the room neat. Here, the state of the house gave her something to do.

Maybe it was because she hadn't seen it in two months, but the place looked worse than she remembered. She hadn't been here to scrub away the mold taking root near the toilet or the smell of stale milk in the fridge. She wondered how long it had been since they shopped and, absurdly, she felt a swell of protectiveness. This used to be her job, making sure everything ran smoothly. She shook herself and tried to push away the thought.

Mr. Moreno sidled into the kitchen and stood perhaps two feet away. Dee felt her body jump, quivering like Gremma's Camaro when she shifted gears too quickly.

For a long minute, he didn't say anything. Dee continued to wash the dishes, adding in the cups and cutlery, going to work on them with a sponge. Maybe it would be different this time. Maybe he would comment on her willingness to work hard, to try to stay at school. Maybe—

"You think you're too good to come home?" he asked.

His expression had changed. Gone was the semblance of control. It had been replaced with something sloppy and ugly and terrifying. Suddenly, she was all too aware of his nearness, of the heat coming through his cotton T-shirt and the sheer size of him. She held a breath until she felt it burn in her lungs, held it until it wouldn't look like retreating when she took a step back. She reached into the soapy water, eyes on the reflection in the kitchen window. Her fingers touched the edges of a serrated knife and she skimmed downward, finding the handle.

Mr. Moreno leaned against the fridge. "Don't see why the school here isn't good enough for you."

"It's not about it being good enough," said Dee. She tried to talk calmly. "It's about the best shot for my future, for getting into a really good college—"

"Don't see why your future requires you to spend so much time away from your family," said Mr. Moreno. His voice had roughened into a familiar tone, one that set Dee's teeth on edge. She spoke more quickly, voice low.

"It's a good school." Less calm this time.

"That good school doesn't teach you anything you need," he scoffed. "Shakespeare and drama and philosophy. You think that's gonna help you get a job? You think you can survive in the real world?"

It felt like a fist was squeezing her insides; if she were being honest with herself, the real world terrified her. With its unspoken rules and paperwork and threats of never finding a real job. That was why she'd gone to Brannigan—because graduates always went to a good college, any college of their choice.

"It's what I want," she said in a thin voice.

"Daughters don't abandon their families," he said.

Dee looked down at the gray, soapy water. "Fathers don't guilt their daughters over wanting a better life." She spoke the words without thinking. There was a moment of heavy silence, and Dee thought the tension might pass.

Something hit the floor and shattered. A beer bottle or a glass. Dee didn't look. Her fingers tightened around the knife hilt. "Better?" snarled her father. "Better than this? You think you're better than us? We're not good enough for you anymore?"

"Mark?" Then Mrs. Moreno was there, warily edging into the kitchen. "Dee, did you drop something?"

Dee released the knife and it sank beneath the dirty water. Keeping her gaze averted, she said, "Sorry, need to use the bathroom," and hurried out of the room. She strained for any sound to indicate she was being followed, but there was nothing.

Going to the bathroom was an easy choice. It was the only room with a working lock.

Coward.

She was a coward.

She shut the door behind her and sat on the toilet lid. Already, her mother was picking up the thread that Dee had left off.

"—Fucking stuck-up school—"

"—Mark, you cannot tell her she can't go there—"

"___"

"___"

"___"

The words blurred in her ears, became familiar chords in a song she knew all too well. She knew where this would end up, with her father ranting about how hard he worked and how grateful they should all be, about how he never had this kind of life growing up, about respect and family and how spoiled his daughter had turned out, and with her mother eventually going to the backyard, pretending to get some air but smoking hard out beneath the walnut tree.

Dee turned the shower on and let the sound of the water drown out everything else.

FIVE

She lasted two days.

She tried, she really did.

She fell into her old routines; she cleaned the bathroom and tossed the moldy food from the fridge. She took refuge in the backyard, tried to pull prickly weeds from the overgrown lawn—a joke, she thought, since her father kept other yards pristine. Of course *their* lawn would resemble a half-dead jungle.

She slept in late enough so she didn't have to join in at any awkward morning conversations. Once she heard the distinct slam of the front door, she would venture downstairs in pajamas and robe to make breakfast for her mother. Dee knew the basics of cooking, had taught herself with her grandmother's recipe book propped up against a can of lentil soup. It had been simple stuff at first—omelets and pancakes and French toast. But then she'd moved on from breakfast to soups and stir-fries, and by the time she left for Brannigan, she knew how to crack an egg with one hand, how to whip up a meal from nearly any kind of leftovers, and how to judge if she could cut away the mold on a piece of food or if it was a goner.

But now, no matter how she tried, she could not slip back into this old life. She was fine with short visits; she enjoyed her mother's company and the familiarity of the house, but the prospect of living here permanently made her want to scratch at her neck until the skin was raw.

Her mother took the news of Dee's leaving like she always did—with bright smiles, overfull eyes, and hands that trembled.

"Sorry," Dee lied. "It's just, this project is half our biology grade and Gremma can't do all the work. That's why they break us into pairs." She insisted on making breakfast, which consisted of digging out two clean bowls and trying to determine which cereal hadn't gone stale yet. Dee sat at the dining room table, fingers knotted in her lap, filled with a combination of pity and affection.

"At least the coffee's still good," said Mrs. Moreno, smiling as she set down two mugs. Dee took the nearer one and sipped.

Bitter heat flooded her mouth. She swallowed the burn of the whiskey, making an effort to keep her face normal. "I think I got your cup," she said, and pushed it back.

The dorms were startlingly quiet. Dee liked it that way. The only person she spoke to was the dorm monitor when she lied about needing to return for a school project.

Dee sat with her secondhand laptop looking up fellowships, scholarships, jobs, anything. The problem was that while her parents weren't wealthy like most of the students here, they also weren't poor. They were the middlest of middle class, and thus she was disqualified for most financial aid. Her own scholarship had been merit-based.

Looking up summer jobs was next, but there weren't any good ones—at least not for someone who wasn't eighteen. And none of them paid a fraction of what tuition cost.

She did have a college fund—her grandmother had started it when Dee was a kid. "Always have something in the bank," she had said, placing a hand on Dee's tiny shoulder.

Dee had added to the fund long after her grandmother passed away. Checks from distant relatives, odd neighborhood jobs, pet-sitting for classmates—it went into the bank. After all, that was what responsible people did. The problem was, her parents were still technically the holders of that bank account. Dee couldn't make withdrawals until she was eighteen—at the beginning of next December, long after school started up again.

She'd need her parents' permission to access the funds.

Sadness settled heavy in her skull, made her temples ache

and her head feel heavy. Her eyes stung, but she didn't cry; she'd stopped crying years ago. Crying never solved anything. It just made her nose run.

She couldn't go back to that house.

But it looked like she didn't have a choice.

Dee was suddenly so tired she was in a daze, unable to do more than flop down on her bed and stay there.

She recognized the lethargy: a familiar and entirely unwelcome reminder of her old life. Small things suddenly became insurmountable: getting a new pencil off her desk, rolling over in bed, or even blinking. The air felt thicker, as if the world conspired against her every movement.

No, she thought. This wasn't happening again. She wouldn't let it.

She was grabbing her robe when a knock sounded at her door. Dee flinched and for a moment, her mind was overrun with irrational fear. That they'd followed her here, that she'd open her door and her family would be standing there, ready to drag her home.

She considered not opening the door, but a young, female voice said, "Hey, Gremma! You awake?"

All the tension went out of her. Shaky with relief, she crossed the room to open the door.

Dee had never been a very social person. Having a lot of friends meant needing to keep track of every half-truth, of every careful scrap of information…it was exhausting. She tried to limit her interactions. She talked with the same few lab partners, ate with a group of girls that desperately wanted Gremma to be one of them, smiled at the same people, and was polite to everyone.

But despite her attempts to remain aloof, dorm life meant she knew people. The girls in the next room over were named Tabitha and Courtney, and they happily chatted with Gremma sometimes while Dee did homework. There were others—Julia, the local distributor of instant coffee if anyone needed a fix; Nicky, who annoyed everyone by playing her music just a little too loud; and that one girl who always wore the same shirt when she wasn't in uniform.

The girl at the door was Coffee-Distributor Julia. "Is Gremma around?"

Dee blinked. "She's gone for spring break."

"Oh." Julia's face fell, then brightened. "Oh, well. You doing anything tonight? There's a party in Grover. Their dorm monitor has the flu, and from the way the boys tell it, she's so strung out on cold meds that she wouldn't notice if we threw a rave." She beamed. "We figure all of us left behind on spring break should at least have a little fun."

Dee opened her mouth to decline. She didn't *do* parties. But something caught in her throat. Maybe it was the scent of the unwashed sheets or stale popcorn; maybe it was simply the paralyzing knowledge that she wasn't sure what she would do if left to her own devices.

"Sure," she said.

Brannigan had three dorms: Whiteaker, where Dee lived; an all-boys building called Grover; and Moody, the other girls' dorm. Dee never visited Grover—she had no close male friends and she didn't date. On the outside, the boys' dorm looked like the other two buildings, but once inside, Dee wrinkled her nose. "And I thought we were slobs," she muttered.

"The prank wars are legendary here," said Julia. "Even Moody gets in on it sometimes."

"Why doesn't that kind of thing happen in our dorm?" asked a blond girl.

Julia snorted. "Pretty sure the last time anyone tried to mess with Whiteaker, some crazy girl threw a Molotov cocktail into the idiot's room."

"It was a stink bomb," said Dee, surprising herself by speaking up.

"You sure?" asked Julia.

Dee would know; it had been Gremma who'd devised the counterstrategy with stolen chemistry equipment. Their room hadn't smelled right for a week.

The party was being held in one of the larger dorm

rooms—the kind meant for four kids. Someone had pushed the bunk beds against the wall and made a diligent effort to shove the mess of dirty clothes under them. Even so, the room smelled distinctly of teenage boy and stale chips.

The dorm had been set up with twinkle lights and mirrors, and with the overhead lamp flicked off, even Dee had to admire the effect. The small room suddenly looked larger, and the small crowd was amplified by the mirrors. Dee found herself gravitating toward a corner. She could tell the party had been going on for some time; there was a sense of charged energy, of anticipation and restlessness. Already, she found herself longing for the security of her own dorm. But she knew the moment she returned, so would her depression.

Without the constant vigilance of the dorm monitor, plastic red cups were passed from hand to hand. Dee took one, accepting it the way she would a prop in her drama class. It was a thing to hold. Nothing more.

She watched the swell and tide of the small crowd, the few people who had begun dancing—but it was just an excuse to grind against someone they liked. Dee watched with half annoyance, half longing. She couldn't imagine letting someone stroke the line of her back, to grasp her hip or press a kiss to her throat.

It wasn't that Dee didn't want sex or kissing or any of the other things her classmates always seemed to be doing. It was just—she was afraid. She tried to imagine speaking to a boy, flirting with him, taking her clothes off—and her mind just went blank.

She wasn't attached to her virgin status. As far she was concerned, it was like a mole on her forearm—it was simply there, visible for all the world to see, and sure, it would be nice to be rid of it, but when was the time? Or the opportunity?

Besides, she would probably do it wrong.

Dee found herself near a desk—its contents cleared away and replaced with a hastily assembled assortment of snacks. She considered the bowl of pretzels, wondering how many people's hands had been in that bowl, when someone joined her.

Dee sensed the girl before she saw her. She must have been someone's friend, smuggled on campus. There were seniors who swore it was easy to sneak people in if you knew the security routes. This girl was pretty, with lush dark hair and heavily lined eyes. She was the kind of girl who wore a lot of makeup and wore it well. But that wasn't what drew Dee's attention.

Her red cup was held in a prosthetic hand.

Dee froze. She knew better than to assume. People lost limbs for all sorts of reasons. Maybe she'd been born that way. Maybe she was a cancer survivor. She could've gotten her left hand stuck in a garbage disposal for all Dee knew.

But it still didn't stop her mind from racing. Because there was one sure way to lose a limb these days.

To trade it away for something else.

"You think the pretzels are any good?" said the girl. She spoke slowly, as if the syllables were difficult to pronounce.

Dee shrugged. "I don't think you can get food poisoning from a pretzel." Her eyes were fastened to the girl's sleeve, to the place where the metal and plastic prosthetic disappeared.

The girl cleared her throat, and Dee's gaze snapped to hers.

The girl smiled—half defiant, half mocking. "See something you like?"

Dee's eyes fell to the table and she shook her head. "Ah, no. Sorry. I mean—I shouldn't have stared. Sorry."

This was why she hated parties; inevitably, she would do or say the wrong thing and the memory would haunt her for weeks to come.

The girl's face softened. "No problem." She dug into the pretzel bowl and offered Dee a handful.

Dee took them, if only so she'd have an excuse not to talk. For a moment, the silence hung between them. Dee considered moving away, finding Coffee-Distributor Julia or making an excuse about going to the bathroom, but then the girl spoke.

"I'm used to people staring," she said. Her breath smelled like sugar and vodka. "It's the first thing most people see. So long as it's not the only thing they see, I'm fine with it."

"Ah." Dee had no idea what to say. She felt as if she stood upon a minefield, and one wrong word might destroy her.

The girl gave Dee a shrewd look. "Are you drunk?"

"No," said Dee honestly.

The girl laughed and her cheeks colored. "You're the only sober person here. I like you."

"I get that a lot," said Dee. "The sober part, not the people-liking-me part."

That made the girl laugh again, and she put her drink down so it wouldn't spill. "You come to a lot of parties, then?"

"No," said Dee truthfully.

The girl beamed at Dee, as if they floated together on some sea of alcohol-fueled goodwill. "You want to know, don't you?" She traced her fingers down the metal of her left hand.

"No," said Dee. Too quickly.

The girl smirked. "It's not just you. Everyone wants to know. I usually tell them I was in an accident." She leaned in closer, and Dee knew how drunk the girl must have been—drunk enough to let slip truths she would have otherwise held close. "People get really judgey when they know you've done a deal."

Dee inhaled sharply. "So you did...uh...?" She gestured vaguely at the girl's left arm. "I thought—well, I thought people under eighteen couldn't..."

"Demons don't make covenants with anyone under

sixteen," the girl said, picking up her drink again and taking a swig. "I was seventeen. Last year."

Dee bit the tip of her tongue, trying to hold the words in. Her resistance lasted only a few seconds. "But what—I mean, if you don't mind me asking. What did you...?"

"Ask for?" The girl flashed her a bright smile. "It's nothing scandalous. I didn't ask for bigger boobs or a perfect memory. Which, looking back on it, might have been more useful."

Dee waited, and sure enough, the girl shrugged. As if this was just another drunken confession.

"I wanted my parents together," she said. She wobbled on her high heels and she gripped the side of the desk. "But demons can't make people love you. That's part of their thing, right? They can't affect emotion...and they won't kill people. Not can't, but won't. My demon, she said that it's too much trouble for what they get out of it." The girl laughed.

"So I asked for my parents not to divorce," she continued. "And guess what happened—there was a loophole found in my granddad's will. Turns out that my dad only inherited if he was married...to one woman. No second marriages for my dear old granddad." She laughed again, and it sounded as if it stuck in her throat. "It was so stupid. Like something out of a romantic comedy. I don't know how the demon did it, but that will made sure my parents never divorced. They'd have to give up over a million dollars to do it.

"The demon kept her word," she said, smiling so that her eyes crinkled at the edges. It was a hard, determinedly happy face. "My parents are together. But they still hate each other, you know?"

"Do I ever," said Dee. Her heart was beating too quickly, and she found herself almost wishing to take a drink from her red cup, if only to settle her nerves. Demons. Demons were supposed to be nearly invincible, capable of granting the most impossible of wishes. People joked about making deals the way they joked about winning the lottery. It was idle fantasy to imagine what a supernatural creature might grant you. She'd never really considered making a deal; she was rather attached to her limbs.

Dee tried to keep her voice steady. "But—was it worth it?"

The girl swayed. "People always warn you about demons, tell you it's wrong and dangerous. And yeah, that's true, but that's not the worst part. The worst part. You know what the worst part is?"

"No," said Dee.

The girl smiled harder. "You get what you ask for," she said.

It would have been quite the philosophical note to end on, had the girl not leaned over and thrown up in someone's hamper.

SIX

There were two kinds of bad decisions, in Dee's experience. The first was due to a lapse in judgment. These were momentary slips brought about by simple emotions—distraction, anger, sadness, impatience. Dee wasn't even sure if they could be truly called *decisions*, these actions made in a moment of error.

But the second kind of decision was far worse.

Actions fueled by desperation. They were the worst kinds of decisions, because desperate people could see the error of their ways and simply not care. They would rush headlong into a bad situation because they could see no other options.

She took the bus to the hospital. Normally, it was a short commute, but today the bus kept stopping and starting, traffic clamping down all around them. Perhaps this was the universe trying to forestall some terrible mistake on her part, Dee thought, then shook her head.

The closer they came to the hospital, the more the cars around them slowed to a crawl. Dee rose from her seat and strode to the front of the bus. "Is there an accident?" she asked the driver.

Then Dee smelled it: the stench of metal and plastic, hot in her nostrils. It reminded her of when a nearby house had caught fire when she was twelve—ash and the stench of burned plastic. Houses were filled with objects that didn't easily catch fire; they melted and smoked and made the air reek.

It turned out, hospitals burned the same. A billow of gray ascended from the hospital's campus, and Dee drew in a sharp breath.

"Let me out here," she said, and without waiting for the driver's reply, she pushed the doors open and squeezed through. A car honked but Dee ignored it, darting across the bike lane and running for the hospital.

A squirming, selfish part of Dee was panicking—and not just for the hospital's patients and doctors. If there was a fire, the demon probably wouldn't be here. Fires meant newscasters and cameras, and demons tended to avoid that kind of attention.

But still—she had to try.

Crowds had gathered on the lawn, gazing up at the smoke

billowing from the auditorium. For the first time, she felt a swell of relief that this was a teaching hospital; the fire must have started in one of those teaching buildings and hadn't spread to threaten any patients yet. Dee couldn't see flames, but firefighters and EMTs were rushing about, talking amongst themselves. Dee rose to tiptoe, trying to peer over taller people. With a grimace, she tried to find a way through the crowd—the smokers' grass was on the other side of the hospital; perhaps that area was untouched, perhaps...

Someone took a step back and Dee stumbled, her toe catching their heel. She fell to hands and knees, a curse caught behind her gritted teeth. Anger welled up within her, but then she shook her head, that anger dispelling into familiar anxiety. She looked down at the grass to see if she'd dropped her purse, and that was when she saw it: a strand of bloodred yarn.

The soft material held between thumb and forefinger, she rose to her feet. She glanced about the crowd, taking care in looking over all the faces.

A demon stood beneath one of the trees.

Between the chaos and the noise, the smoke and the din, no one else seemed to have noticed. Not just *a* demon. *The* demon, the one she'd seen knitting two weeks ago. Dee's heart lurched and she took an involuntary step forward.

It wore the same gray suit, and an umbrella was tucked beneath its arm. It gazed at the flames with an expression it took Dee a moment to recognize. Satisfaction, she decided. It looked upon the chaos with a certain fondness, the way Dee felt herself smile on papers she was sure would garner a good grade.

You did this, she thought, utterly certain.

The demon turned and strode away, Dee following in its wake.

SEVEN

The demon moved through the chaos, unseen and unnoticed, until it came to a neighboring building. There was a side entrance, the kind kept locked from the outside, but it simply reached down and yanked the door open, vanishing inside.

Dee knew where that door led—the hospital basement. *Because of course it did.*

Her heart jolted up into her throat. "Couldn't have lurked on the roof," she said aloud, just to hear her own voice. If she sounded normal, she could fool herself into believing this was normal.

Dee paused, gathered herself. And stepped through the door, letting it click shut behind her.

This building's basement defied cliché. It wasn't dark, creepy, or dirty. Rather, its cinder-block walls were kept free of cobwebs by the ever-diligent janitorial staff. Dee had been here once before, when an orderly needed extra cleaning supplies. The basement was mostly storage, although there were a few abandoned areas that might have doubled as classrooms. White paint flecked off the ceiling. Down here, the shouts and noise were gone; it was utterly and painfully silent.

Dee tried to walk quietly, but doing so in flip-flops was all but impossible. Her fingers were tight on the strand of yarn, and she held it like a talisman, as if it could lead her to the demon. There were stories about this sort of thing—heroes entering mazes with enchanted balls of yarn. But then it was to kill an evil monster, never to make an ally of it.

She glanced in every open doorway, into rooms full of folding chairs and buckets and mops. She tried a few locked doors.

Then she saw a figure in one of the storage rooms. It stood with its back to her, lit up by the pale white of the industrial fluorescents.

It wasn't the demon.

When he turned, she saw he was definitely human, a man or a boy, or something in between.

His mouth was hooked upward in a sly smile, as if he'd been caught doing something he knew he wouldn't be punished for. His eyes were blue—not the unnatural brightness of the demon, but an honest, human blue—and his jaw had a sharp edge. He slouched a little. His features wouldn't have been considered handsome by themselves, but when put together, somehow they made him look good.

For a moment, Dee felt herself flush—and then she saw his clothes.

Jeans with holes in the knees, badly worn shoes, and a secondhand parka. *Do people actually wear parkas in Oregon?* she thought wildly.

She went hunting for a demon and found some homeless boy instead. The demon must have stepped into one of those locked rooms and left her to blunder on ahead.

Dee and the homeless guy regarded each other for a moment.

"You're not heartless, are you?" he said, and Dee had no idea how to answer. Was this his way of asking for a handout?

"Um, no," she said. "Sorry, but you're not supposed to be here."

He blinked at her. "What?"

She tried to think of a tactful way to answer. "I know it's warm," she said hesitantly, "but you're not supposed to come down here. There's a shelter a few miles away—I can tell you how to find the bus stop, give you a little money for it—"

Footsteps rang out and before Dee could react, another guy, probably only a little older than the homeless one, thudded down the hall. He had the blunt, hard-edged face Dee had come to expect from high school jocks. He carried himself with a kind of arrogant assurance. But none of that swagger reached his expression—he smiled at the pair of them like they were all old friends.

"Lancer, you sad bastard," he said fondly, directing a look at the homeless boy. "How many times have people tried to hand you spare change this week?"

The homeless one said, "Counting this time? Three. I don't see why."

The jock snorted. "I *know* you can afford a mirror. Or do you just not care what you look like?"

The homeless boy looked at himself, as if surprised to see clothes there. "My last mirror went into a multimedia piece."

The jock rolled his eyes. "He's not actually homeless," he said, finally directing his words toward Dee. "He just dresses like it." He turned so that he fully faced her. "You new?"

"Not unless the Daemon's started recruiting rich prep school kids," said Not-Homeless. His gaze was fixed on the Brannigan logo on her shirt.

"I'm not a rich prep school kid," she said. "I'm—I—" She floundered, unsure of what to say.

"Lost?" asked the jock, not unkindly.

"No," said Dee. "You—do you know there's a fire outside?"

"Yep," said Not-Homeless, not sounding the least bit worried. "And that's a good thing."

She gaped at him.

"As long as that building burns," said the boy, "no one will come looking down here."

She found her words again. "Who *are* you?"

"James Lancer," said Not-Homeless. His name didn't quite fit him. It sounded straightforward, and this young man looked about as off-kilter as they came. "And this upstanding individual is Carroll Medina."

"Cal," said the second boy, a little despairingly. "Everybody calls me Cal. And you are...?" He squinted at Dee.

"Looking for someone," said Dee. She put her hands on her hips and tried to appear imposing, if only so she wouldn't feel so flustered. "I don't suppose you've seen—I don't know, um, a...?" She hesitated, unsure of whether or not to reveal her secret.

She never managed to finish her mangled sentence.

Something hit her in the chest. A sold *thing* with whiskers and fur and warmth, and she clutched at it instinctively, hands wrapping around it.

It was squeaking wildly, writhing, and when cool claws touched her bare skin, Dee threw the thing to the floor. It was a large, furry rat.

Dee felt a cry lodge in her throat, but she swallowed it down. The rat righted itself, then darted away.

"You okay?" said the jock. It took Dee a moment to remember his name—Carroll. No, Cal. He extended his hands, as if ready to catch her if she fainted. "It didn't bite you, did it?"

A shudder tore through her and she found herself rubbing at her bare arms, her hands, her wrists, trying to wipe away the sensation of fur and flesh.

"It's okay," said Cal. He took a quick step forward, placing himself between Dee and the place the rat had vanished. It was a strangely gallant gesture, but rather than reassure her, it threw her more off balance. What little experience she'd had with boys was enough to know that they didn't do things like that—they made lewd comments and tried to arrange hookups on scribbled notes passed by their friends. She wasn't used to…whatever this was.

"Well, that's interesting," said James Lancer.

Dee whirled, expecting to see her own shock mirrored on his face. But he was staring at something behind her. "Flying rats?" she said raggedly.

"No," said James. "The trajectory." He traced a finger through the air, past Dee, and upward. "It came from up there."

"Oh," said Cal. "Right. Damn." He looked around, then squatted, grabbing something from the floor. An empty bottle, Dee saw. Cal held it in one hand, judged for a moment, and flung it into the air.

"What—" Dee started to say.

The bottle flew high, nearly hit the ceiling, and then it simply *vanished*.

This time Dee did make a sound, more out of surprise than fear. Because that was when she saw it.

Well, she couldn't *see* it. The moment her eyes found the thing, it slid out of her vision. She glanced away and saw it from the corner of her eye. It was like looking at stars—the moment it was fixed in her gaze it vanished. But what she did see looked like a smudge, as if reality had simply blurred.

"What is that?" she said.

"Non-space," said Cal, at the same time James said, "Magic portal."

They looked at each other. "I thought we agreed on non-space," said Cal, sounding hurt. "They're voids; they're not magic."

"Hey," said James, "every time you say 'non-space,' all I can hear is technobabble."

"Well, technobabble has to be better than you peddling your blatant ignorance," replied Cal.

James sighed. "All right, all right. I'll defer to your genius." He turned to Dee. "Living things can't enter the mag— I mean, the *voids*. So when the rats try to get in—that one probably used that high shelf—they get about a few feet and then the void spits them back out. I once saw one splat against a wall."

"Cheery," said Cal drily. "Yes, let's traumatize her some more." He rubbed at his forehead. "Fine, fine. You know where we can find a ladder?" This was directed to Dee.

She opened her mouth, tried to speak and failed.

"Never mind," said Cal quickly. He took a step nearer, hand

held out as if to reassure a startled animal. "It's okay. You stay here—I'll go find a utility closet. There's bound to be one down here." He glanced at the other boy. "Lancer, stay with her."

"Right-o," said James, like this was *normal*. Dee watched as he knelt beside a black duffel bag. He unzipped it, peered about the contents, then nodded in satisfaction. He tightened the strings of his parka hood, rolling his shoulders as if he were a runner preparing for a sprint. The movements were comfortable, almost nonchalant. Another rat was creeping along the far wall, its small eyes gleaming in the dark. Dee shrank back.

"They won't hurt you," said James. "They're just, ah, attuned to the void. Or that's what we think. Like dogs can hear higher frequencies. Or hell, maybe the rats get off on its proximity or something. Whenever we find a void, we always find rats."

"Or maybe they just like to follow you around," said Cal, returning. He waddled backward, clutching a tall ladder in his arms.

"Are you calling me the Pied Piper or something?" asked James.

"Actually, I think they're trying to reclaim stolen property." Cal nodded at the other boy's parka.

Dee's world had suddenly become unrecognizably macabre. Rats creeping along the walls, a smudge of unreality against the ceiling, two teenage boys talking like this happened every day.

"What are you doing here?" she said.

James's smile widened. "We're here to make sure that"—he gestured at the void—"doesn't open."

"What happens if it opens?" She still had no idea what they were talking about, but speaking made her feel better—at least, it drowned out the soft sounds of the rats moving in the shadows.

James shrugged.

"Then what are you waiting for?" she said.

"Three-person team," he replied. "We've got another friend coming... if they don't get stuck in traffic all day."

Something about that statement made her choke out a laugh.

Get out of here, she thought. Whatever was happening, it was *other.* It was *dangerous.* She needed to leave, to go back to the normal world. She turned on her heel, pushing herself forward.

And then she slammed into the demon.

All the breath rushed out of her and she found herself spun around, knocked off balance by the force of the demon's entrance.

It looked just as startled; it gazed at Dee with its unnaturally blue eyes, a line between its brows.

"About time you got here," said Cal. "Where's Cora?"

The demon's attention snapped to the two boys. "I was ensuring that no one finds us," it said, with a bite of annoyance. "As for Cora, I had assumed she would have arrived by now."

Cal slid a cell phone back into his pocket. "Looks like she's stuck on the way here. That's the thing about starting a fire—traffic shuts down." He frowned, but he looked more annoyed than disapproving. "I told you we should've just called in a bomb threat."

"Because *that* would never cause traffic issues," drawled James, but neither Cal nor the demon paid him any attention.

"There was no one in that building," said the demon. "But we should act now." Its mouth pulled tight. "I shall collect Cora."

Cal grinned. "If you're going to do that rip-a-hole-in-reality thing again, can I watch?"

The demon blinked once. "No." And then it glided out of the room.

This was it. This was her chance. Dee couldn't talk to the demon in front of these boys. She took a step forward, and then another, until her feet carried her out of the room and into the hall.

The demon eyed her. It looked exactly the same—dressed in the clean lines of a suit, an umbrella beneath one arm, and its dark hair tucked neatly into place.

"Back for more community service?" it asked.

That surprised her. She didn't think the demon would remember her, to be honest.

"Are you—I mean, are you here to do business?" she asked.

The demon slid its hands into its pockets. "No," it said, face impassive.

She wrapped an arm around her own stomach, trying to make the gesture look natural. "I want to make a deal."

It raised an eyebrow. "Maybe you didn't hear me. Maybe you didn't see the thing that is taking root in that room. I don't have time for this." It started to walk away, and her heartbeat skyrocketed.

"I could help," she said. Her voice was quiet from nerves.

The demon froze. Not like humans froze, but how Dee once saw a stray cat freeze just before disemboweling a bird.

"You need three people," she said. "That's what those boys said. You need a three-person team, but you only have two."

The demon glided toward her. "You didn't want to make a deal before."

Her throat was twisting shut, and she barely managed to croak, "I need money."

The demon's brows rose higher.

She swallowed. "I need money. A lot of it. I can't—I need it. If I help you, if I do whatever you need three people to do—do you still need a...part?"

It was a hopeless sentence, filled with false starts and stops. But the demon understood. "Yes."

She knew this was coming, so she shouldn't have been afraid. She *refused* to be afraid, even as she began to shake. "What would I have to give you?"

"I don't deal in toes or fingers," it said.

The words felt like a physical punch; she was knocked off balance, and she swayed. A foot, she thought. It wanted a foot—or a leg. Could she do it? Could she trade part of herself away if it meant her future was secured?

"What, then?" she said.

The demon turned to face her fully, angling so that the line of its shoulders was parallel to hers. The pressure of its gaze squeezed at her insides. But she stood her ground, even as it answered her question.

"Your heart."

EIGHT

*M*agic did exist.

Dee felt it in that basement. It hung around those two strange boys, around that smudge on the ceiling, clinging to the otherness that was the demon.

Real magic, Dee thought, and wished she could tell her eight-year-old self. But it wasn't princesses and fairies, knights and vows. It was that darker flavor of magic, spools of stolen gold and promised firstborn children. It was the huntsman cutting out Snow White's—

"Heart," she said.

It took a moment to register. And then her heart was racing, thumping so hard it felt like the demon was already trying to take it from her. She pressed a fist to her breastbone.

This hadn't been on any of the websites—they said it was always a *limb*, not a *vital organ*. Or in this case, the most vital of vital organs.

"But I—" she started to say, and then stopped. "I'll die."

It sighed and held up a pale hand. "You'll live. A twenty-four-month lease is my usual price. I take your heart for two years, and during that time you do my bidding."

A laugh snaked up her throat. "You want to lease my heart?"

"Yes," said the demon, inclining his head. Because it was a *he*, no matter how much Dee tried to think of it as alien. It was a beautiful, courteous, absolutely terrifying *he*.

"How will I live without my heart?" she asked.

"Your body will be in a sort of stasis. You won't age or change physically. You will simply…be."

"Be what?" said Dee.

He smiled, and the expression was cool and impenetrable. "That's entirely up to you."

She suddenly felt keenly aware of her own heartbeat, her pulse in her throat, in her wrists, even in her fingertips. Dee glanced over her shoulder, taking in that smudge on the ceiling, the smell of dust, and the rats skirting the room's edges. And the two boys, just out of earshot, conversing quietly.

Something in the room *shifted*.

It was the air pressure—similar to the sensation of someone opening a window, of fresh air spilling into a room. Dee inhaled, smelled hot metal and sand.

"We need to do this now," said Cal, his voice rising in pitch.

Dee forced herself to breathe through her mouth. "What they're doing—is it dangerous?"

The look the demon gave her was almost approving. "Yes."

"Could I die?"

That approval warmed further. "It's a possibility."

She wasn't stupid.

She knew how this would likely end—some cruel twist of fate, a wish turned against the maker.

And then she thought of home.

She imagined that house, the faded carpet and the brown bottles, the sharpness of her mother's collarbone when she hugged Dee, the scent that clung to her father—sweat and something sour and stale. She imagined what it would be like to sleep there, night after night, just waiting for the next blowup. For the shouting that reverberated through the walls and permeated her chest. She remembered when she had been small enough to wedge herself between the wall and her bed, humming quietly to block out the noise, hoping they'd forget she was there.

She wouldn't fit in that spot anymore. She'd have to find a new place to hide.

She would rather die.

That last thought settled into place, and she felt stronger because of it. There was some comfort in knowing that if her life were destroyed, it would be her own decision and no one else's. She met the demon's eyes.

"I am the Agathodaemon," he said.

Dee knew the correct words; the vow had been the first thing to show up in all the search engines.

"I'm Deirdre Moreno and I agree to the covenant," she said, then added, "Agathodaemon."

He didn't move, and the moment dragged by. Dee wiped sweaty hands on her jeans. "So...now what?" she said, when the silence was too much. "Do we sign something or...?"

"No," the Agathodaemon said, and then he was in front of her. "But you might feel a slight pinch." The blue in his eyes seemed to swallow her—she couldn't look away, not even when she felt his hand on the neckline of her shirt, gentle and quick as a thief, and then—

—agony.

NINE

The world was very quiet.

That was her first thought. She swayed on her feet and reveled in the silence. It was so marvelous that she didn't care when her knees began to give way.

Hands gripped both her arms and kept her upright.

And then the world came back, with a snap and a hiss, like turning on a television. Everything returned—sight, sound, even the sensation of saliva building up in the back of her throat.

"Don't you dare be sick on me," said a voice, and Dee managed to look up. The one holding her upright was James Lancer. His face was drawn with nerves. "Come on, now. Good—swallow it back down."

Dee swallowed bile she hadn't known was there.

"Oh, come on," said Cal. He was standing beside them, hands out as if ready to catch her. "It's not like she'd ruin your clothes, Lancer."

"It's more the smell I'm worried about," said James. "Who knows what it'll attract."

Dee opened her mouth. She felt oddly numb, like the time she'd been on narcotics after getting a tooth pulled. The world wasn't quite there—or maybe she wasn't quite there. "I'm all right."

James loosened his grip on her arms, but he didn't let go.

Dee took a moment to glance around. She half wanted to see if it was true—to see if the demon had truly taken her heart. She didn't *feel* any different; there was no gaping hole in her chest and she could still breathe. If anything, she felt lighter.

Cal spoke again. "She'll have to be the doorman. If she can barely stand up, there's no way she's walking into a void."

"That's fine," said James. "It'd be a shame to let the parka go to waste. Hey, Prep School Girl"—she could almost hear the capital letters in James's voice—"what's your name?"

Dee swallowed again. "Dee," she said, still trying to fight through the dizziness.

"All right, Dee," said Cal. "You're going to be the doorman. All you need to do is climb that ladder and push yourself halfway into the void. And then you don't move, understand? You'll stabilize the entrance, keep it open when the void implodes."

"You'll be our living doorstop," said James helpfully.

"Thought that thing wasn't supposed to open," said Dee. She blinked at the smudge.

"When we collapse it, the mouth will be the first thing to go," said Cal. "If there's a person in the entrance, it'll ensure we can both get out. All you have to do is stand there, all right?"

Dee thought about it. Moving sounded like an epically bad idea at the moment, but she waved James's hands away and tried to stand on her own. She'd manage. She'd managed through worse.

"Good girl," said Cal. "You'll go through first."

Dee took a halting step and then another. She reached for the ladder, grateful to have something to steady herself with. She took a few seconds and just breathed. The numbness was beginning to recede, leaving pinpricks of sensation. It felt like the times her leg had gone to sleep and she'd tried to shake off the discomfort.

She put one foot on the ladder and stepped up. She'd never been afraid of heights, but in her current state, a little wariness was only sensible. She took each rung slowly, pausing to test her balance. Finally, she reached the top of the ladder, just beneath the smudge. Closer up, she saw what it really was—a small circle about four feet across, misting in and out of existence.

Dee pressed her palms to the ladder's metal surface and pushed herself upward, into the smudge of unreality.

And the world ripped apart.

Wind tore at her hair; it was flung into her eyes and mouth and she blinked instinctively, trying to push it away with her arm.

She looked to her left and saw dust swirling in the wind. The ground crumbled beneath her left hand, and she thought it was sand until she saw the flecks of black and gray. It was crumbling pavement, almost exactly the same type as in the basement floor. Shadows rose around her like walls—in the same layout as the basement below.

It was the same world, a reflection of it, distorted by time and wind and some otherness that she couldn't place.

A mirror world, she thought. She couldn't be sure how far it went on.

Dee glanced down. Her feet were still on the ladder, in the real world, while her torso was wedged in this place.

Our living doorstop, James had said.

Something moved beneath her. Dee looked down and saw Cal struggling up the ladder, carrying something heavy on his back. She tried to give him room, but there was only so much space on the ladder. Cal eased past her, his foot barely avoiding her hand, and fully emerged into that other place.

He gave her a small smile and extended a hand downward. James grasped it and Cal pulled him up. They sat on the edge for a moment, the wind pulling at their hair and clothes. They nodded at each other, and Cal swung the heavy bag from his shoulder. James took one strap and Cal the other.

They struggled against the wind—James's parka protected him against grains of pavement. Cal looked like he was having a harder time; he had one arm up, as if to ward off the wind.

Then the two of them vanished behind one of the shadow walls.

Dee remained there, half in and half out of reality. The tiny grains of cement stung her eyes and she squinted through the haze.

This all felt *new*. She couldn't have said why, but something about it reminded her of the smell of freshly laid concrete, of buildings with nothing more than a skeleton of metal, of the first rumble of thunder in a storm. It was new, a thing still forming. This dust, this wind, it wasn't tearing the world down...it was building it up.

She wasn't sure how much time passed. It could have been five or ten minutes. The world continued to move around her with dizzying speed. The shadow walls were solidifying, and even the ground felt stronger beneath her palm. She wondered what would happen if this place became whole.

A noise made her turn. It rang out, even louder than the wind. A shout.

Fear cut through the rest of her numbness. Dee's fingers

dug into the ground and she turned, trying to find the source of the noise. It was difficult to pirouette while still balanced atop the ladder, but she managed to twist far enough to see a figure race out of the shadows.

James and Cal were sprinting toward her. Cal barreled through one of the shadow walls, and it shattered like thin glass. Pieces of solid, glittering black hit the ground. He was grinning as he ran, an exuberant triumph in his face.

Something behind him moved. It shifted out from behind one of the shadows, one long limb extending as if in question. Not an arm or a hand—it wasn't anything mammalian. It reminded Dee of things she saw in tanks at the Newport Aquarium—boneless and devastatingly quick. Something that looked terribly like claws extended from the tip.

She stared hard, unable to look away, suddenly caught by the realization that if that thing moved, she wouldn't be able to escape. Not until James and Cal had passed through the entrance.

That's when she truly understood: She stood in a door. And where there was a door, there was something to venture through it.

Cal arrived first. He lunged through the mouth of the void and fell to the ground.

When James reached Dee, he never slowed down. He grabbed her arm and lurched through the barrier. She felt a jerk, a sharp snap of release as if some cord had been broken, and she began to fall. The ladder buckled beneath them and she found herself in midair.

Cal broke their fall. She wasn't sure if it was intentional or not, but he landed on hands and knees and she slammed into his back. His arms gave out and there was one last moment of freefall before everything calmed. The wind was gone and in its place was that odd quiet. Her skin was raw and she felt grains of sand under her shirt. James was beside her, panting, and one of the fuzzy threads of James's parka was in her mouth, and her knee was probably digging into Cal's thigh, but Dee didn't move. Wasn't sure she could move. The moment she moved, she'd have to accept what she'd just seen. James let out a huff of breath, pushing himself to his knees. Cal wheezed, the air driven out of him.

Dee rolled over, eyes drawn to the ceiling, where she caught sight of the smudge. It trembled, turned in on itself, like the last of bathwater being drained away.

"What was that?" said Dee.

"What was what?" James rubbed at his chin and his fingers came away bloody. He grimaced and reached down with his clean hand, offering it to Dee. She hesitated, then let him pull her upright.

She looked around the room, but it was empty.

No demon.

"That," said Dee. "In there—it's not like our world. And what was that thing—"

"Doesn't matter," said James.

Dee breathed hard. Now that the numbness was entirely gone, fear twisted her insides. "But what about—"

Cal shook his head and she fell silent. "Don't ask now," he said, but he said it gently. "It's too new. No answer we can give you will satisfy. Wait a week, then ask us."

Dee was shaking, and it took her a moment to steady herself. "What—what am I supposed to do now? Where's the demon?"

James ran a hand through his hair. Sand fell through his fingers, scattered along the fabric of his parka. He shook himself before looking at Dee again. His face was more composed than hers. "Go home," he said. "Things will look more normal after you've gotten a night's sleep."

She gaped at him. It felt as though her life had begun anew here in this basement, and she was unsure of how to move forward. Leaving, stepping into the world without a heart—how did a person do that?

James's expression softened. "Look, I get it. You're panicking right now." He edged closer, until she had no choice but to look him in the eye. He made a motion as if to touch her arm, but then his hand fell away. "A demon just ripped your heart out. By all rules of the universe, you should be dead. I should be dead. But you know what we're going to do in the meantime?"

"What?"

"Live," he said.

He reached down and took her hand. Gently, he pried her fingers open and placed something soft in her palm, closed her fingers around it. "Keep this on you at all times," he said quietly. "Don't lose it." He gave her hand one last squeeze, then he was straightening his parka, turning to stride through the basement doors. Cal nodded to her, smiling encouragingly, then he left, too. Dee found herself alone; she shifted and found the concrete floor slick with grains of sand.

Her gaze fell on the object in her palm.

She didn't realize what it was—not at first. It was a lump of bloodred yarn. There was a scrap of paper with an address scribbled on it, but that wasn't what had caught her attention. Her fingers stroked one soft edge. She'd seen this before, tangled around the demon's fingers. Now she saw exactly what he'd been working on.

Resting in her palm was a knitted heart.

And that's when she finally realized why the world was so quiet.

There was no pulse in her ears.

TEN

The first time James Lancer lost his heart, he was in Rome. He thought it a bit of a cliché, if he were being honest with himself.

It was early summer and the streets were flooded with tourists. James had been living in an apartment with a friend for several months, paying his way with the crumpled euros he made as a street artist. He joined the other flocks of painters carting their wares to the top of the Spanish Steps, to the view of the modern and the old—the carts selling roasted hazelnuts near thousand-year-old ruins. After setting up his paintings for tourists to browse, he would begin work on a new piece; it was always better to be working on something in view of potential customers. It made him look less like a merchant hawking his wares, and more like an artist who just happened to have his work for sale.

Being an artist was one part talent, two parts illusion.

He had come to Rome on vacation, or at least that was what he told the bored-looking customs official, and he had simply never left. Whether this was legal or not, he didn't know. But he was pretty sure that the Italian authorities had more important things to worry about than a seventeen-year-old crashing on a friend's couch.

And he liked it here; he liked the four buildings that made up the apartment complex, towers with a small courtyard in between. He liked the clotheslines that hung between windows and how everyone seemed to use them; he liked the smell of rain on wet cobblestones, how storms seemed to blow in and out in a matter of hours, how the sunlight cast long shadows across ruins older than anything he could imagine. He even liked how he had to count out his money in coins, how he fumbled through the language and was nearly brained once by a tourist with a selfie stick.

There was a romance to this life, a brilliant chaos, and he embraced it.

But today was about business. James made sure his pieces were carefully settled before unfolding a tiny three-legged stool and seating himself upon it. He had a half-finished piece from last week—a small watercolor the size of a postcard. He returned to the piece, his gaze reaching across the horizon, trying to find the right lines and colors to capture. That was the most difficult part. Knowing what to include and what to leave out, how to take reality and condense it into something eternal. He dipped his brush into the water, then swirled it through a blue paint, and set bristles to canvas.

He painted like he did everything else—with fervor. He thought his own impatience bled into the lines of his work, and that was why he favored watercolor. It was more forgiving than oils. It was less precise, looser. The flaws could be explained away as part of the medium.

A woman stopped by to watch him work. He gave her a subtle once-over—middle-aged, with pressed slacks and a fresh Sephora bag tucked under her arm. "Please browse," he said, in his stilted Italian. Then, when her brows creased, he added in more fluid English, "Go ahead and look, if you want."

Comprehension dawned on her face and she gave him a smile. His watercolors were carefully arranged by size, stacked with the smallest ones at the front. She began flipping through them, eyes flicking over the scenes of the Trastevere, a winding alleyway with a stray cat, the sun setting over the Colosseum, an outdoor scene at a cafe. She smiled down at the painting and seeing her amazement was like a drug, a shot of euphoria straight to the heart.

The only time James felt truly happy was when someone liked his work.

They haggled—it was expected at places like this, and he accepted thirty euros for one of the mid-sized paintings. It was wrapped in tissue paper, slipped into a bag, and he smiled at her when she walked away, taking a piece of him with her.

Another painting in the world; another little scrap of his life that would outlive him.

He tried not to think about the future. He had been told he didn't have one enough times that he believed it. But when he did allow his thoughts to stray in that direction, it was always to years ahead when he would be in some grave and his paintings would live on.

Gritting his teeth, he set his still-drying watercolor beside him, picked up a fresh piece of paper, and went to work. The world drifted on around him, and he listened to church bells and the sound of irate taxi drivers honking at one another.

When his stomach ached with hunger, he packed up his supplies, tucking them into his shoulder bag. He bought *suppli* from a street vendor and ate the rice balls while leaning against the stone railing of the steps.

It was times like these he could almost forget himself; forget the ever-present anxiety that hummed in the back of his mind like a badly tuned radio. He was always keenly aware of his own insignificance, of how he yearned to be more, to do more to—

To just fucking matter, for once.

He was walking down the street, toying with the idea of

working on a new painting, when he felt a whisper of sensation against his left hip.

Instinctively, he glanced behind him and was just quick enough to see a flash of fingers as they lifted James's wallet from his pocket. The thief was probably about James's own age, and his gaze was fixed on his work so intently that it took the pickpocket a second to realize James was staring at him.

A breath. A heartbeat.

Frozen in time, a teenage thief holding his wallet, and then the boy was gone, running, tearing across the street.

Sometimes, James looked back upon this moment and wondered what might have happened if he hadn't given chase. If he had simply let the thief run away with his euros and his American driver's license.

But James did give chase. He sprinted forward, across the street, and into an adjoining park. There were children and tourists, strollers and cameras, but he ignored them all.

The thief made a mistake—he rounded a turn into an alley, where there were two cars parked illegally, cutting off his route of escape. If he had been expecting them, perhaps the thief could have leaped atop the hood and vaulted along in his merry escape, but the sudden obstacle came as a surprise and James saw indecision play out in his jerky, halting steps. The kid glanced from side to side, whirling around to face James, and James was sure this was when the thief would give up and toss his wallet on the ground like some kind of peace offering.

But then a pocketknife was in the thief's hand and James understood exactly how badly he had miscalculated this encounter.

And in that moment the demon stepped around the corner.

It was male, coldly good-looking, and he might have been pretending to be anything from a banker to a supermodel. Despite the sunlight, he had an umbrella in his left hand.

James wondered how this looked—a teenage pickpocket wielding a small knife while some stupid American tourist stood with his hands outstretched, reaching for his own wallet.

The demon eyed James with a lazy interest, like a lion gazing at a gazelle. Only a full belly would keep it from making a move.

The thief looked at the demon and narrowed his eyes. He rattled off something derisive in Italian. James couldn't be sure, but the tone of his voice sounded familiar, like all the times James had told someone to fuck off.

The thief wasn't afraid of the demon.

He looked at the demon as if he were just another wealthy idiot. As if he were human.

He didn't know. He didn't know what the demon was—he thought he *was* human.

James couldn't understand it; the thing's otherness was plain to see. There should have been people flocking around the demon, begging to trade fingers and toes for impossible miracles.

But there weren't.

And then a memory came to him. A whisper at a party, the air filled with sour smoke, a plastic cup filled with beer at his lips. A girl with a prosthetic foot, a girl so beautiful she was almost painful to look at. She had leaned close, her fingers on his shoulder, whispered to him that demons only appeared to those who needed them. Seeing one meant that it was fate—it was meant to happen.

The thief ran. He took advantage of James's distraction and James let him.

The demon watched as the thief darted away. "Did I interrupt something?"

The sun beat on the back of James's neck. Sweat rolled down his stomach, and his fingers were still slick with the grease of his lunch. But he stepped forward without hesitation.

He would not waste this opportunity. After all, every heartbeat could be his last.

Turned out, he was more right than he knew.

ELEVEN

Gremma returned from spring break in a rumpled, mascara-smudged state. She made a sound like a dying animal when Dee turned on her bedside lamp.

"Sorry," said Dee, and flicked off the light. "How was your spring break?"

"Not very memorable."

"Because nothing happened or because you don't actually remember what happened?" asked Dee. Part of her took a perverse delight in her roommate's suffering.

Gremma blinked, as if she didn't know quite how to answer.

Dee said, "Is that ketchup or blood on your shirt?"

Gremma glanced down. "Not mine."

"That doesn't answer the question."

"Ignorance," said Gremma, with as much dignity as she could muster, "is a good policy." She pressed the heels of her hands against her forehead, as if she was trying to hold her brain together. "Next year, we stay in."

"We?"

Gremma's fingers eased apart, and one eye slid over Dee, disconcertingly perceptive. "You look more hungover than I am. So you went out? Met some people? Did something crazy?"

Dee considered several answers before saying, "Ignorance is a good policy." Her fingers went to the soft yarn of the knitted heart in her pocket.

The average resting heart beats between sixty and ninety times a minute. It varies from person to person, depending on age and fitness level. Dee knew her own resting heart rate had been around seventy—she'd had to take her own pulse during her last gym class.

Dee spent hours sitting with the knitted heart tucked into the crook of her elbow. With her left hand, she kept two fingers on her throat. Waiting, searching. For that familiar flutter of sensation, for any hint of movement.

But there was nothing.

She tried not breathing. It didn't hurt, not exactly, but

something about it felt wrong. Stasis, the demon had said. Her body would simply go on without her heart. But did that mean all her other systems were frozen? What about going to the bathroom? Eating? Was she going to spend the next two years without her period?

Actually, that might not be so bad.

But there was a sense that something vital had been taken from her. Which it *had*. She felt strangely hollow.

Two years. Two years of this.

Two years, and then her life was utterly her own.

That thought calmed her when nothing else would. She would never have to worry about going home, about cramming herself into tiny nooks, hoping to remain unnoticed, would never have to force herself to look down and swallow so many hurtful words that her stomach was always in knots.

And with this hollowness came something else—buoyancy. She felt lighter without her heart, without the throb and pulse of it.

It was easy to slip into old routines, to ignore the knitted heart shoved in her purse and the deadened sensation in her chest. She could tell herself everything was fine, everything was normal, and there were stretches of time she actually believed it.

It felt as if everyone should have known just by looking at her. Dee spent her classes feeling oddly conspicuous, waiting for someone to touch her and realize. Surely something like this left a mark on a person, some indelible sign that some part of her was missing.

A week after her encounter with the demon, she woke to a strange text from an unknown number. It contained a bank account and password. When she checked the balance online, she let out such a curse that she woke Gremma from a sound sleep.

Perhaps the demon didn't know how much schools cost these days, because he'd overshot it a bit.

All right. He'd overshot by a lot.

Brannigan was paid for.

So was college. And possibly her first year of grad school.

But she would be damned—*if she wasn't already*—before she informed him of his error. She stared at those numbers and thought: *This is how much a human heart is worth.*

Dee picked up the scrap of paper James had given her at the hospital. She knew Portland well enough to recognize the address's general location—Pearltown, an odd place for a demon to make its lair. Somehow she had thought this paper would lead her to a sewer or a castle.

It was a Saturday. She had a signed permission slip that allowed her off campus on weekends—she had forged her mother's signature herself. If she wanted to check out this address, she might as well get it over with.

"I need to get out of here," said Gremma, as if hearing

Dee's thoughts. She was sprawled across her bed, a chemistry book before her. "You want to come get coffee with me?"

Dee hesitated.

"Can't," she said. "I've got errands to run."

"And you can't make time for a teensy coffee with your roommate in between whatever you're doing?"

Dee didn't bother to think about it. "Nope."

Gremma rolled over. "You're heartless sometimes."

Dee snorted out a laugh. She snagged her purse and her bus pass and hurried out of the room.

The address did not lead to a sewer. Nor a dark tower, a castle, or a cave.

It was one of those warehouses—the kind that had been converted into apartments for young up-and-comers. There was a food truck parked on the opposite curb, and a man in a custom suit held the door for Dee when she walked into the building. It was clean, neat, and everything she had not expected. She took the stairs, too keyed up to stand still in the elevator.

The apartment door was slightly ajar, a sliver of light piercing the gap between wood and frame. Dee swallowed, pushed on the door, and it swung silently open.

Inside was a large space of unfinished brick and concrete.

It looked as though some designer had gotten fed up and abandoned the project halfway through. One entire wall was nothing but windows, crisscrossed with metal. The whole area was wide open, with curtains cordoning off what must have been a bedroom. Closest to the door were two couches and a ratty recliner. There was a kitchen—if she could really call it that—with a fridge, a microwave, a portable camp stove, and a cluster of tables that were clearly being used as counter space by whoever lived here.

"Hello?" she called.

A groan came from the clump of furniture. Dee jumped, ready to flee, but the noise hadn't sounded aggressive.

"Cora?" It was definitely a male voice, rusty and surprisingly familiar. "If we're being sent on another mission, you'd better have brought bagels." A hand appeared, grasping at the back of the couch, and a face followed the hand.

It wasn't the demon. It was Mr. Not-Homeless. *James*, she thought, taking a moment to place the name. His hair was rumpled and stuck up on one side, and his expression was fuzzy with exhaustion.

"You're not Cora," he observed.

"And you're definitely not homeless," she said.

He pushed himself off the couch. He was dressed in an old flannel shirt and sweats. His feet were bare, and something about that made her feel safer. If she did run, he'd have to put on shoes before giving chase.

He rubbed a hand over his eyes. "Dee, right?"

She nodded.

James let out a breath. "All right. All right." He repeated the words quietly, as if they weren't meant for her. "I'll call the welcoming committee. You"—he waved at the couch—"make yourself at home."

She hesitated, unsure about venturing farther into the apartment, but then James was walking away, his gait unsteady. He blindly reached out and hit a button on the coffee machine before tottering into the curtained-off portion of the apartment.

The couch was Ikea-standard, a model made for comfort and sturdiness. There was a gray stain across its red fabric. And sitting at the coffee table was a knitted red heart. She picked it up. It was dirtier than hers, worn, and a few strings were knotted together as if they'd come undone and been clumsily fixed. Papers were everywhere, smudged with charcoal and pencil. Dee set the knitted heart down, picked up one of the papers instead.

It was a drawing that belonged in some art history book. A Renaissance painting before it became a painting.

It was...beautiful.

The sound of running water came from what must be the bathroom, and then James strode back into the living area. He'd put on jeans and his hair was wet, as if he'd run dampened fingers through it. He poured two cups of coffee into paper cups, stirred in liberal amounts of cream and sugar. With a careless little gesture, he pushed the crumpled sketches aside and placed one cup before Dee.

A knock came at the door.

"It's open," called James, taking a swig of his coffee.

A girl around Dee's age strode into the apartment, carrying a paper bag in one hand and a folder in the other.

She was pretty, with dark skin and smooth hair that sent a pang of yearning through Dee. She'd tried straightening her hair a few times, but her stubborn curls refused to flatten. Self-consciously, Dee ran a hand through her bushy hair and glanced down at her own jeans and flip-flops. This new girl wore a blouse and lace skirt, and she seemed to carry herself with a poise that Dee could never manage. But the moment she saw Dee, the girl hurried over and without so much as a greeting, she pulled her into a hug.

Dee went rigid.

"Hey," the girl said, voice close to Dee's ear. She spoke with a gentleness usually reserved for small children or wounded animals. "It'll be all right. Whatever James told you—ignore it."

Dee waited a beat, then pulled back. The girl let her.

"I haven't told her anything, Cora," said James. "So you can stop with the Team Mom routine."

The girl didn't exactly glare at James, but it was close. "She looks terrified. What have you told her?"

"Not a thing," said James. "She's seen most of it for herself already." He sat with his legs in a tangled sprawl. He took up half the couch and he looked comfortable doing so.

"Why did you give me your address?" asked Dee quietly.

"You have questions. The others can answer some of them," said James. "And as I'm the only person with a usable apartment…" He let the thought trail off.

Cora rose and strode to the kitchen. She upended her paper bag onto the counter. Half a dozen bagels spilled out. "Barely usable. Please tell me you have a knife somewhere?"

"And here I thought introductions were going to be awkward," drawled James. "Dee, this is Cora—our fearless and self-appointed leader. And knives are in the second drawer over."

Dee glanced between Cora and James; she wondered if all demons kept teenagers at hand to do their dirty work. "How many of us work for the Agathodaemon?"

"Four of us, counting you," said Cora. She vanished behind the counter and reappeared a moment later. "You've met Lancer. There's also Cal and me." She scowled at something on the counter. "Okay, when I said, 'knife,' I meant something other than the plastic kind."

"You mean those things you have to wash?" James beamed at her.

Cora picked up a disposable plastic butter knife and began cutting a bagel. Well, cutting was perhaps too generous a word, Dee thought. Shredding, maybe.

"Dee's practically an old pro at this," said James. "She helped us in the hospital. Not sure if you need to give her the usual lecture."

Dee glanced between Cora and James, taking in their rapid-fire quips. It was clearly a regular occurrence, Cora coming here and complaining about the cutlery. Even James's and Cora's jibes felt blunted, as if the insults had lost their edge over time.

"How long ago did you make your deal?" Dee asked, looking at Cora.

Cora straightened. "I was the first heartless in Portland. That's why I'm in charge. Seniority."

"And your being naturally bossy didn't come into it at all." James smirked.

"And your being naturally lazy also had nothing to do with it," Cora replied smoothly. She put one mangled half of a bagel into the toaster. "No wonder the Daemon didn't want you in charge."

She pronounced it differently than Dee did, and she could almost hear the capital letter. "You mean the demon?"

"Don't call him that," said James. He walked to the counter, reaching for the bagels. He picked one flavored with dried onions. "He doesn't like it."

Dee felt herself frown. "What's the difference between *demon* and *Daemon*?"

A new voice spoke. "One hard vowel."

Cal strolled into the apartment, his hands shoved in his pockets, smiling at Dee.

"Dee, you remember Cal," said James, waving his hand in a lazy introduction.

Cal sat beside Dee. "You know," he said, "I don't think I ever got your full name. It isn't really Dee, right?"

"Deirdre Moreno," said Dee, after a moment's hesitation. She always felt a little self-conscious; she had been the last person in her first-grade class to be able to properly *spell* their own name. "I was named after my grandmother."

"You have no idea how lucky you are," replied Cal. "Carroll was the name of some dead uncle. And apparently, I was a difficult birth, so my mother decided to curse me with it."

"Seems little has changed since then," said James brightly.

Cal gave him a narrow-eyed look. "And when was the last time you showered?"

James took another bite of bagel.

"Well," said Cora, ignoring the boys, "we're glad to have you, Dee. I suppose you'll need our numbers." Without asking, she reached out and took Dee's purse. It was half open, and before Dee could utter a word, Cora fished a cheap cell phone from it. "I'll give you our contact info and loop you in on the troop texts."

"Troop?" repeated Dee, sure she had heard Cora wrong.

Cora took a delicate bite of bagel, chewed, and swallowed before speaking. "We're the Daemon's Portland troop of heartless. There are other troops, in different places around the country—a few international ones, too."

"Like the one I transferred from," said James.

Cora ignored him. "Dee, if you want the basics, here they are: Three people are needed to destroy the voids. When a void appears—and it doesn't happen that often, maybe once every few weeks—the Daemon will fetch us. Two people will carry the explosives into the void, get them to the center of it, and then set off the trigger. The third person stands in the mouth to ensure that when the void starts to explode—"

"Implode," said Cal. "It does not *explode*, it *implodes*."

"—Implode," said Cora. "The third person keeps the mouth of the void steady so the other two can escape."

A memory came back to Dee—that inhuman leg, there one moment and gone the next. No one had mentioned things *living* in the voids.

"What are they?" she said. "The voids, I mean."

Cora, Cal, and James all went silent. A look was exchanged, one heavy with meaning. "Thing is," said James, "we don't really know that. I mean, we have our theories, but..."

Dee drew in a breath. "And what are your theories?"

Cora spoke first. "I think they're doors," she said. "A temporary portal into another...world, I guess you could say. And the Daemon uses us to close those doors. So obviously what's on the other side is a threat to him." She lowered her lashes, and spoke more quietly. "What is the natural enemy of a demon?"

Oh.

Well.

That wasn't gut-clenchingly terrifying *at all*.

"Angels," Dee said flatly. "You think we're slamming doors on angels?"

But that didn't make sense. What she'd seen in the void wasn't at all angelic, not unless stories about angels had been wildly inaccurate.

"That's one theory," said Cal with a little nod. "*I* still think the so-called demons are actually very advanced aliens. The voids could be a warping of reality used to travel long distances in a matter of moments."

"But then how do you explain the magic?" said Cora.

Cal chewed absentmindedly on the edge of his paper cup. "Well, if you sent us back in time a few hundred years, I'm pretty sure our phones would be considered magic, as well."

Dee looked at James. He had remained silent through all this, watching Cal and Cora with the air of a detached outsider. "And what do you think?" she asked.

He jerked in surprise, as if he hadn't been expecting the question. "Don't know," he said, a little too quickly. "Guess it never mattered all that much to me. We do our job, and we get what we want. It's messed up, but it works."

Dee gazed around the small group—Cora as the leader, Cal as the brains, and James as the...she didn't know. He didn't seem to have an obvious role, other than the Guy with the Apartment.

"So, three people," said Dee. "That's how many you need to destroy a void. But then...why would the Daemon have made a deal with me? I mean, he already had the three of you..."

Her words trailed off.

There had been something inside that void. Something inhuman and quick. She remembered the flash of motion, the sense of a presence. She remembered the grim look on James's face as he sprinted toward the void's entrance.

Three people were required.

But she suspected the demon would want a fourth—just in case one of them was killed.

TWELVE

The second void appeared on a Wednesday.

Dee was striding out of the science building when she saw the Daemon.

She froze—a deer catching the scent of a wolf, and if she had a heart it would have been slamming against her ribs. The demon was framed in the doorway of a fire exit. He looked as cool and pristine as ever, that umbrella tucked beneath his arm, and he watched her with ancient, far-seeing eyes.

Or perhaps that was just her imagination getting the better of her.

Students milled about, half going to after-school activities and the others heading toward the dorms. She gripped the strap of her shoulder bag, nails digging into the nylon, and forced her feet to move. Dee slipped through the crowds, just another student eager to be done with midweek classes, until she stepped into the shadow of the science building. And then she was standing beside him.

"Yes?" she said.

The Agathodaemon smiled. "Walk with me."

The Daemon led her away from the buildings and the sidewalks and the comfortably crowded paths. The edge of campus bled into untended trees—brambles and thick under-growth made passage impossible. Some students thought it might be deliberate, to discourage anyone sneaking away through the trees.

The smell of rain drifted up from the damp grass, and Dee tried to focus on that—on the familiarity of her surroundings. It felt as though she had stepped into yet another fairy tale, but then again, if she could stay grounded in the here and now, perhaps she would remain with one foot in the real world. She tried to look at him as if he were what he pretended to be—a thirtysomething, absurdly good-looking man with dark hair and bright blue eyes. She thought of him as human and nothing else.

"I see you are still functioning," said the Agathodaemon.

Well, that thought lasted a good two seconds.

She forced herself not to scratch at the back of her neck. "Shouldn't I be?"

The corner of his mouth turned up. "It does not take,

sometimes," he admitted. "Some people hold their hearts quite closely, and without them they simply... stop."

His voice carried a trace of admiration, as if there was something noble to be found in the bodies of those victims he left behind. But were they truly victims? If they made a deal, knowing fully what they were trading for a wish—but then again, could a person ever truly know the consequences of giving away their heart?

The Daemon surveyed her with a small smile. "That is why I take the younger ones, you see. You already give parts of your heart away so easily—little fragments attached to celebrities, to hobbies, and to ill-fated love affairs. Your kind have the best chance at survival."

Dee felt her hand rise to her chest. She had never placed any true importance on bands or television shows or even boyfriends. Her own heart had remained locked tightly behind her ribs—at least, until she allowed a demon to take it.

"You have your knitted heart on you?" asked the Daemon.

Dee felt the lump in her pocket. "Yes."

"Good. Good. I would hate to lose such an... intriguing investment so soon."

There were so many questions that Dee could have asked—why a knitted heart mattered, why she was an investment, and an *intriguing* one at that—but what came out of her mouth was, "Why are you here?"

She wanted to *know.* Why a demon existed in a place

like this—if he was in fact a demon. Why he needed to be in Portland, in Oregon, in this world. But he seemed to take her question quite literally.

"There is a void," he said. "It is forming on the outskirts of a place called Beaverton."

That startled a laugh out of her.

He looked at her, a silent question forming in his unnaturally bright blue eyes.

She shrugged. "I know Beaverton. But let's just say no one would miss it."

He regarded her coldly. "You would not care for it if a void opened there. Nor anywhere within a hundred miles." A tilt of his head. "At least, you would not care for it in the few moments you had left to live."

She didn't quite *gulp*, but it was a near thing.

"Here is the address," he said, and held out a business card. On it was a scribbled address. "Call the others."

And then, before she could answer, he simply vanished.

〰〰〰〰〰

If she'd imagined James's car, she would have conjured up images of a brown clunker—probably held together by paint and duct tape. She would have been wrong, it turned out. When James pulled up to the curb, it was in a very sedate, very normal blue car. A Mom Car.

He met her on the curb, smiling as if this was something they did every day. There were rough edges, a rawness to his face that she appreciated more after seeing the flawless Daemon. She never knew she'd long for rumpled hair or scruff, but James was so human she nearly relaxed.

She didn't, though.

She was still Dee.

"I can't leave campus," she said, glancing up the sidewalk. "It's not a weekend."

Cora gazed at her, peering from her seat behind the steering wheel. It appeared that even though it was James's car, Cora insisted on driving.

"This is kind of required," said Cal, from the backseat. He had a magazine half-open on his lap, and he'd cranked the window down all the way. "Can't you just sneak away?"

Dee glanced about the parking lot. Sure, there was no one watching—odds were good that she could get away with it. But the dorm monitor would patrol the halls around seven—and it was five now. Two hours felt like too short a span of time.

And this school was what she'd sold her heart for.

Then again, she had a perfect record. Even if she was caught, she might just get a detention or a warning. And if she was truly late, maybe she could text Gremma, get her to stage a diversion.

She met James's eyes; they were crinkled at the corners in

a gentle smile. "I could call the school," he offered. "Pretend to be your dad or something, say there's a family emergency."

She answered without thought. "Oh, no. That'd get the school's attention, probably. My dad never calls."

A lift of his eyebrows; she had said too much. "I mean," she said quickly, "it's just—you know—parents are busy and all that."

Flustered, she hastened around to the other side of the car and yanked the door open. She slid into the backseat quickly. "Drive," she said, keeping her gaze lowered. "Please."

Once James was in the passenger seat, Cora hit the gas and yanked the car toward the main road. Dee glanced once over her shoulder, at the shrinking buildings of campus as they drove through the gate.

"Are we all set?" asked Cora. She was looking down at something near James's feet. "Car, check. Rocks, check. First-aid kit, check. Emergency rations, check."

"Emergency rations?" asked Dee, alarmed. "I thought we were just going to Beaverton."

Without so much as looking at her, James reached over and pulled open the glove compartment. Inside was a paper sack filled with half a dozen bagels.

"Check," said James.

"Cell phones?" said Cora.

"Check," said Dee, feeling her own phone in her pocket.

"Check," said Cal.

"C-4?" asked Cora.

"In the trunk," said Cal.

Dee went rigid. "Is that—is that safe?"

"So long as no one rear-ends us," said James cheerily.

⋙⋘⋙⋘

The drive to Beaverton took about thirty minutes. Cal had a map and called out directions from the backseat, guiding Cora into what looked like a half-deserted neighborhood. Dee caught a glimpse of a wall that was more spray paint than concrete, and newspapers sagged in the sewer drains. Despite her quip to the Daemon, there were good parts of Beaverton. This just wasn't one of them.

Cora took a sharp right, pulling down an alley. Then another left turn, and she slowed the car to a halt. They parked beside what looked like a decrepit brick building.

Fear fluttered in Dee's chest like a caged animal, struggling to get out. But something was strange, off; it was because there was no thudding heartbeat to accompany her fear. She was used to feeling it throb, set aflame by adrenaline, and she had never felt its absence more keenly.

James was whistling an off-key tune when they trudged toward the broken building. It was an old garage, if the struts and large glass door were anything to go by. But the place was deserted—the glass glittered upon the ground and a heavy layer of dust covered the interior.

The old building smelled of gasoline and rust, and small flickers of movement darted away from the beam of Cal's thin flashlight—more rats.

The explosives were in a duffel bag. Cora hefted the bag over one shoulder, ignoring any offers of help as she strode through the broken door without any hesitation. Dee froze.

What would they say if they were caught? Four teenagers, breaking into an abandoned building, a duffel bag full of C-4. They wouldn't be let off with a warning. They'd be branded hard criminals, maybe even terrorists—

A hand touched her elbow. Dee looked up, saw James looking at her. "We don't get caught," he said, so quietly that the others wouldn't be able to hear. "Trust me. The Daemon makes sure of that. We'd be useless to him in jail." He held out a thin flashlight, smiling just a bit. Not as if he were mocking her, but as if he understood.

Silently, she took it and switched it on.

The beam of the flashlight swept around another corner, and the sound of small, skittering claws intensified. Dee felt something pass over her foot—luckily, she was wearing her uniform-standard loafers rather than flip-flops, but the sensation made her shudder.

There were still old tires, flat and useless, piled around the room, and boxes of old steel bolts and shelves of other detritus not deemed valuable enough to be stolen.

And there was a void. A shimmer, a ripple, like heat rising from the pavement on a hot summer's day. It hung just a few inches off the grease-stained floor.

The others saw it, too, and they moved forward with an ease born of practice. Cora knelt before the shimmering patch of air and reached into her pocket. She came up with a small aerosol can of spray paint. And before Dee could ask why Cora was suddenly into tagging, Cora shook the bottle once, twice, then sprayed the air just in front of the void.

The paint misted through the air, then swerved right. Before Dee's eyes, the red paint simply vanished—but not before she saw the clear outline of the void's mouth. Well—it was certainly a more precise way of finding the void's entrance than tossing an empty bottle at it.

Dee glanced about the room, trying to take in everything at once. It seemed there was only one way in or out—the door they'd walked through. The broken windows were too high up for escape. She turned in a circle, and her foot hit something.

She stumbled, her flashlight falling to the concrete floor. She scooped it up, hands shaking, and aimed the beam down.

The light fell upon a rat. Unmoving, still, and dead.

It had been impaled—a thin metal rod shoved through it the way a child might pin a butterfly to a corkboard.

And then she saw what the creature had been killed with.

It was a knitting needle.

"He's been here," said Cora quietly.

Dee jerked in surprise. The other girl had approached while Cal and James talked between themselves.

Cora's cool gaze slid over the needle. "You see what he is, right?" There was a low, almost confidential tone to her voice. As if she were sure she spoke to an ally. "The others forget that he's a demon, but you don't. I know you're scared of him—and you should be. They're not right; they're not like us. We have to stick together."

Dee looked at Cora and for the first time wondered what she was doing here. Cora belonged in some high-powered internship, holding a clipboard and ordering people around—not standing over the body of a rat. "You made a deal with him, too," she said. It wasn't a question, but at the same time, it was.

Cora looked away. "I made a mistake," she said curtly.

Before Dee could ask what she meant, James called over. "Charges ready and timer set!"

"You mean, *I* readied the charges and set the timer," said Cal. "While you stood there and critiqued how fast I did it."

"Well, my part comes now," said James, smiling.

Cora straightened, ran a hand over her perfect hair, and said, "Dee, since you're the newbie, you watch. Cal will keep the void stable while James and I go inside."

Cal squatted down, then did a sort of crab-walk into the void.

Dee watched with fascination. She hadn't seen what being the human doorstop looked like from an outside view. Half of Cal simply vanished, like he had been sliced down the middle by a mirror. He glanced to his left, one eye seeing something Dee couldn't. Then he nodded, gesturing, and James and Cora stepped forward. James first, angling sideways to slip past Cal, and then Cora. They vanished, one after the other.

And then there was silence.

Dee felt her fists clench. She was too hot; whatever magic kept her in stasis did nothing for the feverish sweat that broke through her skin. She could feel it dampening her shirt.

She had not counted on the seconds dragging by like hours, the agony of waiting for the others to reappear. Cal appeared calm, crouching with his elbows on his knees and gaze resolutely forward. With only half of him visible, he reminded her of one of those statues with pieces missing, the eyes old and face worn.

Dee paced back and forth, checked her cell phone for the time. "How long does this usually take?" she asked.

One of Cal's eyes—the only one visible to Dee—flicked toward her. "Depends," he said. His voice warbled oddly, an echo of an echo.

"On?"

"If there's trouble."

At once, she remembered that creature. None of the other heartless had mentioned seeing anything like that, and she had not dared to mention her own glimpse of it—for fear of drawing attention to herself. She was still new to this, after all.

But still—the thought of what might lie beyond that flicker of unreality…

She needed to see.

"Could I look inside?" she asked.

She expected Cal to argue; it was what Cora would have done.

But Cal smiled slightly. "You won't like it."

"I want to look around," she replied. "I'll just be a moment. You can watch me the whole time, right?"

He nodded. "Go on and try it."

She ventured closer, hand reaching for the void. It felt like touching the surface of water—a slight resistance against her fingertips before it caved inward.

Fingers extended, she stepped past Cal and into the void.

It was like stepping through a door into a sandstorm. Wind flung her hair out of its ponytail and she found her breath yanked free of her lungs.

She stepped into this non-space, this half-formed world and—

—It knew her.

That was the only way she could describe it. This void knew her, tugged at something inside of her and then she was falling to her knees, sand and grit digging through the material of her uniform and—

—She is ten years old and trying to clean the bathroom. Her legs are too short, arms too stumpy, and she can't quite reach the mold behind the faucet—

Dee yanked herself free of the memories. It felt as if the void were pulling at her own mind, feeding on her memories.

—She is eight and so excited about a new cartoon, but then there is a voice telling her, "Only losers watch cartoons every day. You don't want to be a loser, do you?" And she is ashamed because she does want to watch cartoons—

—She is six and the house is quiet, heavy with silence; her mother has told her that Dad is feeling ill today and Dee does not know why—

She scrambled back on hands and knees. She hit Cal's leg and scooted to one side, until she felt cool pavement rather than hot sand, and she was panting as if she had just run a mile.

Cal looked down at her, smiling ruefully. "The void has hallucinogenic properties that kick in when you fully immerse yourself. Which is why I prefer to remain here, as the human doorstop."

"W-what?" she gasped.

Cal's face softened. "Voids make you see things," he said, with the calm benevolence that someone might use when trying to explain calculus to a golden retriever. "We don't know why or how."

Scrambling to her feet, she backed away from the void. It felt as if some of the grit were lodged in her throat.

"It's disturbing," said Cal. "It'll show you things you don't want to see. That's why the same people usually go into the voids. You get used to it, I guess. Cora and James are the old team. At least until Cora gets her heart back in a few months, and then the dynamic will change again."

The way he spoke was so normal, as if this were just another after-school job to him.

"W-what did you trade for?" she said raggedly. It was probably a rude question—she shouldn't have asked.

Cal shrugged. "Someone's life. It seemed fair." The words came so easily to him, as if he were utterly at peace with the fact he stood half in, half out of some piece of unreality. He checked his watch and then let out a sigh. "I hope this is all the Daemon needs done tonight. I've got an eight a.m. class tomorrow."

She blinked. "Aren't you still in high school?"

"Grad school, actually." When he caught sight of Dee's stare, he let out a little laugh. "Prodigy," he said, as if the word embarrassed him. "Studying physics—although I might fall back on astronomy if I get bored."

Her jaw dropped. "You're some kind of science genius?"

He flushed. "I wouldn't put it quite like that—but yeah."

"How do you..." Dee gestured at the void, at Cal himself, and then her hand dropped to her side. "How do you reconcile all this? Magic portals?"

Cal snorted. "It's not magic. It's...just something we don't understand yet. Which is why I'm going to unravel it." He said the words so matter-of-factly, as if explaining the unexplainable were something mundane. "Once I get my heart back, I'm writing a paper on this."

Dee rubbed at her hair. Small grains of sand scattered along the pavement and a moment later, Cora and James sprinted out of the void's mouth. They were windswept but grinning, and James high-fived Cal as he ducked into the real world.

"See?" gasped James. "Everything's good."

Dee watched as the void flickered. It curled in on itself, like water draining from a tub, and then it was gone.

As if it had never been.

THIRTEEN

Carroll Medina did not sell his heart.

He traded it on Craigslist.

When he was seventeen, he spent many days in a hospital room. His attention was torn between a stolen doctor's chart and a cardiovascular medical textbook. He did not know the right vocabulary, not at first, but after several days of reading, things seemed to settle into place.

Congestive heart failure.

Inoperable.

Cal overheard the doctors speaking to one another; a teenage boy seemed invisible to them, particularly when he sat quietly in the hall, his knees drawn to his chest. Perhaps they thought him asleep or ignorant, but he heard every word. When they were gone, Cal rose to his feet and strode back into the hospital room.

His grandfather was quiet and still—two words that Cal had never associated with his grandfather before. He was a robust man, even in his sixties, always working on their small garden or on home repairs.

Cal looked down at the older man, at the delicate lines around his eyes. At the slight rise and fall of his chest. At the work-worn hands, the same hands that had given Cal his first physics book. "You can do anything," Grandpa had said with a smile. "But whatever you do, I'm sure you'll be great at it." He'd stopped trying to tutor Cal years ago, when Cal had been given the title "gifted."

Gifted—or cursed, as he would have called it in middle school. He was too smart for his own peers, too young for those older kids he went to school with, and the weight of perfection seemed to drag at him. But through it all, Grandpa had been there. A stillness in a chaotic world, always smiling with his whole face.

Inoperable.

The word sounded so clinical. It was a detached way of stating the obvious.

Dying.

And all at once, Cal couldn't draw breath. His lungs felt hollow, his throat too full, and he found himself walking quickly, that walk shifting into a jog, then a run. Worn rubber soles slapping against the linoleum floor, past nurses and rolling beds, until he saw a door leading into a stairwell. He burst through it. The air was colder here, but it was still not enough. He nearly tripped over his own feet in his haste to get down the stairs.

He only slowed when he reached the parking lot. His chest heaved, every breath rasping through his throat.

Inoperable.

The word felt as if it had taken root inside of him, grown like some poisonous thing.

He gazed up at the stars, tried to comfort himself with his own insignificance. He was little more than a tiny ape, standing on the surface of a rock—one of many such rocks in this galaxy. His own grief would be a blip in time, there and gone again in a moment. Humans were helpless creatures, he thought. Good with tools and problem solving, sure, but they couldn't even fix a heart. They couldn't—no one could—

Well, he thought, no one human could.

Cal took a moment to consider it. Only a moment. Because his mind was already racing ahead, weighing cost and gain. A limb for a life. A limb for a life.

He could do it.

He would do it.

So he pulled his phone out of his pocket, and did the only thing he could think of.

He placed an online ad.

In the ensuing hours, he received countless e-mails—most of them spam, a few rather terrifying. Cal sorted through them, deleting them one by one, until he came to one that stood out.

It was three lines long.

A heart for a heart.
A life for a life.
Yes/No?

It was a joke. It had to be a joke. But Cal clicked the reply button and typed a single word.

Yes.

When he looked up from his phone, a man stood before him. He wore a dark suit, an umbrella tucked beneath his left arm. A thread of red yarn was caught on one of his lapels.

And he was smiling.

FOURTEEN

Dee was getting dressed when Gremma pushed into the room.

"Your dealer's here," she said. "He's lurking outside of the building—he's going to get the cops called on him if the dorm monitors see him."

Dee froze in the act of clipping on her bra. "What?" Her robe hung loose around her shoulders, and any moment now it was going to slip off, exposing her damp and chill back to the air.

It was a Saturday—and she had planned on spending her day alternating between an English essay and watching old episodes of some medical drama with Gremma.

"Your dealer," said Gremma. "He's out by the courtyard, asking anyone who passes by if they know a Dee."

Dee remained frozen, her robe slipping down one shoulder.

Gremma heaved a sigh. "He's got brown hair that really needs a cut. He probably hasn't shaved in a day or two. Kind of looks like a hot homeless guy. Any of this ringing a bell?"

Dee's stomach bottomed out. "James."

A light lit behind Gremma's eyes. "You *do* know him." She said the words with an almost childlike glee, as if overjoyed to have found Dee's deep, dark secret.

Oh, if only.

"Yes, but he is not my dealer," said Dee.

Gremma squinted through the window. "Really? Then... I don't know. Bookie? Secret crime lord?" She wriggled her hips in a vague motion. "Man of the night?"

"We...sort of know each other through an acquaintance."

Gremma's face spoke volumes. "*Sure.* Well, I'd recommend putting on a shirt before you go out to meet him."

Dee was wearing a shirt when she ventured out of her dorm. She also put on her second-best cardigan, skinny jeans, and flip-flops—hoping that perhaps if she dressed normally, maybe she could trick the universe into acting normally. Her knitted heart was shoved in her cardigan's pocket.

The courtyard was a small stretch of concrete and potted plants between the Whiteaker and Grover dorms, mostly used by the seniors to try to sneak a smoke. The flower beds smelled of old ashes.

James leaned against an overlarge flowerpot, checking his nails. When he heard her approach, he offered her a friendly grin. "Glad to see word reached you. I forgot my phone and somehow throwing pebbles at random windows seemed like a losing strategy."

"My roommate thinks I'm running drugs," said Dee flatly. "And that you're my dealer."

James blinked. "At least she thought I looked enterprising."

"She said you looked homeless."

James straightened the sleeves of his orange leather jacket. "It's vintage."

"You're going to get arrested for loitering," she said. "What are you doing here?"

He nodded at the dormitory. "You free to leave?"

"It's Saturday," she replied.

He tilted his head. "You know, that's not really an answer."

"This is boarding school, not prison," she said. "It's the weekend—I've got parental permission to leave."

"Ah." He flashed her a grin, one that was far too chipper for eight in the morning. "Perfect." He offered her his elbow, as if this were some old movie, but she made no move to take it.

"What are you doing?"

"At the moment, attempting to be gallant and gentlemanly. And apparently failing at it." He dropped his arm and instead ran a hand through his rumpled hair. "Look, I've got to run an errand for the Daemon and this particular task is easier with more than one pair of hands. It's not dangerous or even particularly interesting."

She crossed her arms. "What is it?"

"Rock collecting," he said, utterly deadpan. "Now, you don't have to come with if you don't want to. But I thought you might have questions you didn't want to ask with Cora and Cal around. This would be an opportunity."

She was about to refuse him—but James was smiling, so *hopeful,* and it suddenly occurred to her that he didn't want to run this errand alone. He wanted someone with him.

Dee was too well acquainted with loneliness not to recognize it in another.

She sighed. So much for her relaxing Saturday.

〰〰〰〰〰

They drove out of Portland. She watched the familiar sights slide by, in hues of gray and blue and green. Portland was a sprawl of city encroaching on tangled suburbs, but she liked it. There was a quiet hum of activity, a sense that there was always something going on beneath the surface. She rapped her fingers absentmindedly on the car's door as James drove. He was a restful car companion—he didn't blast the radio or try to roll down the windows.

"Where are we going?" Dee asked.

"A park," he answered. "Don't worry, I'll have you back long before curfew." He slid her a look, then his gaze went back to the road. "Speaking of which—you managed to get into your dorm all right after that void?"

Dee grimaced.

She hadn't, actually. Cora had dropped her off at the gate and Dee had snuck through the brambles and bushes, and slipped on a patch of moss. Knees muddied, hair even frizzier than usual, she had nearly managed to get into her dorm— until a teacher spotted her.

Dee had made up some quick story about needing samples of pond water for a biology experiment—and thankfully she'd been let off with a warning.

She explained as much.

"Ah, boarding school," said James, smiling. He glanced over his shoulder, then merged into a faster lane. They were southbound, heading down I-5. "That's kind of cool. The only boarding school I know about is Hogwarts."

"You are aware that Harry Potter isn't real, right?"

He shrugged. "Well, I mean, in the movies the dorms looked cool."

She shook her head. "I've never seen the movies."

"You read the books, then," he said, with a knowing little nod. "You would be a book reader."

"I do read. But I never read Harry Potter."

His fingers jerked on the steering wheel. "But everybody's read those books."

"Not me."

He made a sound of distress. Actual *distress*. "I can lend you the books if you want them."

She made no attempt to hide her own skepticism. "I don't read fantasy." It was too close to fairy tales. Trying to change the subject, she said, "So, are you a big reader, then? You in school?"

He laughed. "I dropped out when I was seventeen. And don't look at me like that, I got my GED. It's just...I didn't really like school all that much. I went to quite a few of them. Moving around as a foster kid will do that to you."

"Foster kid?" she repeated.

He nodded. "Parents gave me up. No idea who they were. It wasn't terrible—I mean, I'm sure other kids had it worse. Some of the parents were fine, and others...well. It's hard to feel like you're wanted when you're told you're only there to up their paycheck. And I think I went to five different schools in as many years. After a while, I gave up. I ended up getting my GED and leaving."

"How old are you?" she asked, confused. He didn't feel that much older than her.

"Eighteen. Nineteen in two months."

He pulled off the highway, taking them to one of the many state parks that bordered the Willamette. This park was situated with a parking lot and a long concrete ramp, leading into the river. Clumps of trees were clustered near several picnic tables, and there was a familiar large sign over a wastebasket, reminding them to keep Oregon clean.

James parked the car, then reached into the back and snatched up two burlap sacks. Dee frowned, confused. "And what are we doing with those?"

"I told you we were collecting rocks," he said.

She took one of the bags and gazed at it. "I thought you were kidding."

James began to laugh. "Come on. It's easier with two people."

She got out of the car and followed him toward the river. It was a rather nice day to be outdoors—streams of sunlight lit up the billowy clouds, and the greenery was still damp and fresh. The scent of the river hung heavy in the air. It being a Saturday, the park was already occupied. That made her feel safer; nothing truly bad could happen while there was a herd of toddlers trundling about like slightly drunken wildebeests. A bedraggled woman was attempting to corral them onto a worn blanket laid out on the damp grass. There was another person, a man with one of those large cameras, snapping pictures of birds in the overhead trees. And two twentysomething girls were perched on the rocks near the river, passing a cigarette back and forth.

James trotted down the inclined pavement, reaching to unlace his shoes as he went. He kicked them off, wading into the river with bare feet.

Which, considering this was the Willamette, was inadvisable. But Dee wasn't going to lecture him on tetanus.

She kept her flip-flops on, her jeans rolled up to her knees. Stepping into the water was an act of will—it was painfully cold, and the pebbles felt unsteady beneath the rubber soles of her shoes. She kept wobbling, trying to stay upright despite the current and uncertain footing. "This is your idea of an easy errand," she said, following him out until they were knee-deep in the water.

"Hey, we're working for a demon," James replied. "We could be disemboweling virgins or something."

"That's...a good point, actually," she said reluctantly.

He beamed at her, then bent over at the waist and began scrabbling around in the water. "Try to find rocks about the size of your fist. Any smaller and they won't have any effect. Any bigger, and whoever is carrying the load will get tired faster."

Dee frowned, confused, but began fumbling about in the water. It was murky and a greenish brown, and the current flowed between her fingers, tugging at her. Her hand closed over a rock and she dropped it into the burlap sack.

It was...rather peaceful work. There was a rhythm to be

found in bending down, rummaging through the riverbed, placing rocks into her sack, and then moving to a new place. The sound of the rushing water relaxed her, drowned out the nearby noises of traffic and children. Even the chill of the water seemed to dissipate, but she knew that was simply her skin going numb.

As she worked, she watched James.

He did not attempt to make awkward conversation or even look at her; he was consumed by his own thoughts and his task—picking up rocks, studying them, and then deciding to keep or toss back. He was more discerning than she was, but then again, she had no idea what these rocks were for.

She asked him as much.

"Oh," said James, once she voiced her question. "I'm bad at explaining this part."

One of Dee's brows twitched. "You're not going to tell me."

"Oh, no," he said cheerfully, "I'll tell you. It's just, you're going to get different answers depending on who you ask." He straightened, then reached into his burlap sack and pulled out one of the rocks. "All right. So when we explode one of the voids, it's a two-part process. The first part is...well, the explosion. We have C-4 for that."

She felt her mouth twist. "I know. I remember that harrowing car ride."

"It's fine," said James. "It's one of the more stable explosive materials. At least according to Cal. He's the only one brave enough to prep the stuff. He sets it to a twenty-second timer—any shorter and we don't have time to get out. Any longer and…whatever's in the voids might have time to dismantle it. We place the explosives directly at the center of the void—and the explosives themselves are packed with these rocks." He held up the rock. "Something about the explosion and the introduction of solid rock makes the voids go boom."

"Is it like shrapnel?"

James grinned. "This is where it gets interesting. Technically, the rocks shouldn't do anything other than get blown about. But according to the Daemon, we can't destroy a void without them. When we asked him why, he refused to explain. Said we were mere humans and couldn't grasp the finer details." He shook his head ruefully. "Cal theorizes that the voids themselves are simply non-space and they cannot create their own matter. When the explosion goes off, there's nothing to explode. The rocks are there so the explosion can actually be destructive."

Dee nodded. "Is that what everyone thinks?"

"Cora disagrees." James dropped the rock back into his sack. "She's of a more…well. She thinks that the element of stone disrupts the energies of the voids."

He gave her a significant look. "The voids only started appearing after the demons declared themselves. Cora thinks… well, she thinks the voids are here to counter them."

"Angels," said Dee, for the second time. "So Cora thinks there's some kind of...supernatural war going on?"

"And that by doing the Daemon's bidding, we're on the wrong side, most likely," said James, his cheerful tone at odds with his words.

"But Cora works for him anyway?" said Dee.

James gave her a look. "The Daemon has her heart. He has all our hearts. Tell me, are you simply going to tell him to eff off?"

Dee considered it. "No," she admitted.

She'd thought when she made a deal with a demon, that would be it. Lose a limb, gain a wish, and be done. Isn't that what other demons did? But this drawn-out contract, this taking of hearts and sudden introduction of a war—it was far more than she'd ever expected.

A laugh burst free of James. "Yeah, but there's still no disemboweling, remember? In comparison, rock collecting and setting off explosions in magic portals seems tame. And besides"—he slid her a knowing smile—"it's not like we're doing it for free."

That was also true.

"You look green," James told her. "Take a breath. Go...sit on that boulder or something."

She wanted to tell him that she was not going to throw up; she was fine, she was totally fine—

But her fear became a knot in her throat, choking back anything she might have said. She'd managed to stave off the fear, to ignore the implications of it all, but now it felt as if her empty chest was filling with panic.

She tried to recall the old stories, to remember any scrap of wisdom that might get her out of this. People who panicked in fairy tales ended up doing something stupid and getting themselves devoured by wolves or making bread crumb trails or chopping off body parts. In those stories, the survivors were those who managed to keep a cool head, who could outwit the villains.

The problem was, she still didn't know who the villains *were*.

She needed to stay calm, to think this through. Her hands fisted, nails biting into her palms. She took a deep breath of air and then another, gulping as if she might never breathe again. "Hey, hey," said James, hastening over to her. He reached out as if to touch her, then appeared to think better of it. "Look at me. No, look at me."

She looked at him.

"I've been at this for a while now," he said, "and I'm still here. You will be, too, so long as you're smart about this." He held her gaze, intent and focused, and when he spoke, it was with the cadence of one talking someone off a high ledge. "You want to know a secret?"

He obviously expected an answer, so she forced a nod.

"Whenever I panic, I think to myself, *I chose this*," he told her.

She stared at him. "That's it. That's your self-affirmation right there. *I chose this*? Not *Everything's going to be all right* or *all things pass*?"

"I've never been all that good at lying to myself," he replied, smiling. "Somehow I think you're the same."

She huffed.

He looked out at the river and the rocks at their feet. "Most people feel like their lives are out of their control. Like everything could change in a moment, depending on luck or chance. And while that's probably true, I like to think that I was the one who made the choices that brought me to this moment. They may have been bad or good choices—I don't know. They might have been mistakes. But all I know is that I'm the one who made them. I brought myself here. I chose this."

"And that makes you feel better?" she asked, intrigued despite herself.

"It means that I can't blame my life on circumstances or chance," he said. "It also means I could make another choice, make another change. It keeps me in control." He looked around, as if searching for a way to help her. "What do you do when you panic?"

"Generally, I just panic," she said, her throat tight. "But—my roommate vivisects teddy bears when she's stressed."

He blinked. She had a feeling that people didn't surprise him all that often. "Your roommate. Vivisects. Teddy bears."

The look of shock on his face snapped her back to reality. "No wonder you haven't panicked until now."

I chose this, she thought. *I chose this.*

And something in her stomach settled.

That was unexpected. But not unwelcome.

I chose this.

She thought the words again and again, held them like a talisman against her missing heart, and slowly she felt herself unwind. The panic faded.

James watched her. She looked up, expecting to see pity or even disgust for her cowardice. But rather he looked...satisfied. "Better?"

Wordlessly, she nodded.

He took a step back, as if to give her space. "You know, I think we've collected enough. You want to get out of here?"

She could not feel her feet anymore; she wriggled her toes beneath the cold water, thought it might be a good idea to stand on dry land again. She followed him up the concrete incline, past the toddlers and the college students, to the parking lot. He didn't press her to speak, even when he vanished around the back of the car and reemerged with a towel. She used it to dry her feet and ankles, then passed it back. Once inside the car, he cranked the heater to full and directed it at their legs.

It took several minutes, but she began to thaw.

FIFTEEN

The last time Dee was invited to a family Thanksgiving was when she was fourteen. It was held at one of her uncles' homes. In a small suburb outside of San Jose, the Morenos clustered into the house—a tent erected in the backyard for the children. Dee was just old enough to merit a couch, but she elected to sleep outside with the other kids. She liked listening to the sound of the traffic and the neighbors, liked breathing in the air that smelled of sunlight and freshly mown grass.

There were about twelve cousins running around, and she found herself intimidated by their height and experience; they talked too quickly and used slang she didn't know. There were three dogs: two large mutts that seemed cowed by another relative's Pomeranian. Adults gathered in the kitchen, cracked open beers on the counter and argued jovially about whose turn it was to use the oven. Someone ended up cooking the turkey on the barbecue outside because there simply wasn't enough room in the kitchen. One of Dee's great-aunts kept asking for those "good, home-cooked rolls" and Dee watched her uncle pull out a tube of the instant-bake ones when he thought no one was looking.

The dinner was chaotic and loud and Dee liked it.

She ate with the other kids in the living room, with some cartoon on that she didn't recognize. The adults carried dishes into the kitchen, made towers of dirty plates and did some creative rearranging in the refrigerator, trying to fit all of the leftovers.

As they worked, some of the men went out into the backyard to smoke cigars and open a bottle of something stronger than beer. Dee watched as they poured small tumblers of the brown liquid. Dread curled her stomach into knots; she talked a little more quickly, as if trying to outpace her own fears.

It was a family gathering. She was safe here, among the others.

That night, as dusk began to creep over the horizon, Dee was on the back porch with three cousins and the Pomeranian. They were tossing the dog little scraps of turkey—and every so often, they would try to sneak a brussels sprout in there. To the kids' delight, the dog would chew it a few times, then spit the vegetable onto the porch. It was clear proof that mammals were never meant to eat such things, one of the cousins declared, and this set off laughter.

A shout broke into their conversation.

Dee cringed; she shrunk in on herself before she was even truly aware of the noise's source.

A fight had broken out. Half-smoked cigars littered the lawn, and two men were at each other's collars.

Dee did not need to see her father's face to know he was one of them. The familiar bellow turned her blood to ice.

She never learned what the argument was about—it could have been anything from an old family argument to politics to which football team should have won the Super Bowl in '87. That didn't matter—what did matter was the argument itself. It was like setting a match to tinder.

She watched her father slam her uncle into the fence, heard the crack of the wood breaking. A snarl of profanity, tangled up with her uncle's name.

Two men managed to break up the fight, yanking the brothers apart and coming to stand between them. "Stop it, Mark," said one of them. "Walk it off."

"You fucking walk it off," snarled Mr. Moreno. And threw another punch.

Dee never saw if it connected; she was already walking

quietly inside, to pick up her things. "Come back when he's sober," said her uncle.

Within an hour, she was sitting in the backseat of their car. Her mother was in the driver's seat, and her father the passenger's. At some point, his anger had burned itself to ashes, leaving him apologetic and weeping, trying to pull each of his brothers into a hug, only to find himself shrugged off.

It was a thirteen-hour drive back home; thirteen hours that dragged by, punctuated by her father's sobs and the sound of the car's fuzzy radio.

Dee sat in the backseat, headphones clamped firmly over her ears and a magazine on her lap. She tried to lose herself in the glossy pages, reading about makeup and clothing she didn't truly care about. It was a distraction, and that was all she wanted.

She turned a page and saw the next headline: INTERVIEW WITH A DEMON.

Her mouth twisted into a frown. People were still obsessed with these things masquerading as demons. It was stupid—it wasn't as if—

But then her eyes fell upon the picture. A woman, smiling at the camera, her blond hair carefully arranged around her perfect face. But it wasn't a woman.

Dee looked down at the photograph, startled by the certainty settling within her. Not human. She couldn't figure out what had changed—but something had. She knew it wasn't human; she could see it in the lines of the woman's face, in the curl of her mouth, in the too-perfect brightness of her eyes.

After that Thanksgiving, Dee had no trouble recognizing the demons. She thought something about them must have changed. Perhaps the demons decided to unveil themselves to more people. It wasn't until years later that she understood the demons themselves hadn't changed.

She had.

SIXTEEN

*S*he got the call on the way back to Brannigan.

It was her home number and something inside Dee froze when the call came through. It couldn't be her father; he would still be at work. Hesitantly, she answered. "Hello?"

Her mother's voice. Ragged and worn, and just a little hopeful. "Dee?"

"Hi, Mom." Dee angled the phone closer to her ear, trying to block out the sounds of traffic. "What is it?"

A pause.

Horrible pieces fell into place and she said, "Mom, what's wrong?"

"I—I'm bleeding." The admission came in a voice tentative, ashamed, and just a little self-deprecating. "There was a can and the lid—and, dear, do you remember where the bandages are?"

Dee gritted her teeth. The ache spread through her jaw, into her skull, settling in her temples. She closed her eyes for a moment, forced herself to answer. "They're in the bathroom, under the sink."

"Ah." And then the phone clicked off.

Dee wondered if pain was written clearly cross her face, because James looked at her with something like concern. "You all right?"

She began to scratch at the back of her neck. "I—do you mind if we make a stop?"

She expected questions—and knowing him, they'd likely be impertinent ones. But he simply nodded. "Sure. Where do you need to go?"

The word tasted bitter in her mouth. "Home."

She left James in the car when they reached her house. She didn't tell him the reason for this visit; that was one conversation she really did not need to have. "I'll take the bus back to Brannigan—you don't need to stay."

She found her mother in the living room. She sat with her foot propped up on a stool, her left hand fallen into her lap. A cigarette burned between the fingers of her right hand, and it idled over the couch's armrest, ash falling to the carpet. An empty glass tumbler sat on the coffee table, ice cubes melting into nothing.

"Dear," said Mrs. Moreno. Her face lit with a kind of exuberance, and it was worse than anything because Dee knew it was genuine. She tried to stand and wobbled.

"What did you do?" Dee sighed and took her mother's hand. The blood was mostly dried—it looked as if she'd neatly sliced open the side of her palm.

"I was making lunch," said Mrs. Moreno, with all the dignity she could muster. It was rather difficult to take her seriously when her breath reeked of bourbon. The scent of it was nearly enough to make Dee dizzy. "There was a can—the lid—"

"I'll take care of it," said Dee quickly. "You stay here."

The first-aid kit was indeed beneath the bathroom sink—behind a fresh bundle of toilet paper. Dee fished it out and strode through the kitchen. There was a can of tomato soup sitting on the counter, half-open. Several red splatters decorated the blue countertop. Dee wondered how much of it was actually soup.

Dee returned to her mother, sitting beside her. It was a simple matter to clean the wound, wipe it down with single packets of rubbing alcohol, then press fresh cotton to the cut. Dee covered it with tape, then sat back to survey her work. It was good enough.

"I miss you," said her mother, a mournful note in her voice. "You should come home more often."

Dee hated the word *should*. It implied all sorts of things, and every one of them hurt. *Should* was a measure of something she'd never live up to—comparisons to other parents' children, report cards with not enough high marks, activities she'd never shown any real interest in. She *should* be more grateful, she *should* be a straight-A student, she *should* have more friends, she *should* have different friends, she *should* be—

She should not be here.

She rose to her feet. "I'll make lunch, Mom." It was a small gesture, but it helped soothe her conscience. She returned to the kitchen, dumped the can's contents down the sink, and began rummaging around in the cupboards. She found a packet of instant noodles, flavored with herbs and chicken, and put on a pot of water for boiling.

Her parents had not always been this way. She'd seen them in pictures, decades ago, both bright-eyed and smiling and more alive than Dee had ever seen in real life. They'd met in their early twenties, when her father was just starting his landscaping business and her mother was taking poetry classes at a local college. He'd been assigned to work on the campus when they'd met; a leaf blower tore papers from her mother's hand and she went scrambling after them, until the man turned off the machine and hastened to help. When he handed the crumpled papers back to her, she smiled and called him her knight in shining armor.

Dee had heard variations of this story over the years.

She wondered when the sweetness of their story had turned sour; she wondered if all happy endings turned out this way, if the Happily Ever After only lasted until there was a kid born, until the mother was laid off and the father worked harder to compensate, until there were bottles tucked away beneath the sink and bloodied napkins on the counter-top and their child—*not a child*—trying to figure out how to hold things together.

She automatically turned in the direction of the bus stop as she left the house, but quickly stumbled to a halt.

There was a blue Mom Car still parked at the curb.

James was sitting on the trunk of his car. He swung his legs back and forth, oblivious to the stares of the neighbor kids.

Dee gaped at him, then hurried over. "I said you didn't have to stay."

James threw her a grin. "Yeah, I know. But what kind of gallant gentleman would I be to simply desert a friend when they still might need help?"

She opened her mouth to reply, then went silent. Because she didn't know what to say. A wave of almost embarrassing gratitude swept over her.

"You want coffee?" she asked. "I could use coffee."

He beamed at her.

They found a local cafe. There was no shortage of them in Portland, and there was a place with fresh baked goods and a glut of local college students—all with shadowed eyes, typing away on cheap laptops and sipping organic espresso. Fresh rain left a fog of condensation on the windows, and the air had a thick, damp quality to it.

When they ordered their drinks, James pointed at a multi-grain bagel, ordering two.

"What is it with you heartless and bagels?" asked Dee.

"You say that like you're not one of us," he replied. He gestured to a free table near a window and she went to claim it before any college students could. The chairs and tables were dented, heavy dark wood, and her chair squeaked when she pulled it back. A few minutes later, James appeared with the coffee and bagels. James pushed one toward her, along with a miniature packet of cream cheese.

"I thought you might be hungry," he said. "Besides, food is one of life's great pleasures. And we should live for the moment."

She picked up the cream cheese and frowned.

"Are you lactose intolerant or something?" he asked quickly. "Because I can grab jam."

"No," she said. "I just like the light cream cheese."

He gazed at her. "Is this a diet thing?"

"No." She shrugged, although she could not shake off the words of her father, telling her she needed to take a PE class.

He made a clearly skeptical noise. And with a deliberate sort of care, he pushed another one of the cream cheese containers toward her.

"Is this some kind of subtle comment on my weight?" she said tartly.

He shook his head. "Whatever you're worried about, ignore it. There's no sense in limiting ourselves," he said. He took a huge bite of the bagel and spoke around the mouthful. His words came out gummy. "Live now."

"And for you, living means full-fat cream cheese?" she said flatly.

He swallowed. "I like to keep my dreams attainable. Eat cheese, sleep on a nice bed, have my work in the same museum as Rothko—the usual."

"Yes," she said, face deadpan. "That's what everyone dreams about."

He ducked his head, a smile pulling at his mouth. "You don't agree?" he said, nodding at Dee's food.

"Anyone can be a hedonist. Self-control is what keeps us human."

"See," said James, taking another bite, "that's what I don't get about you. You come off all tight-laced and pleated skirts and you look like you could behead someone with a ruler, but your price was *money*."

She cut him a sharp look.

"I eavesdrop," he said, unashamed. "Cal thought we shouldn't listen, but I heard you in that hospital basement. You could've asked for anything and you asked for money. Not exactly what I'd expect from someone like you." He slid a pen from his pocket and began doodling on a napkin. As if he needed something to do with his hands.

She clasped her own hands around the cup of coffee, glad for its warmth. "The money wasn't for anything stupid. I'm not going for a wild time in Vegas or anything."

"Good plan." He took another bite of bagel, then went back to sketching on his napkin. "I hear it's full of demon hunters these days. So, what is the money for?"

She smiled briefly, then looked down. "You're very curious all of a sudden. I could just lie. Or refuse to answer."

"Either way," he said, "I'll learn something about you."

"Ah. Well." She considered wildly for a moment telling him. About the bottles and the cigarette smoke and the scar on her foot. "It's for school."

"School," he repeated. "...That's—that's it?"

She sipped her coffee serenely. "You thought it'd be something more interesting, didn't you?"

Another small shake of his head. "Nah. It's just...why is your school so important to you? That place looked pretty fancy, so I can see why you'd want to stay. But...I mean. There had to be another way to pay for it other than a deal with a demon."

She felt her smile fall. She picked at the bagel, tore its edges into tiny pieces. "No. There wasn't."

She felt his eyes on her and when she finally gathered enough courage to look up, she saw something she hadn't expected. It wasn't curiosity or pity. It was...recognition. Like seeing someone he thought he'd never see again.

She waited for him to comment, to ask the obvious question. But he remained quiet, sipping his coffee and finishing off his bagel—and then hers.

"I needed out of that house," she finally said. "I couldn't be what they wanted me to be."

His tone was gentle. "And what was that?"

A crutch. A carbon copy of her father. Someone who could fix things.

She looked down at the crumbs scattered across her plate. Uncertainty became a weight in her mouth, and she couldn't have spoken if she wanted to. The silence dragged on, until James leaned back in his seat.

"You can ask me," he said, with the breezy air of someone changing the subject.

Dee latched on to his question, grateful for his not pressing. "Ask you what?"

"What I sold my heart for."

She had wondered that; she did not know what attractive, fearless boys sold their hearts for. *Girls*, was her first thought, but James didn't seem to have a girlfriend. *Money*, was her next guess—but then she gazed at his clothes. Beyond that, she did not know.

"All right," she said, "what did you sell your heart for?"

He smiled and slid the napkin across the table.

She had been half-wrong. He had been doodling, but... but the word *doodle* hardly did it justice.

He had sketched her. A girl with a squared-off jaw, bushy hair, hands clasped about her coffee cup. But he'd done something—smoothed out the imperfections of her skin, made her lips seem softer, her eyes lowered and mysterious. Heat flooded her cheeks and her stomach went tight. It was undeniably beautiful, and for one brief moment she thought, *Is that how I look?*

But one glance in the reflection of the window reassured her that no, she had not suddenly transformed into a model. It was simply a trick of the art, a subtle flattery of her features.

When she could speak, she said, "Art talent."

He inclined his head in acknowledgment. "I was always talented, and I could get by on that talent when I was in school or living with my foster parents. But out here, in the bright and cold real world, talent is all too common. You need skill, and that takes years."

"You weren't willing to wait?" asked Dee. "Get skilled the normal way?"

His smile dropped. "Why'd you trade your heart for money? Couldn't have earned it another way?"

"There wasn't time," she said.

He smiled. "There never is."

SEVENTEEN

After their coffee, they did not immediately return to Brannigan.

Turns out, the Daemon really did have a lair. But it was not in the sewers.

Dee found herself standing on the curb, eyeing a dilapidated building with some amount of unease. It stood among several other condemned structures, and the whole street looked like a mouthful of rotting teeth—all gray and caved in, with a few solid pieces still standing. Dee eyed the building that James pointed at. Above the door was a sign, and the only words she could make out were EDIT UNION.

She cocked an eyebrow. "A bank?"

"An abandoned bank," corrected James. "I doubt a demon would set up camp in a working credit union."

He walked up to the bank doors—they were chained shut, and a large red KEEP OUT sign was hung in the window. Ignoring it, James slid a key into the lock and the chains snapped free. He dropped them to the ground and pulled open the door.

"What are we doing here?" Dee asked, making no move toward the open door. All she could see was darkness and a thick layer of dust on the floor.

James smiled. "After you," he said, and held the door open.

She remained rooted to the spot.

There was an awkward pause.

James's mouth twitched, as if he were trying to hold back a smile. "Why are you looking at me like that?"

"Because," said Dee, "this is the moment when the girl gets offed by the seemingly nice hobo hipster because she was gullible enough to walk into the creepy building." She had a flash of mortification, wondering if she'd angered him, but then James burst into laughter.

"Fair enough," he said. "But I'm the least scary thing in this building. Does that help?"

"It doesn't," she told him.

Another rueful laugh. He stepped through the door and Dee had a moment of indecision—to stand on a deserted street corner with a burlap sack, or to follow a boy she barely knew into what looked like the set of a horror movie.

Eff it, she thought, and followed him.

The interior of the bank was about what she expected: rusted-over hinges, layers of footsteps through the dust, and illumination filtered through a dingy overhead skylight. Mold crept along the walls and she covered her mouth with a sleeve, trying not to inhale too deeply.

"This is where an all-powerful demon lives," she said. "A condemned bank." Her voice bounced off the walls, coming back to her in eerie little echoes.

"It's the last place you'd look for one," said James. He strode through the hall as if he knew this path well, following the line of old footprints. He walked past the clerks' desks, down a corridor that must have been offices, and finally came to a halt before a large, circular door.

A vault.

"And this is why he took up residence here," said James. "The decor may leave much to be desired, but the security is unequaled.

"We'll leave these here." He placed the burlap sacks before the door. "Everything gets stored here—the duffel bags, the C-4, the rocks. It's a safe location, no pun intended, and the Daemon probably figures that if something ever goes wrong, nobody will miss this building."

She gazed at the vault, taking in the clean hinges and

heavy lock. She took a step forward, palms out, and rested her hands on the door. She felt its solid weight, the bedrock strength of it behind her fingertips.

"This is where he keeps our hearts," she said quietly.

James's small, conspiratorial smile was her answer. "Rumor has it that if you can outsmart a demon, they can't renege on their deal," said James. "Meaning, if you could get your heart back fair and square, he couldn't take away your money."

"What is that?" said Dee. "The Rumpelstiltskin clause?"

He laughed. "Something like that, I think. It makes sense, though. Throughout history, there have always been tales of deals like ours. Most of the time, the human ends up dead or wishing they were. Fairies stealing firstborns or cursing princesses and all that. But once in a while, the human gets the better of the immortal—and for whatever the reason, they can't get back at the human. Maybe they respect intelligence."

"Or maybe the story wouldn't have as good an ending if the human died," said Dee.

"Such a cynic." James gazed at the door, then cocked an eyebrow. "You think you could break in?"

She leveled a flat stare at him. "Do I look like a supercriminal to you?"

He laughed. "All right, then."

Dee couldn't help but ask. "Did you bring me here hoping I could break into the vault?"

"Naw," said James. He looked at the door with a breezy unconcern. "I thought you'd want to know where your heart is, but I'm not all that attached to mine. As far as I'm concerned, the Daemon can have it for now."

She touched the door a second time, running her fingertips along the seam, as if she could pry her nails into the gap between door and frame and somehow yank it open—the metal was cold, smooth, and perhaps the only clean surface in this whole building. She wondered for a moment exactly how the Daemon kept the hearts. How did one hold such precious cargo?

With her luck, her heart was likely in a red-and-white barbecue cooler, surrounded by cans of Pepsi and melting ice.

They left the bank empty-handed. No rocks, no burlap sacks, and no stolen hearts. Dee stepped up to the edge of the curb, balancing on the balls of her feet while James threaded the chain through the bank doors and snapped the padlock shut. He was whistling some song she didn't recognize, and when they returned to his car, he unlocked her door and held it for her.

She stared at it.

"Oh, come on," said James. "You suspicious of gallantry, too?"

"Gallantry is dead," she replied. "Or maybe you hadn't

noticed the lack of knights and horses running around Portland."

He laughed. "That would be a sight." But he continued to hold the car door open until she sighed and slid inside. He carefully shut it behind her before striding around to the driver's side and seating himself.

"You're weird, you know that?" she told him. "You dress like a hobo, talk about being gallant, and you act like this is all some kind of weirdly themed party."

"Life is a weirdly themed party," he said, with all the solemnity of someone reading from a fortune cookie.

"No, really," she said. "How are you so...chill about all this? I mean, even Cal and Cora looked a little stressed when I met them."

James shrugged and slid his key into the ignition.

"I want the life I want," he said simply. "If that means I'm going to die for it, then so be it."

She shook her head.

"You don't agree?" he asked, curious.

"I just want to live," she said. "That's why I made my deal."

"So you took a deal that might kill you," he said. "You know, you're kind of a walking contradiction."

She took a breath. "I made a deal because I—I just couldn't go back. To the way things used to be."

"Ah," said James, as if he understood.

But she had one last question. "You called yourself a transfer. When you introduced me to Cora. Does that mean...?"

"I was with a different troop," he said. Calmly, but something in his tone set off warning bells. "I started in Italy."

"Why did you transfer?" she asked. "I mean, going from Italy to Oregon must have been a step down."

James looked away. "I was the only one left in my troop. Can't have a troop of one, and the voids were finished in Italy, so the Daemon asked if I would move. I didn't mind. Portland's got a good art scene."

He had been the last person in his troop. For a moment, she wondered who he had been teamed with before, if he had gotten along with them, if perhaps he'd dated one of them, if they'd been anything like Cal or Cora or Dee herself.

She didn't ask if they'd gotten their hearts back.

She wasn't sure she wanted to know.

EIGHTEEN

Dee was sprawled on her bed, working on an essay about the New Deal, when her phone made an ugly buzzing noise, like an insect trapped in a jar. She stared at it suspiciously; very few people called her. Everyone texted these days. Calls were reserved for emergencies, for parents, for pranks. None of those appealed to her.

But it was Friday, after classes, which meant Gremma was in the room. And she would notice if Dee suddenly started avoiding her phone. With a mental sigh, Dee picked it up and checked the caller ID.

It was James. Fear made her tighten up; she'd been dreading another void, but she accepted the call. There was no point in hiding. "Yes?"

"Do you have a car?" he asked.

She squinted at her phone. Of all the weird questions, she hadn't expected this one. "No," she said.

A pause; a muffled curse. His voice was taut, and for once she could hear none of his usual breezy demeanor.

Dee didn't like the strain in his tone. "What happened?"

James let out a frustrated growl. "Someone came through the parking lot and slashed my tires, well not just mine, lots of people's, but I've got a show tonight and I was supposed to have had my stuff there by noon."

"A show?" It must be something to do with his art. She glanced at the clock; it was half past three.

He sighed. "Listen, Dee, I'll talk to you later."

And then he hung up.

For a moment, the sound of her own name rang in her ears.

Dee glanced over at the other side of her room. Gremma had a pair of white earbuds plugged into her phone, and she was reattaching one of her teddy bear's legs with tight, neat sutures.

"Hey," said Dee. Said it twice more, and then Gremma finally heard.

Gremma yanked out her earbuds. "Huh?"

"Were you planning on using your car today?" she asked.

Gremma had never been stingy about the use of her Camaro, but then again, Dee rarely asked to borrow it.

"Not really," said Gremma. "Why?"

Dee looked down at her phone. "I think a friend might need help."

Something in her voice must have tipped Gremma off, because suddenly her green eyes went bright with interest. "Would this happen to be your dealer? The reason you broke curfew a few weeks back?"

"For the last time, he is not my dealer. Nor my man of the night."

A grin spread across Gremma's face. "But you don't deny the curfew thing."

Dee hesitated. "He's got a problem."

"Gang war?"

Dee threw her a despairing look. "Not everything in my life is sordid and criminal. In fact, nothing in my life is sordid and criminal."

"I would argue," said Gremma, "but my SAT verbal scores weren't as high as yours and I have no idea what *sordid* means." She swung her legs over her bed and gave Dee another smile. The kind of smile that birds saw just before a house cat swallowed them whole.

"You can use my car," she said, ever so sweetly, "but only if I'm driving."

Dee grimaced and hit the call-back button on her phone. It rang twice, then James's harried voice said, "Yeah?"

155

"My roommate has a car," she said, without preamble. "But she would have to come along. My roommate. Um. You know. Teddy Bear Girl."

"Have you *warned* him about me?" said Gremma. She sounded as if she were trying for offended but was delighted instead.

She expected James to hesitate, to think about it, but the words left him in a rush. "Seriously? Oh, thank you. Thank you, thank you. How soon can you get to my apartment?"

"Pretty soon." Dee glanced over; Gremma was pulling on a jacket.

Dee pursed her lips, heaved a sigh, and hoped she wouldn't regret this.

※※※※※※

The last time Dee had been inside James's apartment, it had looked normal. Well, relatively normal. It looked transient and half put together, curtains serving as walls, and a kitchen made out of portable shelves and counters and a camp stove.

Now, when Dee pushed the door open, she felt her jaw drop. It wasn't an apartment, not anymore.

It looked like a museum.

Paintings. Paintings everywhere. Propped up against the counter, the couches, laid flat on the floor. Oil paints were cast across canvases, swirls of color that might have come from the hand of any master painter. Several of them were covered with brown paper—Dee supposed these were marked for the gallery.

"All right," said Gremma faintly. "Not a bookie, then." She paused. "He still could be a dealer, though. Imagine all the drugs you could slip inside one of these frames."

James was counting out canvases. "Will these fit in your trunk?"

"Not safely," said Gremma, recovering. "But we'll manage."

"Good." James went to the first pile of paintings and picked up two. There were wires attached to the back of the canvas, and he brought two small ones to Gremma and two slightly larger ones to Dee.

It was cumbersome work; the paintings weren't exactly heavy, but they were unwieldy, and Dee found herself having to angle oddly through doorways. Once they were in the elevator, Gremma dragged a sharp breath between her teeth. "Your boy is an artist," she said.

"He is not my boy," replied Dee. "He is a friend. An artist friend. Whose tires were slashed."

Gremma managed to hold her silence. Until the elevator doors pinged open and Dee waddled out to the first floor, trying to heft the paintings without bumping into anyone. Gremma's car wasn't exactly built for carrying storage, but the trunk was just large enough to slide the paintings into.

Dee carefully set one on top of the other, trying not to damage anything.

"He's hot," said Gremma abruptly.

Dee threw her a look.

"What, because I'm gay I can't comment on the attractiveness of boys?" said Gremma with a half shrug.

"He is not my type," said Dee. "He's…"

"Da Vinci reincarnated," said Gremma.

"I'd say I'm more Delacroix than Da Vinci," said James as he passed by. It must have been an art reference, but it went right over Dee's head. She was too busy trying not to look mortified.

The art gallery was one of those trendy, up-and-coming deals—designed to look fashionable without being stuffy. There was something distinctly hipster-esque about the way all the employees were dressed. A woman wearing thick-rimmed glasses and a worn cardigan spoke to James for a moment, then unclipped the velvet divider for James to step through. Dee hesitated, then followed. The room was dimly lit, with spotlights shining on the paintings. The walls themselves were draped with linen and it gave the room a strangely muffled quality. When she spoke, it felt as if the air swallowed up her words, blunting their sounds.

"Where are we supposed to put these?" she asked. She had a painting in each hand. James took one from her and stepped through the gallery confidently, toward the back.

Near the back of the room, Dee saw where the polished gallery frayed into something half-built and slightly panicked. There was a man with a clipboard trying to count a number of sculptures, a thirtysomething woman trying to reattach a wire to the back of a painting, and a teenager with a pencil jammed behind his ear was on the phone, saying something about a liquor license. There were clumps of sawdust on the floor, and unstrung twinkle lights had been lumped near one of the doors.

"Lancer," said James, smiling in that breezy way of his. Clipboard Man paused in his counting and heaved a sigh.

"Thank god, I knew we were missing someone."

"Sorry we're late," said James, and they shook hands, falling into an easy conversation about local vandals and flat tires. Dee stood awkwardly to one side. Gremma was still unloading paintings from the Camaro—parked in a wildly illegal spot on the curb—so Dee had no immediate person to talk to. She considered fake-texting someone, so she wouldn't look so woefully pathetic, but then James was saying, "And this is my personal savior, Dee."

Dee looked up, realized that she was being introduced, and hastily shoved her phone away. Clipboard Man was smiling in a vaguely disinterested way, but when he saw the painting leaning against her thigh, his eyes brightened.

Gremma appeared a few minutes later, having charmed the bouncer by the velvet curtains into carrying the rest of the paintings for her. "Remember," Clipboard Man was saying to James, "the show starts at eight. We would love to have you make a personal appearance, Mr. Lancer." He turned his smile on Dee and Gremma. "As well as your lovely guests, of course."

〰〰〰

They left the gallery in its half-finished state. Gremma immediately strode to the car. A meter maid had pulled alongside the Camaro and was scribbling out a ticket.

James glanced at Dee; there was an expression on his face she hadn't seen before. It was almost embarrassment. "You can come, if you want," he said. "To the opening tonight. I mean, I was invited and you pretty much saved my ass today. Getting a cab over here would have probably cost me a limb and I'm already pushing that envelope."

She laughed. She couldn't help it. "Do I look like I'm dressed for an art opening?" She gestured down at herself.

Green Old Navy flip-flops, skinny jeans, an oversized sweater, and some necklace she'd found in a dollar bin and liked. Her curls were little more than frizz, forced into a braid that kept threatening to break free.

James deliberately looked down at his own hipster-hobo clothing.

"Point taken," she said. "But I still don't look like I belong in there. Everyone's wearing heels and slacks and those chunky glasses."

"And you're going to let that stop you?" He was smiling now, embarrassment apparently forgotten.

She crossed her arms. "And what does it matter to you if I go or not? You can still make an appearance, and it sounds like they want you to."

"Of course they want me to," said James sourly. "I rarely show at these events and it drives them crazy. If my paintings didn't sell so well, I doubt they'd put up with me. Young artists are supposed to be accommodating."

"Then why aren't you accommodating?" she asked.

His gaze drifted to the gallery, then away. "It's a waste of time," he said, with more seriousness than she expected. "I could be working on something new. Creating something, putting another piece of myself into a painting. In two hundred years, no one will remember if I came to these things or not."

"You've got a thing about immortality," she observed. "Being remembered and all that."

"Is that so bad?" said James. "I want people to know my name long after I'm dead. I want future art students to have to memorize the year I painted a man with a mechanical heart and I want those students to hate me because they're going to have to write some essay on whether I painted it because I believed that hearts are useless things, easily replaced by machines, or if I just had my heart broken, or if this was simply the part of my career known as my mecha period." There was a fervor in him she hadn't ever seen before. "We're all just moments and most of us don't matter. We study less than one percent of all humanity in our history books."

"And you're going to be part of that one percent?" asked Dee.

"I just want to matter," he said, unsmiling.

It was like pulling a curtain back, peering behind a mask made of smiles and quips. This was the real James, this young, bright, desperate thing. There was a burning intensity to his eyes, and she saw for the first time a boy who would sell his heart—not for some hobby, but because he thought it was the only way to live the life he wanted.

They had that in common.

Some of his fire burned away, and then the normal James was standing before her, in his leather jacket and wearing a breezy smile. "You helped me," he told her. "I'd like to pay you back with a night of culture. It would be the gallant thing to do."

Her mouth twisted. "Culture?"

"There's also free booze," he said. "And—I don't know. I thought you might have fun."

Before she could reply, Gremma's voice rang out. "Come on! I just talked us out of a parking ticket and I'm not sure if I can pull that off again." Gremma stood next to the Camaro, hands on her hips, tapping one foot expectantly against the ground.

James laughed quietly. "She's…"

"Forceful?" asked Dee. "Confident? Attractive?"

"I was going to say a budding serial killer, but those work, too," he replied. "Don't think I've forgotten the teddy bears."

She shook her head. Somehow, the silence between them felt easy, comfortable. Perhaps it was the fact that he knew a secret about her, and she knew one about him. In the presence of others—those like Gremma—their temporary alliance seemed to strengthen.

"Why'd you call me?" she asked, before she could lose her nerve. "I mean, I don't mind that you did. But…there had to be someone else you could've asked for help."

He shrugged, suddenly appearing self-conscious. "I thought that's what you did with friends?"

Friends. The word felt strange. But perhaps that was what this recognition was, this strange connection. Friendship. An understanding.

She'd never had anyone ask her for help before. Well, besides her parents, but those requests were always tangled up with guilt and obligation and a stomach-churning need to do something.

Gremma's car horn rang out and Dee flinched. "Come on," she said, and she found herself taking James's arm, pulling him toward the car. "She will leave us if we take too long."

NINETEEN

They ended up going out to eat. Gremma had no compunctions about staying out after curfew, so they found a Thai restaurant and conquered one of the corner tables.

They ate spring rolls and stir-fried vegetables and some kind of coconut milk soup. Gremma ended up using one chopstick like a spear, and when Dee picked all the cashews out of her veggies, James scooped them onto his plate.

Gremma and James regarded each other like cats—seemingly unsure if the other was friend or foe. Gremma made a few cracks about James's wardrobe, and James only replied with a grin, which seemed to annoy her.

Somehow, this relieved Dee. Gremma had a way of

dominating a room, of drawing the eye, and Dee seemed to shrink in her shadow. That James appeared immune to Gremma's charisma was reassuring.

It wasn't as if Dee had a claim on him or anything, she thought, but it would be disappointing to realize that whatever connection she felt with him was something he forged with everyone he met. She knew people like that, who bonded as easily as breathing, but it seemed James wasn't one of them.

When they left the restaurant, Gremma forced a path through the gathering crowds on the sidewalk; James slowed, fell into step with Dee. "Thanks for doing this," he said. "I usually spend weekends alone. It's kind of nice going out with people."

She looked at him. For all his hobo clothing, James carried himself with a breezy confidence. He spoke easily, smiled frequently, and laughed at his own jokes. He could have had any number of friends or half friends, or even acquaintances. "Why?" The question slipped out. "I mean—it's not like you're truly a hermit or terrifying or anything. Why don't you go out?"

"No family," he said simply. "And too busy for friends. I sort of count Cal and Cora, but Cal is busy with his research, and Cora—well. She'd probably chew her own arm off before spending an afternoon with me." James looked remarkably uncomfortable for a moment. "And...you're easy to be around."

She wasn't sure what he meant by that, but she liked it.

The gallery had transformed itself in a matter of hours. Long gone were the catering trucks and the harried-looking employees. Tea candles were set up along the walkway, and when Dee, James, and Gremma strode up the sidewalk, it was to find a crowd trailing from the front door.

Gremma went first, like the bow of some warship, cutting her way through the tide of people. Dee trailed in her wake, with James taking up the rear. They managed to navigate the crowds until they were at the wide-flung front doors. The receptionist had smoothed her hair and donned a fresh shade of lipstick, her fingernails glittering in the dim light. She recognized them instantly, and she pushed Gremma aside, reaching for James's arm. "Oh, good. My boss will be so glad you decided to show up."

The receptionist took his arm in what was likely meant to be a polite gesture, but somehow it reminded Dee of a person clinging to the leash of a badly behaved show dog. James reached for Dee's arm—Dee reached for Gremma. They were pulled around the velvet rope barrier, and Dee found herself in the gallery proper.

All the sawdust was gone; the floors were polished and the strings of lights were hung overhead. The drapery along the walls still muted the sound, giving everything an intimate feel.

A man in a pressed black jacket had champagne flutes balanced on a tray. James took two, handed one to Dee.

She sniffed; it smelled crisp and sharp, but she did not drink. Even so, it was nice to have something to do with her hands.

Gremma was already talking to someone—an old lady who had paused in front of a statue that was…rather anatomically correct. Dee choked back a laugh and turned to James. He was walking around the edges of the room, eyeing the paintings. "These ones are mine," he said, and nodded to the five before him.

The first was a painting of an old woman. The left half was all oils and elegant colors—a traditional painting. The detail was incredible; Dee could see the wrinkles in the woman's face, how her skin was thin as parchment in some places, the way the sunlight caught in her far-seeing eyes. But the woman's right edge began to bleed away into charcoal lines, into muted colors until it was all black-and-white sketches. They faded away into blank paper. It gave the whole painting a deliberate, unfinished look.

A HALF-LIVED LIFE said the plaque beneath it.

"It's a very interesting piece," drawled James. There was a middle-aged man eyeing the painting critically.

"Yes," replied the man. "A deliberate statement about regret in old age. It's very well done."

"I don't know," said James, grinning. "It looks like the artist was trying a little too hard. You can see where he left off the brushstrokes—like he got bored and gave up."

"It's a metaphor," said the man. "Didn't you see the title?"

"Right." James nodded as the man trundled away.

"For the record," said James, "I did get bored."

Dee gazed at him. "Do you do this often? Show up at places with your art and pretend not to be...well, you?"

He grinned, unrepentant. "I'm a ghost," he said, leaning into her ear. "I drift in and out of these functions, unseen and unheard." He gestured at the gallery and Dee followed his gaze.

A woman strode by; her heels clinked against the hardwood floor, and the sound was muffled, swallowed up by the swaths of fabric. The twinkle lights sparkled off someone's champagne glass, and she imagined for a moment that she felt as he did. An observer, as untouchable as one of these paintings.

"No one really sees me here," said James. "They don't have to—they're all staring at my work. I like seeing how people react to it, seeing how it affects them." James smiled at her, the lights catching his white teeth. "Haven't you ever wanted to change someone's day? Alter the universe just a tiny bit? See if you could leave a mark on the world?"

Dee thought of the times she had tried watering down her parents' bottles, of learning how to unscrew a cork when she was eight, her small hands strangling the neck of a wine bottle, dribbling in white grape juice, all the while hoping that if the drinks weren't drinks at all, things might change.

They never did, though. People didn't want to change.

But maybe a person could.

Dee swirled the champagne around in her glass. All the bubbles were nearly gone. "So, what were you thinking?" she asked, and nodded at the half-finished painting. "If it wasn't a metaphor for a half-lived life."

"Oh, it was definitely a metaphor," he said. "Just because I got bored halfway through doesn't take away from that. But I mean…" His eyes slid over the painting, brows drawn and mouth pulled up to one side. It was a focused look, one she had never seen him wear. Perhaps, she thought, this was what he looked like when something truly mattered to him.

"I saw an old woman on a curb that day," he said. He spoke the words slowly, as if sorting them out while he said them. "She looked…well, she looked like that. Sad, somehow. She was waiting for a bus and she was all alone and I just kept thinking, *I don't want to end up like that. I don't want to be old and sad and alone.*"

Dee frowned. "So what's the alternative? Party it up in a retirement home?"

He laughed. "Somehow, I don't think that's the kind of life I'll lead." He tilted his head back, smiling at the painting. "I figure I'll live for now, as much as I can. And if I crash and burn before I'm old, then I won't regret it. There are worse things than living hard and dying young. Byron certainly recommended it."

Her stomach twisted in on itself. "There's nothing romantic about dying young," she said firmly. "A life is not diminished by the fact that it wasn't romantic or short-lived."

He looked taken aback. "Ah. That's...one way of looking at it."

Gremma found them by another one of James's paintings—one depicting a teenage girl stepping into a river. The angle was from the back, the sunlight pouring around the girl so she was nearly all silhouette.

It took Dee a good thirty seconds to recognize the frizzy hair, the cardigan, and the flip-flops.

It didn't take Gremma nearly so long.

"Oh my god," she said, mouth gawping open. She had a miniature sandwich in one hand and a champagne flute in the other. "That's Dee."

James swallowed the last of his champagne. "It...might be."

"It totally is," said Gremma.

James slid Dee an anxious glance.

"All right," he said. "Tell me now. Is it nice or creepy?"

Dee studied the painting again. It was a gorgeous depiction of the river: She could see the little flows and eddies of the current. The girl looked beautiful from the back—strong and carefree. And it wasn't like the painting was perverted or anything. The most visible skin on the Dee in the painting was of her ankles and calves, her jeans rolled around her knees.

She found herself catching smaller details, as well. The way the girl's curls seemed to catch the sunlight, shining like embers; the play of shadow across the water; and something in the girl's posture gave the impression of determination, of stepping into freezing cold water. She would have been lying if she had said having an attractive boy paint her wasn't flattering. She'd never had anyone pay attention to her like this, and it made her feel too warm.

For the first time, she wondered if that trip to collect river rocks had really been about having another pair of hands. Perhaps it had been an excuse, a way to talk to her without the awkwardness of asking her to coffee. But her mind shut down at the idea.

"If I was naked, it would be creepy," said Dee. "This is just…well. I mean. Artists get inspiration from real life, right?"

Relief broke across his face. "Yes."

But even so, it made her feel odd. He must have been watching her more closely than she realized.

"Come on," said Gremma, taking her hand. "I need to pee and I need company." She flashed James a bright smile before pulling Dee away.

They made their way through the crowds, and Gremma dragged her into the small private alcove, before releasing her.

Gremma crossed her arms. "All right," she said. "Talk."

Dee squirmed, glancing at the single-occupancy restroom not far away, wondering how annoyed Gremma would be if she simply ran and locked the door.

"Your boy painted you," said Gremma. "I thought people didn't even do that outside of cheesy romantic flicks."

"For the last time," said Dee, "he is not my boy. And he doesn't want me."

Gremma gave her a look.

"He doesn't!" Dee insisted. "Trust me—I'm not that kind of girl!"

She snorted. "What kind of girl is that?" said Gremma. "The breathing kind?"

"The datable kind!" Dee waved her hands uselessly about herself, trying to gesture. "I'm—I'm—"

Not worth it.

But there were some words a person didn't say—couldn't say. In real life or in fairy tales, there were some things that could not be uttered aloud. And this fear, this deepest fear of hers, was something she dared not even whisper.

With that, she turned and strode into the bathroom, leaving Gremma with her mouth open in a reply. Dee slid the dead bolt shut, stood in the darkness for a moment. This was one of those old-fashioned restrooms without automatic lights, and Dee was glad for it. It was almost a relief to stand in the dark, alone with herself. When she thought she could breathe again, she fumbled for the switch.

The light came on.

And someone was already in the restroom.

Dee choked back a shriek. Her hand reached for the doorknob, ready to yank it open and run, but then she recognized the figure standing between the sink and toilet.

The Daemon.

He gazed at her, his face unreadable. "Hello."

"You are in a girls' restroom," said Dee, once she had caught her breath. Very observant, she thought. Very astute. She would likely win some kind of award for intellect. "You are not supposed to be here."

"Well," said the Daemon, "I would have done this outside, but that would have drawn attention."

He reached for her.

Dee jumped back. "What—what are you doing?"

"There is no time," said the Daemon, and despite the stoic expression, she saw something flicker in his eyes. Unease.

"Something's gone wrong, hasn't it?" she asked.

"Yes," he said curtly. He reached for her arm. His long, pale fingers closed around her wrist and—

It was like when he had taken her heart.

There was a *yank*.

There was the sensation she was falling, falling through the floor, gravity pulling her downward—

Her feet slammed into pavement and she wobbled, blinking at the sudden darkness and the cold night air.

She stood alone on a dark stretch of pavement.

TWENTY

Dee's stomach rolled, and she felt as if she had just stepped off a particularly turbulent roller coaster. She fell to her knees, found herself crouching on oil-stained pavement.

She forced herself to look around, to take in where the Daemon had brought her.

A parking lot. It was huge, and in the distance she thought she saw the dim lights of a strip mall. A cold wind cut through her clothing and she shivered. The sounds of distant cars meant she was not in the middle of nowhere, but she was not in Portland, either. She turned in a circle and cried out in shock.

A figure sat on the pavement. A figure that had not been there a moment ago. She fumbled for her cell phone, fingers clumsy with panic, and when she managed to find the flash-light app, the sudden illumination spilled over—

"Cal," Dee gasped.

Cal was cross-legged, sitting beside a large duffel bag. "Deirdre," he said with a grin. "Fancy meeting you here."

"W-what are we doing out here?" snapped Dee. Her voice was sharp with fear. "How did you—"

"He must have grabbed me after he dropped you off," said Cal, shrugging. "The Daemon did his little 'folding reality' trick."

Her stomach was still in knots. "That was—what the hell just happened?"

"Did the Daemon grab you from your dorm?" asked Cal.

She shook her head. "Women's restroom in an art gallery."

"Ah." Cal nodded knowingly. "Well, if it makes you feel any better, I was at the gym. Coming out of the showers. Wearing nothing but a towel. Luckily I'm a fast talker or I'd still be dressed like that."

A little laugh escaped her. Cal looked pleased at this, as if making her more comfortable had been his goal. He was a nice guy. A bundle of contradictions—a genius who looked like a beefy jock—but nice.

"So you were at an art gallery?" he said. "I don't suppose… Lancer took you there?"

She nodded.

"Ah." Cal appeared impressed. "Well, good for you.

Haven't ever really been able to get past his defenses. You know how it is—he's all smiles until someone asks a personal question, then he clams right up."

Perhaps Cal and James weren't as close as she assumed. When she'd seen them in the hospital basement, they had been joking and comfortably insulting each other, but perhaps they weren't truly friends. Half friends. Dee had plenty of those herself.

She took a moment to look around the parking lot. "The Daemon," she said, then hesitated. She still remembered the stark, pale lines of his face. "Did you notice—was he...?"

Cal glanced at her, then looked away. "More curt than usual? Yes. I assume it means there's a void that's further gone than it should be." He pushed himself upright, brushing the dirt from his jeans. "I hope this doesn't take too long. I promised a buddy that I'd lend him my telescope later tonight. There's some supernova he wanted to chart."

She studied him—of all the heartless, Cal seemed the most level-headed. "So demons can just pop in and out of places?" she asked him. "I mean—if they can do that, why doesn't he magic us to every void?"

Cal shook his head. "It isn't magic. It's...some kind of quantum entanglement, I think."

She gaped. He grinned.

"Teleportation," he said. "It's not magic. It's just not explainable by our tech yet. *Yet*," he repeated, as if for emphasis. "As for not doing it all the time, I asked the Daemon about that. He isn't big on answering questions. All he said was, 'Fold a paper enough times and it will never be flat again.'"

Dee frowned. "And that means...?"

"I think he folds reality to bring us places," said Cal. "And he can't do it too often without the risk of messing things up permanently. So he only does it when it's really needed."

The chilled night air settled into her skin and she shivered. "Like now."

"Like now," Cal agreed.

"What do you think—"

She never finished.

There was a sensation of displacement, a ripple of air, and then—

The Daemon popped into existence again. He had James by the collar, the way one might drag an unruly pet. He released his hold and James fell to his knees. And then the Daemon vanished again.

Hurriedly, Dee scrambled to James's side. Her hand fell on his shoulder and he looked up, his eyes searching for hers. "You're all right?" he asked.

It was touching, especially considering he looked on the verge of vomiting. "Fine," she said. "You?"

He swallowed audibly. "Shouldn't have had that second glass of champagne." He rose to his feet. "Where are we?"

"Woodburn," replied Cal. "Something's wrong. The Daemon

came to me, and he had the duffel bag with the load in it—said there wasn't time for us to drive or stop by the bank. He just took my arm and brought me here."

Another shiver went through Dee. She wrapped her arms around herself, wishing she had her hoodie. But she'd left it at the art gallery.

The art gallery.

Her stomach plummeted.

"Gremma," said Dee. "Oh, hell. We just ditched her." She reached for her phone; they had only been gone maybe five minutes, so it was likely that Gremma wouldn't have noticed yet.

"Just tell her you had to run because of…I don't know," said James. "What do normal people use as excuses these days?"

"Illness," replied Cal. "Family emergency. Statistically those are the two used most often to get out of something."

Dee considered. "You know, those excuses might have worked if I hadn't just vanished from a room with only one door."

Cal looked thoughtful. "Were there any windows?"

Dee opened her mouth to reply, but before she could say a word, the Daemon appeared again not two inches away. She staggered backward, arms flailing wildly. James caught her around the waist, pulled her back.

Cora yanked herself free of the Daemon's grip.

"What the hell?" she snapped. Her hazel eyes were lined in smoky gray and she wore a pencil skirt and frilly top. Even her shoes were dove-gray pumps. She looked nearly as put together as the Daemon himself.

"Whoa," said James. "You look…"

"…Whose secretary are you?" finished Cal.

"I came from my internship," Cora said. She stood in those heels far more comfortably than Dee could have ever managed. "Now, if someone would—"

"Not now," said the Daemon sharply. "Follow me."

And without another word, he picked up the duffel bag and strode away from the strip mall. Dee exchanged a glance with James, then Cal. James shrugged and was the first to fall into step behind the Daemon. Cal was second, and Dee went third. She glanced back, saw Cora hesitating, then the girl made an angry sound and followed, her pumps clicking against the ground.

The lights of the parking lot faded away. Despite the other heartless around her, Dee felt very alone as she walked after the Daemon, away from the mall and the sound of traffic, into a field. It was probably farmland—grass seed was big in this area, she knew. The dry dirt crumbled along her flip-flops, catching between her toes.

They walked and they walked, until the night closed in around them. Dee could barely see the outline of the Daemon in the pale light of the half-moon. A hand touched her arm and she jumped, only to see James next to her. "Sorry," he whispered. "Just making sure you're still there."

And then, the Daemon went still and the teenagers stumbled to a halt behind him. Glimmers of light shone through cracks in the air, catching on motes of dust, making it look as though reality had cracked open and bled starlight.

A woman stood beside the void, stopped so still that Dee did not notice her at first. She was slim, with a shaven head and dark skin. Like the void, like the Daemon, she was ethereally lovely.

A demon, then.

"Heart-Monger," the woman said. "What are you doing here?"

The Daemon answered smoothly, "Taking the pets out for a walk."

"Do not trifle with me." The female demon's voice sharpened. "They are not needed."

The Daemon sneered. "Your tools have failed."

"You can't know that."

"Then why is the door still half-open?" he replied. He nodded at the void. "Let me use mine."

"Hey." This time it was Cora who spoke. Dee felt a thrill of fear for her, and she wished the other girl had the sense to remain silent. No good ever came of interrupting feuding adults—she'd learned that young. "We are not his," said Cora. "We don't belong to anyone."

The female demon gave Cora a flat look. "He holds your memories, your very *core*, hostage, and you say you are not his?"

James drew in a breath. His fingers wrapped around Dee's wrist, as if he needed something to anchor himself—or perhaps he thought she might say something.

"Fine, then," said the female demon. "Send your hollow creatures inside. See how they fare against a burrower."

The Daemon inclined his head, as if in mocking thanks. Then he looked back at the four teenagers behind him. The glimmer of the void's light reflected in his eyes. "Come along," he said quietly.

Like they truly were his. Animals to be collared and ordered about. For a moment, they all balked. But Dee realized the futility of it. She was the first heartless to step forward. James hastened after her.

Cora stepped closer to the void, wobbling on the unsteady ground. In her heels, she was nearly as tall as Cal. She glanced about the small group. "Let's get this done. Cal, you're the doorman. Dee, you stay out here—"

"No." The word broke free of her.

James and Cora looked at her.

"I—I can't stay out here," said Dee. She would rather face whatever lay inside that void, terrible memories and all, than remain out there.

"We could use the backup," said James gently.

Cora looked as though she wanted to protest, but then she shook her head. "All right. James and I will take the duffel bag. Dee, stay close and keep an eye out. If that demon already sent a team in, we might run into them. If we can help them, we will."

Dee could smell the void—the scent of sand and burning metal joined that of dried grass and earth. The edges between this world and the void were blurring, and she thought she could see past the blur and the ripples, into the void itself.

Cal was the first to get into position; he stepped into the void, turned so that he was half in, half out. Then he held up his one visible hand and motioned for the others to go through.

"Come on," said Cora. She had one strap of the duffel bag and James took the other.

Dee shook her arms, as if readying for a run, and stepped forward. If she'd had a heart, she thought her pulse would have been ripping through her. As it was, the fear was bad enough. It tasted bitter on her tongue and she felt her body draw in on itself, readying for fight or flight.

"Listen," Cal said, seeing her face. "I've only had to go in there a few times, but—try to center yourself. Don't lose yourself to the memories. The void will yank out anything close to the surface. Try to stay calm."

She nodded at him. He was trying to help; it didn't matter

if the words slipped through her like water through cupped fingers.

Dee watched as Cora and James strode through the mouth of the void first.

The world rippled, and they vanished into nothing.

TWENTY-ONE

It was like last time—she felt the sweeping gusts of the wind, the grit of sand in her hair, the raw newness of the world and—

She is fourteen, home for Christmas break from her first semester at Brannigan. Her father is screaming, about how shit their life is, how he was cheated, and she goes outside and sits in the yard, lets the freezing rain lash at her face and hands, sits beneath the oak tree and waits for her parents to fall asleep—

Dee shook. Frantic little trembles ran through her. Her hands were clenched so hard that her nails had broken skin. Blood stained her left hand.

She is five and she cannot understand why her mother won't stop crying—

This must be why the demon took their hearts. Because it was the only way a human might survive this—by hollowing themselves out.

"I chose this," she said, and the wind whipped the words from her mouth.

She forced herself to look up, to wrench herself away from the memories.

It was lighter here—as if this new world hadn't quite figured out what night was. Illumination played off the world's edges, off the half-formed trees and lines of the field.

She blinked through the haze of sand and light and saw James and Cora struggling ahead. James had his arm braced against the wind, and Cora was squinting, struggling along in her heels. Dee hastened after them, forcing herself to concentrate on the rhythm of her own ragged breath. If she could just focus on the moment, she wouldn't see those terrible memories.

Cora stumbled, caught off guard by either her own memories or the uneven terrain. Anger flashed across her face, and then she kicked off her shoes and continued on, barefoot. Dee reached down to pick up the shoes, holding them against her own chest; it was the only thing she could do.

This void was wrong—it was too solid, too bright, too real. The winds were stronger, the taste of metal sharper. The driving gusts pushed against her every step and she found herself panting, sucking mouthfuls of dry, hot air and grit. Every stride felt too slow, as if time had sped up and left her behind, but she knew it was probably all in her head.

When James tripped over an unseen crack in the ground, Dee rushed forward to help. She darted around to the front, taking hold of the duffel bag's strap and heaving it upward. It was heavier than it looked—but then again, explosives would be heavy. Dee walked backward a few steps, until James could catch his footing. She was the only one of them facing the mouth of the void.

And that is how she saw the nightmare behind them.

For the second time that evening, she was glad she did not have a heart. Because she was pretty sure it would have stopped beating.

When it stood, the thing must have been twenty feet tall. For now it was sprawled on the ground, its body canted toward the center of the void.

It looked...human.

Unsettlingly, disturbingly human.

Because it was made of mismatched human parts.

Its ribs were clearly visible, slivers of bone nestled within desiccated flesh, a white cage that was utterly hollow; the flesh hadn't decayed—it had simply dried out, like flowers left to wither and curl in on themselves. The thing's legs were like thick tree trunks, the flesh of many legs bound together, cords of muscle and tendon. But some of it looked as if it had been crafted by the hands of a deranged artist—there were teeth embedded in the thing's hands, jagged little spikes of discolored bone.

Her stomach threatened to crawl up her throat; hot bile flooded her mouth.

This was what the demons did with the body parts. They stitched them together into…these things. Enormous, humanoid things.

It moved with the grace of a toy robot—all jerky twitches as it tried to right itself. It was attempting to stand, but it could not rise. She saw why at once; one of its too-thick legs had been severed at the knee. The thing's head moved. There was no neck to twist; the creature turned its entire torso to look at her with eyes that were mismatched.

And it had no mouth.

Dee felt the dread spread through her body like poison. It paralyzed her, made her freeze in place. *Jack*, she thought, *being sighted by the giant.*

It was a revelation—but it fit. If magic was real, then so were monsters.

Her gaze fell upon something in the creature's hand. It gripped a leg—but not a human leg, not like the leg of any animal Dee could recognize. It was hinged backward, tipped with claws, and there was nothing mammalian about it.

Just like what she had seen in the hospital void.

The leg dripped black ichor, as if it had been freshly torn from its owner.

Breath caught in her throat, Dee glanced at James. He was staggering to his feet, and Cora had her arm braced against the wind; they clearly hadn't noticed the monstrous thing that had collapsed near the mouth of the void. They were blinded by wind and sand, wholly focused on the goal before them.

The creature moved. Dee flinched, sure it would rise to its feet and come after them.

But its fingers only opened, dropping the inhuman leg to the ground. Then its arm lifted and a finger—too thick, made of tens of dozens of fingers sewn together—pointed at something.

Dee looked over her shoulder.

At the center of the void was a shimmer of light. It must have been the door to—to wherever this place led to. The other side. Another world. Heaven. Hell. She didn't know.

"Come on," shouted Cora. "We've got to get the duffel bag to the center of the void."

James nodded. Dee relinquished the duffel bag to him and took several steps back. Her gaze was still on the cobbled-together clutter of body parts. It stared back at her.

Dee looked away, forcing her attention toward James. He had the duffel bag open, and he knelt beside it. In his hand was what looked like a remote control with a wire attached, and he fumbled with it. He twisted something, and his mouth pulled tight. When he looked up and saw Dee, his eyes were hard. He caught her by the arm, nodded.

"Twenty seconds," he shouted, and she understood. They had twenty seconds to get out before the void would implode—taking all of them with it. He started to move, but then skidded to a halt, his mouth gaping wide. "What the—"

Cora slammed into him, but she did not seem to notice; her own attention was finally on the giant, too.

Twenty seconds. There was no time for this. James's fingers were tight on Dee's wrist and she shook him, trying to jolt him back to the moment. He blinked, gaze snapping to her. "Come on," she said, the wind tearing the words from her mouth. She wasn't sure he heard, but he seemed to understand. He took a step, and then another, still holding on to Dee with one hand and with his other he reached out and grabbed Cora's elbow.

And then they were running. Cora was making little sounds on every exhale, a whine in her throat. Dee's attention was yanked back to the hulking creature. It was still on the ground, like some half-fallen statue from ages past. Only it watched them, gaze following the three teenagers as they sprinted toward the mouth of the void.

Dee tried to count the seconds as they ran, but she couldn't tell how much time was passing. It felt like moments were slipping by too quickly.

Then they were at the mouth of the void and Cal was gesturing them through.

Cool air brushed across her face and arms, and Dee gasped, the night air like a knife in her lungs.

They were out.

Out.

Dee tripped and Cora fell, slamming into the grass. James leaned on his own knees, a man trying to catch his breath after a long run. Cal yanked himself free of the void, staggering back.

Dee glanced over her shoulder; sure enough, not five seconds after they emerged from the void, it began to collapse in on itself.

They'd done it.

But there was none of the victory of the last time they had closed a void; rather, a grim silence settled over the group.

The female demon stood over Dee, staring down at her as if she were vermin. Dee scrambled back, tripping over her own feet in her haste to get away. She half expected James or Cal to step in front of her, to take up the role of amateur bodyguards like they had done in the past.

But it was not one of the heartless teenagers who put himself between Dee and the demon.

The Agathodaemon stood there. From what Dee could see of his face, his beautiful features were hard. His umbrella, which was always tucked carelessly beneath his arm, was in his left hand. He held himself loosely, and it put Dee in mind of the fencers she had seen when she passed by a gym at Brannigan—legs spread apart, ready to lunge.

Did demons fight demons? She did not know.

"You will let them be," said the Daemon very quietly. "They are not yours."

"They left my servant behind," the female demon snarled. "Do you know how many years it took to build that homunculus? No, of course you wouldn't." Her face twisted in a sneer. "Heart-Monger."

"Better a monger than a cobbler," replied the Daemon. "And at least I give back what I take."

The female demon's gaze slid past him, to Dee and the others. "Your servants are weak."

"And yet they can hold a conversation," replied the Daemon, "whereas yours...well, it's difficult to do such a thing without a mouth."

The demon rounded on him. "There is too much at stake to rely on inferior models. How would your servants do up against a burrower?"

"So I should rely on your methods?" replied the Daemon silkily. "Of cobbled-together monsters and half-formed creatures? Tell me, how well did you fare in Pompeii?"

The demon took a step back. "The others will hear of this."

"Oh, I'm sure they will." But the Daemon was relaxing, shifting back into a stance of nonchalance. "But the difference between my methods and yours is that everyone will now still be alive to hear about it."

The demon retreated, keeping her gaze fixed on the Daemon. Then she turned on her heel and walked away. She took two steps before Dee's ears popped and the demon simply *vanished*, leaving the four teenagers on the ground and their keeper standing before them.

TWENTY-TWO

For a long minute, nobody moved.

Dee remained still; she felt that if she moved, the world would shatter. The female demon would return, the void would reopen, that nightmarish thing of cobbled body parts would crawl back into existence—

The quiet seemed tenuous and Dee dared not break it.

It was James who spoke first.

"What," he said, "the hell?"

Which seemed to sum up the situation quite well, in Dee's opinion.

Cora rose unsteadily to her feet. She was visibly shaking, her gaze fixed on the place the void had been.

The Daemon did not answer. And somehow, his silence

gave Dee the courage to move. She pushed herself upright; dirt clung to her jeans and she could feel tangled pieces of dead grass between her toes.

"What was that thing?" said Dee. "That giant...thing."

The Daemon slid a look toward where the female demon had gone, and his lips pressed into a thin line. "The voids need to be destroyed," he said. "We living, feeling beings cannot enter them. We have found ways around it. And trust me when I say your kind would fare no better than ours, should one of those doors open fully."

"She called it a homunculus," said Cal. "But—I know what that word means. It's a miniature human construct, but that thing was enormous..."

"Well," said the Daemon, "we built them smaller at first."

Cal let out a snort.

"Come now," said the Daemon, looking at all of them. The betrayal they felt must have been clearly written on all their faces. "Nothing has changed. Surely you must realize that."

He was wrong, though. Dee felt in her bones—everything had changed.

She half expected the Daemon to use his magic to teleport them all home, but he did something far more mundane: He led them back across the field, to the large strip mall parking lot, and then he broke into a car. Well, breaking in sounded far more physical than what he actually did, which was to twitch his fingers at a Mercedes and the car came to life.

Cora all but lunged for the backseat, apparently wanting as much distance between herself and the Daemon as was possible. Dee slid into the middle of the backseat, and James pushed himself in beside her. It was Cal who pulled open the front door and settled himself only a few feet from the Daemon.

No one spoke.

The silence felt heavy in the car. Dee stared out the window, at the city lights as they rushed by. She was trying not to think about that...thing. The enormous creature made of human body parts, the reason that demons took people's arms and legs. It was too horrific to contemplate.

But she couldn't really think of anything else.

And apparently, neither could anyone else. Because just as they were heading across a bridge, Cora said grimly, "Pull over."

"What?" said the Daemon.

Cora's voice was tight. "Pull over. I think I'm going to be sick."

The Daemon threw her a look over his shoulder and if Dee didn't know better, she would have thought it was *anxious*. Worried for the state of his charges...or the upholstery, perhaps.

The car left the bridge and pulled onto the shoulder of the road. Gravel crunched beneath the tires, and then Cora was clawing at her door, shoving her way outside. She headed for a clump of trees; Cal hurried after her. James hesitated, glanced between Dee and the others, then opened his own door and half jogged after them both.

The Daemon remained in his seat. "This is how it always goes," he murmured. "I told the others. Revealing ourselves has never turned out well for our kind. Give humans the slightest bit of knowledge and they cannot handle it."

Perhaps he did not realize she was still in the car. Or perhaps Dee simply didn't register enough as a person to him.

"You've...revealed yourself before?" asked Dee. "Before the press conference?"

His eyes met hers in the rearview mirror. "Many times. When we have a need, we deal with your kind. Then we disappear, let our stories return to myth, and let the truth fade from memory." He exhaled sharply. "I suspect, with this new technology of yours, we will not be able to vanish this time. We are here. And we shall never go unnoticed again, not with cameras on every street corner.

"But," he said, his voice a little stronger, "there are worse prices to pay to keep this world safe." He lifted his chin in a slight nod, angled to the right of the car. "I do not see you chasing after your own kind. Is it fear that keeps you here—or courage?"

Fear. Always fear.

She gazed at him, a rabbit caught in sight of a wolf, frozen in the seat of a stolen car.

"You should go to them," said the Daemon. "Bring them

back." His attention drifted to the darkened car windows, to the trees illuminated by the headlights of passing traffic. "There are more dangerous things in the world than myself."

Dee swallowed. She was hyperaware of the closeness of the car, of the sound of the Daemon's breathing, and the lump of a knitted heart shoved in her pocket.

She scooted from the backseat and tentatively stepped out of the car. The gravel was uneven beneath her flip-flops, and again she mentally berated herself for not investing in better shoes. But then again, at least she wasn't barefoot.

Cora stood on the fringes of the trees, her arms wrapped around herself. Her feet were still bare, her shoes left in the car. She looked strangely younger, vulnerable without them. An argument had broken out amid her and James and Cal, and it took Dee a moment to pick up the thread of the conversation.

"...not getting back into a car with that thing," Cora was saying.

"What are you going to do? Walk home?" But there was no mocking edge to James's reply; it was a matter-of-fact question. "Hitchhike? Trust that some other kind of demon doesn't pick you up?"

Cora turned away. Dee could just make out the nail polish on her toes. "Cora," said Cal, all sympathy. "Listen. I get it. You saw something bad—"

"You don't get it," snapped Cora. "You didn't see it. That

thing. What those demons do with the body parts—" Her voice cut off, and it sounded as if she might be choking back a retch. Cora bent over herself, scrabbling at her own jacket as if it were suffocating her. She threw it to the ground, and a red knitted heart tumbled from one of the pockets.

James caught sight of Dee for the first time. He nodded to her. "You all right?"

For the first time, Dee wondered if her own past was working to her advantage. Cora was sick with fear—but Dee had never known a time when she wasn't afraid. For Cora, this was a horrible revelation. For Dee, it was a Friday.

"I'm fine," she said. Not entirely a lie. "I—I never wondered what the demons did with those parts," she added, more quietly. "I feel...stupid somehow for not questioning."

James's mouth twitched. "If it makes you feel at all better, I came up with a few wild theories and they were all wrong. Perhaps not wondering was better."

"Cora," Cal was saying. "Breathe. Just breathe."

Cora whispered, "This is wrong. We're wrong."

James pressed a hand to his forehead. "We should get back to the car," he said. "I don't like our odds if the Daemon gets impatient and drives away. I'd call a taxi, but I don't have my phone."

"We're not getting in the car without Cora," said Dee, but then she remembered the cell phone still in her back pocket. "I—I have a phone. We could call—someone."

She was not sure whom to call. Her parents were out of the question, and Gremma...well. She had no idea how she was going to explain this to Gremma.

Dee glanced back at Cora and Cal. Cal had taken off his jacket and draped it around Cora. He was murmuring quietly, as if speaking to an injured person. But Cora pressed a hand to her mouth, looked at them. Her eyes were frantically darting between each of them.

"We're not alive anymore," Cora said, and her voice was stronger now.

Dee went still. "What?"

Cora rose to her feet. She looked a sight—barefoot, hair still windblown, Cal's jacket around her shoulders.

"That thing." Cora spat the word. "That homunculus. It could enter the void. Because it was built of parts, but not human. Rats—rats try to enter the voids but they can't. Nothing living can enter the voids." Cora's gaze whipped to the car. "That's what the demon said. 'We living, feeling beings cannot enter them.' *They* can't enter the voids—but *we* can? What does that make us?"

Dee's reply died on her lips.

She—she hadn't thought about that.

She didn't want to think about that.

She wouldn't think about that.

"Calm down," said James. "Nothing's changed. We're still here, and your deal is up in two months!"

"And then what happens?" Cora paced back and forth, a caged animal behind bars she had only just discovered. "When we get our hearts back, who's to say what—"

Her eyes suddenly widened.

"What happened to the rest of your troop?" she said. "You transferred into this one, but you never told us why."

James's face was as still as a mask. "I was the last of my troop in Rome."

"Because they got their hearts back?" Cora's hands were balled. "Or because they were dead?"

James narrowed his eyes and for the first time, Dee saw a sharp sliver of anger in his gaze. She was so used to thinking of him as harmless and good-natured.

Cora took another step toward him. "That...thing we saw. Have you ever seen anything like it before?"

He hesitated, and Dee went cold.

"James," said Cal, sounding hurt.

James threw him a look. "I never saw one moving, all right? But—in Rome. There was a void that...there were parts. I saw body parts. Unmatched fingers, holding a crate of explosives." His gaze darted to Dee, then away, as if he didn't want to meet her gaze. "I didn't know why, but I think—I think most demons use those things, instead of people like us. They explode the voids using a Franken-giant, like we saw in there."

Cora's lips pulled taut. "Walking corpses. That's what can destroy the voids. People like us." She turned on her heel and strode away from him, gazing down at the river below. She shivered violently, then pushed her arms through the jacket, pulling it tightly around her.

Cal took a hesitant step toward her. "Cora…"

"Shut up," she snapped. "It doesn't matter. Nothing we do matters, don't you see? Because it killed us. That thing tore out our hearts and killed us and we're just walking corpses that don't know we're dead yet.

"We gave up our hearts, we sold our souls for wishes, and look where it got us! We're thralls to a demon."

"Speak for yourself," said James, with an obvious attempt at levity. "I'd say I'm more of a willing minion."

"This is wrong," said Cora. "All of this. We shouldn't have to do this." She shoved her hands in the jacket's pockets, and her face went strangely still. When her right hand emerged, she held a knitted heart.

Her fingers dug into the soft red yarn.

"I must have left that in there," said Cal quietly. He held out a hand, reaching for it. But Cora did not move.

She gazed down at the thing with a terrible coldness. "Why do we even carry these around?" she said, her voice shaking.

There was the slam of a car door and Dee looked up. The Daemon was striding toward them, all but skidding down the gravel in his haste.

Dee glanced between Cora and the Daemon, her stomach

drawn tight. It felt as though an ax were about to fall, some terrible fate about to come crashing down. "Cora—" she began to say, but the other girl was faster.

With a terrible snarl of fury, Cora pulled her arm back.

She threw the knitted heart. Out over the river.

Dee watched it; the red speck flew high, hung suspended in the air for one impossibly long moment, and then plummeted.

"No," said the Daemon, and then he just *vanished*.

Dee blinked—wondered what had gone wrong.

Nothing happened. James breathed hard, his gaze boring into Cora, and Dee finally recognized the strange emotion on his face.

Panic.

Utter panic.

But she didn't understand. Cora was fine, she was standing there, glaring down at the river, and—

There was a soft thump behind Dee. She heard it the way one hears all terrible things: with childish ignorance, a certainty that Cal must have dropped something, that this odd sound couldn't be—it couldn't be—

Cal was sprawled on the pavement, unmoving and silent.

Cora froze.

"No," breathed James, and he scrambled to Cal's side. He fell to his knees, felt the space around the young man's mouth and nose. James let out a curse, placed his hands on Cal's chest, and began pressing down.

Dee's mind felt as if it were mired in thick, slow-moving water. She couldn't understand why James was doing that; people only did that in movies when a person's heart had stopped. But Cal had no heart, so chest compressions were laughably useless.

Still, James didn't let up. He pressed a shaky breath against Cal's mouth, then went back to the compressions.

"Come on," he said, voice ragged with panic.

James rocked back on his heels. He was shaking, visibly pale, and when he looked at the bridge, he swore. He picked up Cal, dragged him toward the pavement, onto the shoulder of the road. "What are you doing?" asked Dee, appalled.

"Someone will find him here." James reached down, gently stroked his thumb over each of Cal's eyes. Closing them.

"Humans cannot survive without a heart," he said. "We cannot—we need one. Even a fake one. That's why the Daemon gives those to us. So long as we have something representative of a heart, we're still functional."

Dee took a step back. "W-what?"

Cora had not moved. She stared downward at the river, at the place where she had last seen the heart.

"I saw it happen once before," said James. "That's how I knew—but never mind."

Dee reached into her pocket suddenly, desperately afraid. And—yes. Her own fake heart was still there.

Her life was knitted through this thing, stitched with imperfect red yarn. It was impossible—

But then she remembered another fairy tale, something Russian, about a man who breathed a fragment of his life into a finger bone and left it in a cave so he would never die.

She heard a curse, followed by the sound of gravel crunching beneath patent-leather shoes. The Daemon strode up the steep hill; he was soaking, as if he had leaped into the river, and there were splatters of mud across his face.

In his left hand, he held a soggy mess of red yarn.

It had unraveled—it looked as though it had snagged on something.

"A waste," snarled the Daemon. His gait was smoother than before, somehow even less human, and he stalked toward Cora.

James took two steps, placing himself in the Daemon's path. "She didn't know," he said quickly.

"She cost me my most valuable piece." Every word was edged with icy anger. He took another step toward Cora, but James didn't move. He had his hands up, as if in supplication.

Demons didn't hurt people. They had repeated that over and over in the first few months—in every interview, every public word—they never hurt anyone. There was no proof they hurt people, not even when people attacked them first.

The Daemon's attention remained firmly on Cora. She

knelt on the gravel, gazing at Cal's unmoving form, and she looked as though she might never move again. Dee darted around the Daemon, around James, and she grabbed Cora's arm.

"Come on," said Dee, and tried to pull her upright. Cora rose like a sleepwalker, staggering and unsteady. If there was one thing Dee knew how to do, it was escape. She kept Cora moving, her own gaze fixed on the Daemon, even as she navigated the gravel. And all the while, James stood his ground.

It was a flimsy defense. Dee knew that at any moment, the Daemon could simply push James aside, teleport Cora away, do whatever he pleased. But for some reason, he did not.

Dee maneuvered Cora into the backseat and shut the door behind her. Gravel crunched behind her and she flinched, but it was only James; he jogged up beside her, gesturing for her to get into the passenger seat.

The car was still running. Exhaust fumes hung in the cold, damp air and Dee was glad to slide into the warmth of the car. She glanced through the window and saw the Daemon.

He stood over Cal, gazing down at him.

Fear bloomed in Dee's stomach; they should have brought him, too. Some irrational part of her didn't want to leave Cal behind, to see him splayed out on that dirt and gravel, alone but for the creature that took his heart.

James put the car in drive and hit the gas. Dee jerked in her seat as he drove away, hastening to get back on the highway, to take them back to Portland, back to civilization and lights and humans.

But just before the trees blurred around them, Dee saw the Daemon kneel beside Cal, placing the tattered remnants of the knitted heart on Cal's empty chest.

TWENTY-THREE

Cora Meyer had met three demons before she decided to sell her heart.

She had gone to several states in search of them—a nightclub in LA. A casino in Lake Tahoe. And a coffee shop in Seattle. But the only thing that ever came of it was a few more thousand miles on her hand-me-down Toyota. She walked away from the encounters with all her limbs.

Cora knew she was pretty. Her body was lean and muscled and she had good skin. She was vibrant and healthy, an ideal candidate for a demon. And that was why three different ones had approached her, asked her price.

Every single demon's eyes flashed with alarm when they heard her answer.

They would decline, either with a look or a curt no, and then they would depart.

But Cora was determined—and she kept listening. And when rumors of a place to find demons in her own hometown arose, she followed them to a transitory farmers market. MEPHISTO MARKET read the hand-printed sign.

It was a bright spring day, and the booths were full to bursting with strawberries and lettuce, and at first Cora was skeptical. This couldn't be real. All the other places she found demons were darkened rooms with heavy, sweet smoke. She could not imagine finding a real demon in this sunlit, open space.

She bought strawberries and ate them sitting on the hood of her Toyota, watched as the passersby came and went. There were many hopefuls—people who scrawled their prices on the limbs they were willing to offer up. With a sigh, Cora tossed a strawberry stem over her shoulder.

And then a man behind her cleared his throat.

Cora whirled around so quickly she nearly fell off her car. She reached for her purse, but then she froze.

The man was in his late twenties or early thirties—pale with dark hair and scorchingly blue eyes. Chiseled cheekbones, clean-shaven, and he wore a suit. An umbrella was tucked beneath his left arm. And a strawberry stem stuck to his lapel.

With a flicker of disapproval, he took the stem between thumb and forefinger and dropped it to the ground.

"Please be careful where you throw things," he said, then began to walk away.

She knew what he was; she'd recognized him the moment she'd turned. She slid off her car's hood and hastened after him. "Wait!" she said, catching his arm.

He paused. Looked down at the place where her fingers were roughly digging into his sleeve. She released him.

"You're wrinkling my suit," he said with a resigned sigh. "You know what I am, don't you?"

"Yes," she said. "And you're here looking to buy."

His voice was distant, uninterested. "Am I?"

"Of course you are," said Cora, looking around at the market—with its dirty pavement and the smell of freshly churned earth. "Or else you wouldn't deign to be in a place like this."

A small smile flashed across the demon's mouth. "True." He turned to face her fully, gazing at her as if she had caught his interest. She gazed back, unafraid. "Tell me," he said silkily, "what did you come here for? What price would you ask for a limb?"

There was no hesitation in her answer.

"I want you to kill someone for me," she said simply.

He blinked. It was the only sign he was surprised; the rest of his face remained impassive. "Is that so?"

"Yes."

He looked at her—studied her as if she were an anomaly.

"Girls like you don't ask for death," he said. "You ask for a larger bust or perfect skin or a talent of some kind."

She gave him a grim little smile. "My boobs are fine, my skin is great, and I'm all right with the talents I have. I want someone dead."

"Then why don't you do it?" he asked. His eyes flicked down to her bag. "Demons have no monopoly on violence. Or are you going to lie and say there isn't a gun currently in your purse?"

There was, of course. Cora was eighteen—and on her eighteenth birthday, she had gotten her concealed carry license.

It made her feel safer to carry the weight of the metal against her hip. And besides—her clearest memories of her father were of a hunting range, of a kind man with a worn voice, teaching her how to shoot clay pigeons.

"I don't feel like spending the next few lifetimes in prison," she answered. "I have sisters and a mom I need to take care of."

The demon tilted his head. His eyes were so intent that it made a prickle of discomfort run over her skin. "He hurt one of them," he said. "This man you want dead."

Her stomach turned over.

"I never said it was a man," she answered, her voice still hard.

"Statistically, it's always a man," said the demon, with a little scoff. "What did he do?"

Her back teeth ached as she ground her jaw. "Something he'll never be punished for—at least not in any court of law. Which is why I need to take care of it."

"By asking me to do it," replied the demon.

"I'm not asking, I'm bargaining," said Cora. "There's a difference."

"That there is." The demon let out a small breath. "No demon will kill for an arm or a leg," he said. "You should know that by now. Demons won't kill. It's bad press."

She met the demon's bright blue eyes. "You said demons 'won't' kill. Not that they can't. Is that true?"

His perfect mouth turned up at the corners. "You're asking the wrong questions."

This was the longest conversation she'd had with one of the damned creatures, and it gave her hope. "If a demon wouldn't kill for an arm or a leg," she said slowly, "what would they do it for?"

It turned out, that was the question he wanted to hear.

TWENTY-FOUR

Dee wasn't sure how she got through the next few days, if she were being honest with herself.

Gremma wasn't speaking to her. It seemed that after the Daemon had teleported Dee from the bathroom, the room had remained locked and empty so long that Gremma was sure Dee had died and ended up using a fire ax to break in—only to find the restroom empty. She'd assumed what any normal person would have: that Dee had snuck out through the narrow, high window. Choosing to risk injury rather than speak to her roommate again that night.

Dee tried apologizing, but Gremma waved her off, said that if Dee needed time to go run drugs or smuggle goods through some art gallery, that was her business.

Dee probably should have felt bad about Gremma's anger. But she didn't.

All she truly felt was panic.

Utter, mind-numbing panic.

Cora was right. She shouldn't be alive; she wasn't alive, not really.

She was a girl held together by knitted yarn and magic.

Terrified, Dee had taken one of the jam jars from the dining hall. That evening, she washed out the jar in the dorm bathroom, swirling it with hand soap and rubbing out the specks of seeds with paper towels. When she was sure it was clean and dry, she dropped her knitted heart inside.

It was stupid. Probably ineffectual. But she felt better with the heart protected.

But the more time passed, the more she became aware of the hollowness in her chest. She was empty, carved out.

She couldn't do this. She needed her heart; she needed out.

I could get Gran's money, she thought. *Try to get it without my parents. The bank might let me have it.* She could give the Daemon's money back, shove the username and password for that ridiculous bank account into his hands and demand her heart back. She'd never heard of a demonic refund, but she wouldn't let him refuse.

And with Gran's money, she could pay for one semester of Brannigan. After that . . . well.

She'd figure something out.

James had been texting her since Cal's death. Little texts, the kind that she didn't feel obligated to respond to. They were simple little statements like, **Apparently I'm banned from that art gallery because one of my guests took an ax to a restroom door?**

And the next day he texted, **Sold all the paintings at the gallery. Apparently I'm not banned anymore because I'm the first one to sell out.**

And then, the day after that, **Spilled oil all over my leather jacket. I don't suppose you know how to get paint out of leather?**

This time, she did text back. **Fire**, was all she sent, and that was met with a smiley face.

Nearly a week later, she got another text.

I went to Cal's funeral.

The words appeared on her phone. Simple, small words. But then again, all the worst statements were like that, weren't they?

It was always the small words that did a person in.

She texted back. **I'm sorry. Was it bad?**

It was a stupid thing to say. Of course it was bad. Funerals were never good.

Yeah, was James's reply. **His grandfather was there.**

Dee closed her eyes, felt her throat close up. She had to escape this. She would not be another Cal, mangled from the inside out, dead because she made the wrong deal.

With shaking fingers, she hit James's number on her phone.

He answered after only two rings.

"Yes?" said James.

She breathed. Forced herself to count to three on the exhale. "Is your car fixed yet?"

No hesitation on his part. "Yes. Four brand-new tires. Got the good kind, too. We could take the car up Mount Hood if you like."

She tried to smile, but her lips only twitched. "Um. Would you—would you mind driving me to the bank?"

It was four forty-five when they pulled in front of her bank— a local credit union she hadn't visited in ages. The sky was overcast, and the light felt dim despite sunset being a few hours away. Dee pulled her jacket around her. Her skin felt too tight, stretched over her bones, and she knew she kept scratching at the back of her neck.

"Do you need me to come in?" James asked. He had remained silent throughout the drive, as if sensing her unease.

"No," she said.

A pause. "Do you want me to come in?" he asked.

Another pause, this one longer. "Yes," she said, barely a whisper. It was stupid, but having someone at her side made her feel braver as she stepped from the car.

I chose this, she thought, and pushed the bank doors open.

With the exception of the damp mildew of the Daemon's building, banks all smelled the same to her—clean and sterile, with just a hint of metal. The clerk was a woman, her eyes worn and smile just a little weak. It was the end of the day, after all, Dee thought.

Dee slid her bank card under the glass barrier and said, "I'd like to withdraw all the funds from my account, please."

This was the hard part. Waiting. Waiting to see if the bank would let her have the funds without a parent's signature, if this trip was all for naught, or if she would walk out of this building with money enough to secure her future for just a little longer.

The woman typed away, and James murmured, "Making a withdrawal?"

"Rumpelstiltskin clause," she replied. "I give back what he gave me, I get my heart back."

He tilted his head. "I don't think that's how the Rumpelstiltskin clause is supposed to work. That's a straight refund, not a tricksy back door."

"Well, whatever," said Dee. "I'm going to try."

James smiled. "And that's what I like about you."

She didn't have an answer to that, but luckily that was when the clerk turned back to her. "I'm sorry," she began to say, and Dee's stomach plummeted. This wasn't going to work—she'd need a parent's permission.

218

"I'm sorry, but you cannot make a withdrawal. This account no longer exists," said the clerk. She looked sympathetic, rather than impatient. "It was emptied three years ago."

Dee's lips felt numb. "But—but the account was. Was mine. Only I could have..."

The clerk hit something on the computer, then looked at Dee. "Since the account was made for a minor, it required a parent's name to be on it, as well. The account was a joint one, which means that either owner could have—"

Dee felt dizzy, as if she'd stepped up to a high ledge and looked down. The world teetered beneath her, gravity threatening to take hold at any second. Her breath caught between her teeth.

She knew who had taken the money.

And she felt something snap inside of her. It was a release, like popping a cork on a champagne bottle—something bubbled up inside of her, something she had kept tamped down for years.

Before she was aware of it, she was leaving the bank. Her legs moved of their own accord, and James was beside her, his face pinched with worry. "Dee—Dee, are you all right? You look—"

"We need to make one more stop," she said. The anger bled into her voice, roughened her tone in a way she had never heard before.

James pulled the car keys from his pocket and didn't ask any questions.

The drive took less than twenty minutes, but Dee drummed her fingers on the car door the whole way. She yearned to move, to speak, to do something. She was buoyed up by righteous anger; this was deserved, this was earned. She finally had a legitimate grievance to air, and her anger kept her from fear. She was just angry enough to be foolish, and she wanted to ride that for as long as she could.

Dee shoved her key into the door and stepped through. The house smelled like it always did—of the oil from her father's work boots, cut grass, and unwashed dishes. Dee walked into the house, found her mother on the couch watching the news, and heard the distinct sounds of someone foraging in the kitchen. Her mother had a microwave dinner sitting on her lap.

"Dee?" asked Mrs. Moreno, startled. She was smiling, though, thinking this was a nice, surprise visit.

Dee ignored her. Her feet carried her through the living room, to where the kitchen and dining room connected. Sure enough, Mr. Moreno was there. He was chopping what looked like the leftovers from a rotisserie chicken; his sleeves were rolled up, revealing the corded muscles of his forearms.

"You," said Dee.

Mr. Moreno looked up. His gaze was steady, focused.

Not a bad way to start.

"Ah," said Mr. Moreno, also smiling. "Did you deign to

grace us with your presence for dinner? I'm afraid it's mostly leftovers—"

"You emptied my bank account."

She threw the words out between them, like a grenade without a pin, and waited for the world to explode.

But it didn't. For nearly ten full seconds, there was utter silence.

Mr. Moreno finished slicing through the chicken, set the knife down, and picked up a dish towel. He wiped the grease from his fingertips.

"My bank account," said Dee. "The one Gran started for me. Where—is—my—money?"

His face took on a new strength; he was arming himself, gathering the right words to say. "It wasn't your money," he said calmly.

"It was my money," said Dee. "I earned it babysitting and doing those stupid little jobs for your company. I raked leaves, I—"

"You're a minor," said Mr. Moreno. "That was our money, too. It was family money."

"Family money?" She took a step forward. It felt as if she were on fire, as if she could do anything and it wouldn't matter. Nothing mattered—he'd taken her one last chance at surviving.

"It was for school," she snapped. "It wasn't even for

something stupid, like other kids might have used it for. I never bought new clothes or purses or a nice cell phone—every cent went into that stupid account. For my future."

"And what kind of future is that?" He edged forward. She could see him getting angry, see the storm clouds gathering behind his eyes. "You want to go to college? To go somewhere far away and get some fucking useless degree for thousands of dollars?"

"Yes. Because that's what people do." Her hands were balled into fists. "That's what responsible people do. They go to college and they get good jobs."

"I never went to college," he replied with a sneer.

"And look at all the good it did you." She should have done what she always did; she should have kept her mouth shut.

But all her numbness vanished. She was abruptly aware of the churning in her middle, the flush creeping up her neck, the sudden fire racing through her veins. Anger. Raw fury clawed at her rib cage, as if the hollowness inside of her had been taken up by some wild creature.

"You can still go to college," he said, sliding back into that calm, arrogant demeanor that made her want to strike out. He was always so self-assured, so confident. "You'll just have to earn your own way. Like an adult."

"I was earning my own way!" she snarled. "I got into Brannigan, I put that money away, I—"

"That was Gran's money," he said, and suddenly his

expression darkened. "Though why she gave you a handout, I'll never know."

"Give it back," she said, and she hated that her voice trembled. "Just give it back. I need it."

"For what?"

She opened her mouth and closed it again.

"See, I don't think you want that money so you can go to college." Mr. Moreno's voice dropped, and she realized belatedly that there was a half-empty beer bottle in his hand. He brought it to his lips, drained it. "I think you just don't want to come home."

Hearing those words, those forbidden words, spoken aloud felt like some kind of betrayal. There were certain things people didn't talk about in this family and her desire to escape was one of them.

But if he wanted to open that door, she would let him.

"Family money," she said, mouth twisting with fury. The anger running through her felt like heat and pure force; in this moment, she was invincible, reckless, and the words flew from her mouth. "You took it for yourself." She strode to the bathroom, to the secret places she knew she wasn't supposed to know about. To the plastic brown bottles—half of them empty, half of them not. She snatched up two empty jugs and threw them onto the floor.

"Look what you bought with my future," she snapped. "Was it worth it? To numb out the world for a while?"

A half-formed thought, ready to catch fire, flew from her lips. "Did you ever care about me at all?"

A beer bottle smashed against the floor. And then he was in front of her, a wall of muscle and sweat and everything was too close and too loud.

"WHAT DID YOU SAY?"

Mrs. Moreno ventured into the kitchen with her hands extended as if entreating, but Dee ignored her.

She refused to retreat; she was afraid, but anger still kept her back straight. "You're a fucking addict. And I'm sick of it—I'm sick of watching you get drunk and scream at each other. I'm sick of you screaming at me, telling me I'm defective just because I didn't turn out the way you wanted!"

His hands closed on her arms and he shook her so hard her teeth rattled. "You will not talk to me like that! Children respect their parents."

She tried to wrench herself from his grip, her teeth bared. "Why? You never respected me! I spent half my life trying to fix things and I couldn't!"

"You're an ungrateful little shit." The words spewed from his mouth. "Fucking arrogant little bitch who thinks she's too good to do manual labor."

"At least I'm not a drunk loser," she snapped.

Crack.

The world went white.

She blinked several times, tried to orient herself. She was

on the floor, legs sprawled out before her. He'd thrown her down. The back of her head throbbed where she'd hit the wall.

"I never wanted this life!" he roared at her. "I never wanted you."

Simple words.

It was always those small, simple words.

This was what it felt like to fall apart. It began somewhere in her hands—they were cold, unfeeling, and the numb sensation seemed to travel up her arms, into her chest. It felt like her organs were shutting down; she was cold, but she wasn't shaking, wasn't reacting like living people did when cold. She wondered if she *had* died—if Cal and Cora were right, if she was a soulless zombie wandering around. But wouldn't she have felt something, she thought. If she was dead, there should have been a sign, a way of knowing.

Or maybe she'd been dead long before a demon ripped out her heart.

"Dee?"

It was a new voice that spoke. A familiar voice.

James.

His faded plaid shirt and absurd leather jacket were so familiar and comforting that she felt her eyes well up. Seeing him made the whole thing real. Pain spiked through her chest. She didn't want him to see this, see the ugliness of her past behind her carefully constructed facade.

This—this wasn't fair.

She didn't have a heart. She didn't have a heart. It shouldn't be able to break.

"I heard shouting," James said, uncertain.

Mr. Moreno stared at him, at his clothes, at his mussed hair. "Who the fuck are you?"

James's gaze flicked between Mr. Moreno and Dee, still on the floor. He seemed to change. It wasn't that he grew taller or more intimidating, but something in his face hardened. One of his hands balled up. "Dee?"

Dee opened her mouth, ready to tell him it was fine—it was *fine*—it *was* fine—

Nothing came out.

"Dee," said James. He walked to Dee, but Mr. Moreno angled forward. James took a step, shifted so that he squarely faced the older man. He didn't say a word, but the challenge was there.

"No," she whispered. The word came out so quiet she wondered how anyone heard it, but James did. He glanced back at her, questioning. Waiting for her to take the lead.

She didn't want them to fight. For one thing, she wasn't sure James could win.

"I need to leave," she whispered. She heard a noise from the doorway, where Mrs. Moreno lingered.

James knelt beside her and then his hands were on her, gentle and warm, helping her stand. She shuffled toward the door, her gaze fallen to the floor. She knew it was James who angled himself between her and her father, and she hated how grateful she felt. She shouldn't have let him—she should've handled this. She'd been handling this, she was the only one who knew how to handle this—

"Dee," pleaded Mrs. Moreno, and it nearly broke her.

Not my responsibility. Not my responsibility.

She couldn't be responsible for them anymore. Not when she could barely see straight.

James kept his hand on her back until they reached his car. She slid into the passenger's seat, but she couldn't feel it. She couldn't feel anything. Not James's hands running over her shoulders and arms, as if searching for injury. When his fingertips probed the back of her head, she drew in a sharp breath and he murmured an apology.

"Dee," he said, and she didn't answer. Couldn't answer.

"Deirdre," he said, his voice low and insistent. It was the first time he had ever said her full name.

She looked at him, saw he was studying her intently. "Follow my finger with your eyes," he said, and then his fingertip dragged through the air, back and forth. After a moment, his hand dropped. "All right. Looks like nothing's too badly rattled in there."

He strode around the car, slid into the driver's seat, one hand on the steering wheel and one reaching out, hovering over her shoulder. She sucked in a shuddering breath and then another.

She felt so heavy. Dragged down by the weight of despair. Such emotions threatened to unravel her from the inside out; she was beginning to fray, a sound building at the back of her throat.

She tried to hold it back, but then her eyes were stinging; she was shaking, and all the grief she had held pent up for so long began to escape her in little sobs and gasps.

James did not reach for her, for which she felt impossibly grateful; she could not have borne anyone's touch in that moment.

Minutes passed. She could not be sure how many. They simply sat in the car, on the curb, outside of the house she grew up in—that house where she couldn't untangle the good memories from the bad. And suddenly, she could not be there anymore; she had to leave, to look away. It simply hurt too much to be there.

"I can't," she said, when she could speak again. "Go back. There. I can't."

This probably made no sense to him, but he nodded as if he understood. "The dorm?"

She shook her head and the world swam. "Away," she said. "Anywhere." She expected him to inquire, to ask for more information, but he remained quiet.

She barely noticed when he put the car in drive and pulled away from the curb.

He drove.

She wasn't sure where they were going; the world faded into the quiet hum of the engine, the sound of air rushing by, the gleam of headlights, and the familiar cologne-and-paint smell of James's coat.

He had draped it over her legs at some point.

Probably because she was shivering. He had noticed, even if she hadn't.

"Where are we going?" she asked.

"Does it matter?"

She thought about it, which was harder than it should have been. "Not really."

"Do you care about missing a day or two of school?"

"Not really."

"All right, then."

TWENTY-FIVE

J ames pulled the car onto a freeway and drove east.

If they'd never left Portland, if they'd never gone to her house, Dee realized things would've been different. She'd be calling James a hipster hobo and a weird artist and he'd be smiling and taking it. But here, in this car, it felt like she'd shed her skin—raw and exposed.

No one had ever seen her like that. Cowering and weak, in that house that seemed to sap the life from her. She half expected him to ask questions, to probe at the raw memories.

But he never said a word. He simply drove, his fingers flicking down to the radio when the silence became oppressive. There was something soothing about the sound of pavement beneath the tires, of the low hum of the radio, the voices that occasionally fizzed in and out of audibility, of the taste of stale water when Dee found a bottle in the glove compartment.

They drove for hours, until evening crept in and all she could see were headlights.

They drove.

Because she could not bear to remain still.

It was sometime after night had fallen that James pulled off the interstate, found a dark nook of a gravel road. "I need to sleep," he said. "You should, too."

Dee curled up in the backseat, under a thick woolen blanket James pulled out of the trunk. James took the passenger seat, cranking it to a nearly horizontal position.

She should have protested. Sleeping in the same car as a boy.

But when she thought of him, she didn't think of him as a boy—not exactly. Boys were terrifying in the abstract, all long legs and too-loud shouting and boisterous energy. They were lewd comments and creatures that cowered before the high-heeled terror of self-assured girls like Gremma. Boys were things to be avoided until she was leaner, more confident, until she had actually managed to put together a wardrobe and a life.

When she thought of James, she thought of long fingers smudged gray with charcoal, of notebooks with torn pages, of the way he rolled his jeans up when he stepped into river water, of the pale freckled tops of his feet. She thought of him looking into her eyes and telling her, *I chose this*, and somehow making her feel in control again.

She trusted him.

It was an odd little realization, in the midst of what was most likely a mental breakdown. She trusted him when she didn't even trust herself.

Dee listened to the sound of his breathing. She couldn't see him in the pitch-black, but the occasional whispers of clothing and breath were enough to lull her to sleep.

She woke the next morning, her left arm folded beneath her. She tried to shake off the numbness, sitting up and peering around the car. The sky was light now, white with that predawn glow. James was already sitting up, looking alert but rumpled.

"Where are we?" she said, struggling out from under the blanket. She stepped out of the car in her bare feet, carefully picking her way across the pavement. James had parked on an overlook. There was one other car, a red VW bus with bright yellow curtains.

"Interstate 84," said James. "No idea how far we went, though."

She'd read once that the Columbia River Gorge had spent millions of years being carved out by water and wind. But those descriptions didn't do it justice. Sheer cliff faces rose all around her, the yellow rocks dappled with deep shadows. On her left was a craggy bluff. The wind had scoured away most of the greenery, leaving behind only a few rugged shrubs and bushes. On her right, ancient train tracks stood between her and the wide expanse of the Columbia River. Across the wide river was a sheer, yellow face of naked rock. She felt impossibly small, insignificant next to the towering peaks of raw stone.

"It's beautiful," she said.

James came to stand next to her. Already, the wind had picked up and his tousled hair was dragged across his eyes. "You never came here before?"

"Not really," said Dee. "Not a whole lot of family vacations at my house."

She spoke thoughtlessly, unprepared for how the words would hurt. James knew. He *knew*. Not even Gremma knew. Dee had tucked away her home life, shoved it far out of sight and mind, hoped that no one would ever see it.

But James didn't rise to the bait. He dug into his jeans, came up with the car keys, and offered them to her. "You want to drive?"

※〰※〰※〰※

They continued east.

James pointed out a small town and she swerved onto an off-ramp, drawn in by the logo of a fast-food joint. They didn't bother to go inside—a drive-through breakfast was good enough. Dee found herself holding the steering wheel with one hand and using the other to balance an egg-white sandwich. James tried to order a milk shake, but Dee put her foot down, getting orange juice and plenty of coffee. James ate pancakes out of a Styrofoam box, plastic fork in hand. The food was too oily and salty, and the coffee was so sharp it made Dee's teeth hurt. But the discomfort was the best kind—she sipped the horrible coffee and felt more alive than she had in months.

They returned to the interstate. Driving along I-84 left little room for conversation. The road had sweeping heights and dangerous curves, and they were nearly always in sight of the river. James sat with his feet on the dashboard, his window slightly cracked.

At one point, Dee's phone buzzed.

why did you miss school, came Gremma's text.

"Text back," said Dee. "Just say road trip."

"Your roommate won't rat you out?" asked James.

Dee snorted and waited for Gremma's reply. Sure enough, it said:

WITHOUT ME, YOU BITCH?

"Gremma encourages bad behavior," said Dee simply. "It means she has more company."

James laughed. "I like her."

"Don't get ideas. First off, she doesn't do boys. Second, she would swallow you whole and hack up your bones like an owl." A pause. "Then again, you might go for that kind of thing."

James's grin widened. "Why do you assume I'd go for the scary girls?"

"Because you sold your heart to a demon."

"Fair point."

Part of Dee felt she should have been at Brannigan. She should've been in classes, doing homework, living out her normal life. But she couldn't. She couldn't pretend to be fine—and it was freeing to realize she didn't have to. In this car, she was safely removed from her real life.

They arrived at their destination around midday. James was driving again, and he turned onto 730 East, toward the Washington border. She saw the sign for the upcoming town and raised her eyebrows.

"Walla Walla?"

James shrugged one shoulder. "I like any town that sounds like it could be named after a Muppet," he said blandly.

Dee stared at him. "Really?"

A smile broke across his face. "Come on. Out of all the things I've said, that has to be the most normal. Besides, we need to stop somewhere. I figure this is as good a place as any."

They found a hotel on the edge of town. It was a chain, plain and standard, with the promise of a continental breakfast in the morning.

They ventured inside the room together; neither had luggage, which made Dee feel oddly unburdened. It was clean and neat, with some Western theme to it, all the fabrics and paints in varying shades of orange and brown.

Two queen beds. "I get the one next to the bathroom," said James.

Dee gave him a hard look. "Way to be gallant."

"Actually," he replied, "the one closer to the bathroom is nearer to the door. Should anyone break in, they've got to go through me first."

She fought back a smile. "Are you anticipating a break-in?"

"Hey, that would be tame, considering our lives."

"True."

It should have been weird—she was in a hotel room with a boy. But James kept to his side of the room, remote in hand and flipping through television channels. He found some cooking competition and settled in, tossing his worn shoes off the bed. It was strangely domestic, she thought.

Dee showered. She hadn't brought extra clothes, so she put the same ones back on. But she felt better—the hot water loosened some of her knotted muscles, and she felt clean, lighter.

James was still watching the reality cooking show when she emerged, and she sat down on her own bed. It was strangely entrancing to watch the lives of other people, see them made into dramas. It was a relief to step outside of herself, to lose all sense of identity in the flashing images and sounds.

They went out for lunch.

Walla Walla had a very pretty downtown historic district. The sidewalks were wide and tourist-friendly, with plenty of lamps and benches. Decorative statues rose from the sidewalk like concrete flowers, twisting up toward the sky.

They bought sandwiches from a cafe and ate sitting at one of the benches. The sunlight beat down on Dee's bare arms and she allowed herself to take in the heat and food.

"Thank you," she said.

He looked up over his sandwich. "For?"

"This." She gestured vaguely around them, at the old-time street and tourists. "I mean, you didn't have to. And for—well, not looking at me like there's something wrong with me."

He looked at her. "Do you think there is?"

"I feel like that sometimes," she said, pressing her fingertips to her skull, as if she could push the thought from her mind. "I feel like I'm just this collection of broken pieces I don't know what to do with." It was all too easy to remember the homunculus, that monster of human parts, and imagine herself in such a state.

"What did they do to you?" he asked softly.

She laughed and it came out mangled. "Nothing, really. That's the worst part. It was all little stuff. They never beat me or starved me. But they're alcoholics, both of them. Dad first, and then I think Mom started drinking just to numb him out. Half the time they'd ignore me. Mom tried, but Dad's a mean drunk. He'd go looking for targets to vent at, and I was one of his favorites. Anything I did was wrong. If I was interested in a school subject, it was the wrong one. If I showed an interest in a hobby, he'd tell me it was a waste of time. If I showed any kind of emotion, he'd tell me I was too sensitive. I learned how to deal—how to make myself small or stay hours at the library.

"They used to tell me to keep the house clean," she said. "That if social services ever came by, if they saw a messy house, they'd assume the worst. And I'd be taken away to some horrible place."

"Did social services ever come by?" His tone was deceptively light.

"Once." She ran her fingertips over her jeans. "A neighbor heard one of the arguments. But my parents were always at their best in the mornings, and that's when the social worker stopped by. My father has always been charming, when he needed to be. And he has his own business, and the..."

"The house was clean," said James.

Her throat ached. "Yes. But it wasn't all bad. They had their good points. Which makes this worse somehow—I know they're people. My mom is so kind, ridiculously so at times. She always stopped to talk with homeless people, when most everyone likes to forget they're people. Dad would try, sometimes." She swallowed. "But when I was thirteen, things changed."

"How?"

They had finished their sandwiches by now; Dee stood, tossed her napkins in a trash can made from a vintage barrel.

She bent down and pulled off her boot, carefully placing her sock on top of it. She held up one foot by the ankle, turning so that her back was to James. She heard the moment he saw the scar—the smallest inhale.

"He'd thrown a plate," she said tonelessly. "She was crying in the yard. I tried to clean it up, but I ended up stepping on a piece instead. I tried to hide the blood—I didn't want anyone to worry, so I dug the glass out myself in the bathroom. I was stupid, though. I left bloody towels in the hamper, so it was obvious."

"Was that a wake-up call for them?" asked James.

Dee smiled, felt it crack her face wide-open. She kept her back to him, so he couldn't see her. "The bloody towels were obvious. But they never noticed a thing."

James touched her shoulder. "A wake-up call for you, then."

Dee turned around, eyes on the sidewalk. She let go of her ankle, and her toes brushed bare ground. She hadn't let Gremma paint her toenails in a couple of weeks, so the purple polish had chipped. "It was then that the bad stuff started outweighing the good. I started researching boarding schools a month later."

James looked at her, but it wasn't a look of pity or disgust. It was one of awe. "You saved yourself. And when the money for the boarding school ran out, you did it again. You went out and found a demon."

"More like he found me," admitted Dee.

"Still," said James. "It was brave."

She snorted. "Running away?"

He answered her with all seriousness. "Surviving." He bent down, took her sock, and glanced down at her bare toes. "May I?"

She balanced with one hand on his shoulder. He was still wearing that plaid flannel, the material gone soft with wear. He tugged her sock back on, straightening it so the seam lined up perfectly with her toes. The boot was next. He carefully pulled it into place.

The gesture was such a small thing, but it touched her.

When he stood, he was smiling. "All right. So today is Friday. You're skipping school. Anything you want to do while you're being a delinquent?"

She considered; something had been nagging at her, something she hadn't allowed herself to truly think about until now.

"Can we go to a library?" she asked.

He laughed.

There was a public library. It was well cared for and clean. Everything smelled of old paper and clean carpets and people—students and adults alike, deodorant and sweat and perfume. It was a very lived-in scent, and it was comforting. Dee asked a librarian for the computers and found herself directed around a tall series of shelves.

James trailed behind her, curious but agreeable—his default state, as she thought of it. She went to one of the computers and opened up a web browser. "That female d-thing," she said, stumbling over the word *demon*. There were too many normal people about—students and seniors, browsing the shelves. "She said something. A word I didn't recognize. I wanted to look it up."

"You do realize we have phones for that, right?" said James, smiling.

Dee threw him an annoyed look. "Maybe I feel like not staring at a screen the size of my palm."

That got her a laugh. "What did the demon say?"

"Burrower," she replied. "She asked how we would do up against a burrower."

James's brow creased. "So the demons' mortal enemies are...gophers?"

Dee held back a snort. Her fingers typed the word and at once—sure enough, the first hit was a page on vermin control. "What a terror," said James drily as a picture of a mole came up. "Look at those whiskers. Truly a thing to be feared."

"There's got to be more than one meaning," said Dee as she scrolled down the search page. Pest control, wildlife, a brand of shovel, and then—

Her fingers came up, touched the computer screen. Left little smudgy fingerprints in their wake.

It was a picture of a beast, inhuman, with many legs, rising from the depths of an ocean.

She heard James swallow.

Dee clicked on that page and up popped an info site on Lovecraft.

For a minute, neither of them spoke.

"Old gods," said Dee quietly. "A burrower is a type of old god."

James laughed nervously. "But—but this is fiction, right? I mean, I read that 'Cry of Cathalhoo' thing when I was in high school. The only thing I remember was that everyone who learned about the creature ended up being murdered by some cult. Oh, and Lovecraft was kind of a racist."

Dee pointed at the computer screen. "You mean 'The Call of Cthulhu'?"

James blinked, unashamed. "Literature was never my thing. Name three Impressionists, and then you're allowed to criticize."

"Fair point," Dee said, unable to hide her smile. "But I mean, think about it. The Daemon said that this wasn't the first time demons had revealed themselves. What if…we aren't the first generation of heartless?"

James considered. "That would explain a lot about Bosch's paintings."

"There are tales going back thousands of years about deals with demonic creatures," said Dee. "Faust, Rumpelstiltskin, meeting creatures at crossroads, even blues singers claiming to have sold their soul for talent."

James looked impressed.

"But the thing is, the demons of today aren't buying souls. They want limbs—which they make into homunculi, and use to destroy the voids."

She gave James a steady look. She trusted him. "I saw something," she said quietly, "the first time I was in a void. At the hospital. It was only a moment—and it didn't look entirely like that picture, but it wasn't…well, it's not entirely off. And when we were in that last void, when I saw the homunculus—it had something in its hand. A freshly bleeding leg-like thing." She leaned forward. "Is there anything you haven't told me? About what happened in Rome?"

She wasn't sure what to expect. Perhaps he would look offended or angry, or maybe he would push his chair away from the table and stride out of the library. But he did none of those things. His shoulders slumped, and he let out a breath.

"Rome wasn't like Portland," he said quietly. "I wasn't friends with anyone in my troop. We were simply all thrown together, told what to do and how to do it. The Daemon kept us on a tighter leash; we all lived in the same apartment for a while—except for the Daemon himself. He just popped into the kitchen when he needed us. It was...well, it was one of the best times of my life—but also the worst. I spent my days painting like I'd only ever dreamed of, and I started getting attention, but then at night me and the three other heartless would be in dark alleys, kicking rats out of the way as we tried to find voids. And for a while, it worked. But things...didn't go well.

"We lost one guy inside a void. Something...*grabbed* him. I never saw what it was. I was in the mouth of the void, keeping it open. The girl who was with him swore she saw a monster, but she wouldn't—or couldn't—describe it. I would've gone back for him, but the charges were set and the timer was ticking down." Something like shame crossed his face. "Another girl decided that the knitted hearts were the key to the Daemon's power, so she dissected hers. But the moment it unraveled, she just died. Like Cal. You saw what happened.

"After that," he said, "there were only two of us. The last girl's two years were up, and she got her heart back. I saw the Daemon do it—that's how I know it's possible. He just... pushed it into her chest. Like popping a socket into place. And then I was the only one left, and the Daemon said that Italy wasn't a territory he needed to worry about anymore. He said Portland was the new hotspot, and he told me we would be going there instead.

"When I got to Portland, the Daemon had already made his deal with Cora. Then he recruited Cal, and then it was the three of us for nearly two years." His mouth twitched. "That is, until that void opened up in a hospital." He regarded her almost fondly, as if this twist of fate had been a welcome one.

But she barely heard the last bit; her attention was elsewhere. *Nearly two years.*

"When is your deal up?" she asked. She wasn't sure if she was relieved or frightened to know that he wouldn't always be heartless with her.

James's smile seemed to vanish. "Soon enough." He turned his attention back to the computer screen. Without meaning to, Dee had left the page open on a painting of what must have been Cthulhu. It was a roiling mass of tentacles and teeth, frozen forever in the act of rising from some great depth.

"Old gods," said James quietly. "Here's the thing I'd like to know. If demons are, well... *evil*, then how bad are the things they're fighting against?"

TWENTY-SIX

Dee had never skipped school before. She'd never gone on a road trip with a boy, never slept in a hotel room with anyone besides her parents.

Turned out, it wasn't all that scandalous. That night, they found a boutique and bought overpriced clothes—which James insisted on paying for, saying that the painting of Dee at the river would keep him fed for a year, so he was indebted to her. It was roundabout logic. "I'll accept that," she said, "but only if I get to pick out your clothes."

He agreed.

And they walked out of the boutique wearing clean and vaguely vintage clothing. She'd put him in jeans and a cashmere sweater, and his orange jacket was shoved in the bottom of their shopping bag. He looked—well. He looked good.

They bought Chinese takeout and brought it back to their room, ate it while watching yet another cooking reality show. Dee fell asleep before it was even ten, the TV still flickering in the background.

They spent most of the next day at the library.

If there truly were old gods and demons, there had to be some record of them. Perhaps a clue in one of Lovecraft's stories on how to defeat them.

"You really do not know how to be a delinquent," James told her. But he was grinning and took whatever small task she assigned him.

Mostly, they read. Fairy tales, folktales, Faust, Edgar Allan Poe, Lovecraft, and the authors who had taken up where Lovecraft left off. They read about myths and legends, of deals made and deals lost, about creatures so old they did not have a name. Dee wasn't sure if any of this was useful, but they noted anything that might relate to their current situation. They looked for any mention of a Lovecraftian monster, of burrowers, of holes in reality. While Dee browsed the literature, James invaded the art section. There was a surprising number of paintings that depicted world-ending monsters.

If there were other heartless throughout history, they did

not openly declare themselves. But Dee still wanted to look, to search, to perhaps find some hint that more like themselves had survived their own hollow state.

I chose this, Dee thought, and picked up another book.

It felt inevitable when it finally happened. They were sitting on a park bench, finishing off hot dogs they'd bought from a stand.

Dee was talking about one of the variations of *Snow White* she'd found—mostly because it was one of the fairy tales with literal heart connections. She had a theory that perhaps this was one of the folktales with a grain of truth; perhaps the evil queen had been a demon. It would explain her ruthlessness and her beauty.

"People believed in the supernatural back then," said Dee. "Like werewolves and witches and all that. The queen could've been a demon, but over the centuries the retelling of the story was muddled because modern people don't believe in the supernatural."

"People believe in the supernatural now," countered James. "I mean, hello. Demons."

Dee frowned. "Some people don't. There are entire websites dedicated to disproving them. Cal didn't believe. He told me he thought they were aliens."

James broke into startled laughter. "Yeah. I remember." His expression sobered and he crumpled up his napkin. "So, tell me. What do you believe in?"

"I don't know. It could be supernatural, it could be aliens, or I could simply have lost my mind."

"So you don't even believe in this old gods theory of yours?"

She looked down. "All right. Fine. What do you believe in, then?"

His voice softened. "I believe we're not crazy, for one thing."

"Well, good."

She was gazing out at the park when his fingertips touched her chin. He slowly tilted her face toward him. "I believe I'm glad I met you."

Her skin felt warm where he touched her. She had a wild thought that this was when she didn't miss her heart; because she knew if she did have one, it would have been beating so loud that it would have drowned out the world.

He gave her every opportunity to retreat, but she did not flinch away.

He kissed her. His lips were gentle, as if asking a question, but his fingers were tight on her arm, as if afraid she might suddenly vanish.

It was a sweet, warming thing—like taking a sip of hot chocolate on a misty, cold morning. The world simply tuned out for a moment, and the silence was the most beautiful thing Dee had ever heard.

They drifted apart.

"We probably shouldn't," she said.

His face cleared. "If that's what you want." He said the words without any trace of hurt or disappointment. Again, simple words. But this time they were not intended to wound.

She kissed him.

His lips were warm, soft, and they contrasted sharply with the stubble along his jaw. His hands were soft, too, and he was cradling the back of her neck, his thumb skimming along her hairline, sending shivers through her.

No one had ever kissed her like this. There had been a few parties, middle school encounters with spin the bottle and one memorable occasion with seven minutes in heaven when she and Trevor Farley had not made eye contact until the last thirty seconds, when he said, "Should we just try it?" It had been too wet and had simply felt like two mouths mashing together.

This kiss was soft, tentative. James's lips barely moved against hers—just tiny whispers of sensation that swooped through her stomach.

This time he was the one to pull away, to gaze at her face as if trying to decipher her thoughts. "Was that okay?"

"Why'd you kiss me?" she asked instead. As if she had not just kissed him right back.

His cheeks colored. "I told you before. We could die any day. Might as well enjoy ourselves."

A long pause.

"So you're saying that *I'm* the full-fat cream cheese," she said.

He pressed his lips together, his mouth twitching in an effort not to smile. "I would have given you a cuter nickname, I swear." His mirth faded. "Listen, Dee. I get it. I'm not your type. You like stability and all that, and I'm—well. Me. If you want to just stay friends, I won't hold it against you. Really, I won't."

She was afraid to want this. Afraid to rely on anyone, because she knew how easily they could slip away.

"It's possible I may have trust issues," she said.

"Shocking" was his deadpan answer.

He needed to know why this was such a bad idea. "James," she said. "I—I don't think I can do this. Broken little pieces, remember? I'm not sure I'm capable of loving anyone—not if I can't trust anyone."

His mouth thinned out. "You are not broken," he said. "Dee, you're fine. I like you. You—as you are now."

The breath caught in her throat; she should have just pushed him away—it would have made everything easier. But…she found herself unable to say those words. "Could I just…have some time to think about this?"

She had always thought of herself as *broken*. She had

crafted the word into armor, used it to keep the world at bay, to keep all her little pieces from completely falling apart.

She wondered what it would be like not to carry it around. And maybe this was the first step, maybe letting someone in was how all people did this.

He gave her a brilliant, lopsided smile. "Hey, neither of us is aging at the moment. We've got all the time in the world."

She had forgotten about that—that her life would likely be two years longer than it should have been, thanks to this deal of hers. But then again, that was assuming she lived through this. Perhaps that was the way fairy-tale deals always worked, all or nothing, a long life or one cut tragically short.

"Thank you," she said. For the kiss, for understanding, for simply being him. She wanted to somehow convey that, to tell him that she appreciated him without saying as much in words. She reached down, found his hand with hers. His fingers were dry and warm, his nails edged with charcoal. He seemed to understand; a smile played over his mouth.

Their fingers tangled, wrists pressed together.

No pulse between them.

❧❧❧❧❧❧

Back in the hotel room, Dee thought things might be awkward. But somehow, they weren't. James clicked on the television again, then went to shower. Dee sat on her bed, eating a cold egg roll and half listening to the news.

They couldn't stay here much longer. It was Saturday—and she needed to be back at school by curfew tomorrow. No doubt Gremma would have covered for her in the meantime. Gremma was good for that, even if she was still angry. Dee felt a pang of worry at the thought of returning to her old life; this road trip had been an escape, a way to ignore the pain that would inevitably be felt upon her return. She didn't want to think about it. Not her parents, not the empty bank account, not her tangled friendship with her roommate.

Ah, well. She'd deal with it tomorrow.

Dee was using her chopsticks to eat the last of the fried rice when she heard the news anchor say, "...cause unknown. But the force of the explosion took out half a city block."

Dee looked up.

A blond man stood with his fingers pressed to his ear, the other hand holding a mic. "As you can see, Rachel," he was saying, "the police have roped off the area—but we did manage to get a chopper in overhead. You should be seeing the footage now."

The screen flickered and up came an image of smoking remnants—a building, Dee thought. Or what was left of it. It looked as though a bomb had gone off, ripped the structure to shreds and tossed the cars about. Then the image went back to that of the news reporter. The words flashed beneath his face, as they always did in urgent news reports: SEATTLE NEIGHBORHOOD STRUCK BY UNKNOWN EXPLOSION.

"The neighboring apartment buildings have been evacuated," continued the man, "but we are still unsure as to how many people were affected by the blast. In the meantime..."

But she was no longer listening to the man's words. She dropped the chopsticks and the take-out carton, scrambled across the bed, and gaped at the screen.

There were many people staring at the smoking building, even as the police were trying to ward them away. And among the crowd stood a man. A man with dark hair, beautiful features, and an umbrella tucked beneath his arm.

TWENTY-SEVEN

Dee returned to a world both changed and unchanged.

Unchanged, because when she finally powered up her phone, there were three voice mails waiting for her.

The first two were from her mother. Her voice was carefully neutral, asking if she would like to come home for a Sunday dinner a week from that day. There was a shiver in her voice, as if she were holding back her own distress.

The last voice mail was from her father. He asked if she knew where the extra vacuum bags were, where she had put them. There was no mention of the fight, no allusion to any conflict—likely, he didn't even remember it had occurred.

Unchanged.

Definitely unchanged.

But some things had changed.

Changed because she had not slept last night—she was too busy looking up news of the explosion in Seattle, texting Cora about it. Cora replied with a simple **No idea** and left it at that. James was more willing to talk it out with her—and they settled on one rather uncomfortable conclusion.

Something had gone wrong. With the voids, with the demons—otherwise, why would the Daemon have bothered to stick around? "He wouldn't have been there if it was just an accident," said James darkly, and Dee couldn't disagree.

And the world was also changed, because when they pulled up at her dorm, there was a moment of slightly awkward silence between her and James. She hesitated, unsure of what to expect. This was it—the last few seconds of her Not-Life. The moment she opened the door and stepped onto the sidewalk, things would go back to normal. Or what passed for normal these days.

So she did one last reckless thing.

She leaned in, pressed a kiss to his cheek. His skin was soft, his stubble rasped against her lips. He held very still, as if not wanting to scare her off. "Thank you for everything," she told him, before she opened the car door and stepped into her real life.

When she walked into her dorm, Gremma was waiting. She had a cup in hand, offering coffee in exchange for an explanation. Dee had little energy to make up stories, so she simply said that she couldn't stand the thought of attending school, so she'd begun her weekend early. With James. The boy she'd disappeared with from the art gallery. It was a flimsy excuse, even for Dee.

Gremma eyed her. "You're not telling me everything," she said. Not in an accusing way, but more matter-of-fact.

"No, I'm not," Dee agreed.

A moment's pause.

"This has to do with your drug running, doesn't it?" asked Gremma.

Dee heaved an exasperated sigh. "For the last time, I am not a drug runner."

Gremma narrowed her eyes, her painted green nails thrumming impatiently on her desk. "Organ harvester?"

"Yes," said Dee, straight-faced. "I am an organ harvester. You have gotten the truth out of me. Can I have the latte now?"

Gremma's scowl never lessened, but she handed the coffee over. "You've always been hard to read," she said. "I mean, I know you're a liar. You've always been a good liar. But you're getting better at it and it's driving me crazy."

Dee paused, the coffee halfway to her mouth. Those words coming from anyone else would have sounded like an insult—but Gremma sounded almost admiring, almost fond. The way she spoke about one of her unsolved puzzles.

"I am not a liar." Dee sipped the coffee.

"Only liars say that," replied Gremma. "People lie. It's what they do. But it's about little stuff, like homework and shit. But you—you hide everything. I've never been inside your house."

"I've never been inside yours," Dee protested.

"My parents live in Seattle." Gremma gave her a measured look. "Yours live less than ten miles away. But I know far less about you than you do about me. I didn't even know you were Latino until I saw your last name on a student form. I thought you were just really tan or something."

"Half Latino," said Dee. "On my dad's side."

"See," said Gremma. "I didn't even know that." She tilted her head, eyeing Dee. "You never talk about anything in particular—you've mastered the art of small talk. And for the most part, I like it. I like puzzles. But now you're running around with homeless guys—"

"He is not actually homeless. You know that. You've seen his apartment."

"—and you're missing school, and I swear I smelled something like cordite on you the other day."

Dee took another drag of coffee, if only so she had time to think of an excuse. "Are you going to report me?"

"No," said Gremma. "I just want to know what's going on so I can go back to normal puzzles like how the human body works. This is driving me up a wall. I couldn't focus on chemistry the other day because I spent half an hour trying to figure out your new extracurricular activities."

And for a moment, Dee considered it. She considered telling Gremma everything—about her heart, about her parents, about the Daemon, about that cobbled-together homunculus, about Cal falling to the sidewalk, about Cora's hollow eyes, about the sensation of James's mouth on hers, their fingers woven together, about the fact that her life was some kind of screwed-up fairy tale and she wasn't sure if she was supposed to be reading Faust or Cthulhu or if she was even going to survive all of this—

But the words knotted in her throat, and she found herself unable to speak them aloud.

Gremma saw the distress on her face and she softened. "Fine," she said. "Not now. But later, I swear to everything that I hold dear. Later, Moreno. I will get it out of you."

The text came on a Saturday afternoon.

WE NEED TO MEET, said Cora. **JAMES'S APARTMENT. TONIGHT. 8PM.**

Dee could almost hear Cora's stern voice in the all-caps message.

She texted James. **Did you just get Cora's message?**

yup.

Did she volunteer your apartment as a meet spot?

it's not the first time. u need a ride?

Dee considered; she ran through the scenario of asking Gremma for the Camaro, then quickly typed a reply.

Yes, please.

She met James on the curb. Her stomach was twisted into knots; she hadn't seen him since the road trip and part of her was nervous. She didn't need to be flustered. After all, they were friends. But her mouth went dry when his car pulled up and he stepped out.

And then she froze in horror.

She raised a finger. "No. No, no, no."

James reared back a step, startled. "What?"

Now that they had returned to their old lives, it seemed James had gone back to dressing in his usual wardrobe. With one notable addition.

"You are wearing a *straw hat*." Dee couldn't believe she was even saying the words—but there it was, perched atop his rumpled hair. "You are *not* wearing a straw hat."

"Pretty sure those are two contradictory statements," said James. He was grinning, reaching up to tweak the offensive accessory.

"That is possibly the most hideous thing I have ever seen," said Dee. She was rooted to the spot, paralyzed with disgust.

"You'll work for a demon," said James, "blow up magical

voids, juggle a double life, watch friends get killed…and this is what breaks you?"

"It's got a hole in one side," said Dee, making no attempt to hide her despairing tone.

"Does it really?" James pulled the hat off and poked a finger through said hole. "Oh. Look at that."

Dee snatched the hat from his hands and tossed it into the bushes. "Now look what you've done," said James.

"You said we should live for today," said Dee. "That fedora is not living. That hat is the opposite of living."

"Technically, it was a trilby," said James. "And did you just call my hat undead?"

She laughed and it turned into a snort. Which made him laugh, in turn.

It occurred to her that that was exactly why he wore it. He knew it would distract her, get her to focus on something trivial. And all at once, her nervousness faded away.

"No one else is going to die," said Cora.

James and Dee simply looked at her.

They were still sitting on his Ikea couch, the one stained with paint and charcoal. Her back was to the couch's arm, her feet tucked beneath his thigh. The contact felt comforting. A box of pizza sat open on the coffee table. Cora had declined the food. She had also declined a seat in favor of pacing back and forth, much in the manner of a general at a war council. There was a fire behind her eyes, Dee saw, a burning that had not been there before. Her body was tight with pain, her face rough with sleeplessness.

Cora said, "This is wrong. We're wrong. We were wrong to make deals and the Daemon was wrong to change us. He is going around turning us into these...things." Her fingers touched a lump in her pocket—and Dee thought that must be where she was keeping her knitted heart. "This is wrong. He can't do this to us. We're all being kept alive on a string."

"I think you mean our lives hang on a thread," James corrected, as if unable to help himself.

Cora threw him a heated look. "I have been awake for nearly three days straight. Do you think I give a damn about the phrasing?"

Ah. So that explained her slightly unhinged appearance. "If you do not mind me asking," said James. "Why have you been awake for three days?"

"I'm going to stop him," snapped Cora. "I will not let him take another heart. I've been following the Daemon for three days. Or trying to. I've mostly managed."

"How will you even find him now?" asked Dee, startled out of her silence. "If you're here, and he's out there...?"

Cora's smile was a crooked, triumphant thing. "Demons still think we're helpless. They treat us like livestock, like things to be herded and harvested for their own needs. But humans evolved in the last few hundred years—and we've got technology."

A moment.

Then it hit Dee. Exactly how one might track the Daemon.

"You're following his cell phone?" she said, aghast.

James gazed at Cora in unflattering amazement. "Wow. I mean, I knew you were ballsy, but this is...a whole new level."

Her mouth twisted. "Shut up, Lancer." There was no affection in her words, no blunted insult this time. Her voice was low, utterly serious, and for the first time, Dee did not see a benevolent leader. Cora looked...coldly calculating. She looked like a demon hunter.

This, Dee decided, would not end well.

"So," said Cora, turning flashing eyes upon Dee and James. "Are you both in?"

The ringing silence was answer enough. Cora looked between James and Dee, her own face tight with anger. "You're just going to let this continue?" she snapped.

"I don't see we have a lot of choice," said Dee quietly.

Cora did not say another word. She turned on her high heel and strode out of the apartment.

"I feel like an asshole," said Dee.

"I'm impressed," said James.

She frowned at him. "Because I said no to someone?"

"Actually, it was because you just swore in front of me."

She used her big toe to poke at his leg. He made a squeaking sound and caught her bare ankle in one hand. "Seriously, are we horrible for not wanting to help her?" said Dee, after a moment of thought.

James shook his head. "You're asking me if we're horrible people for not wanting to break a contract with an immortal being, to deliberately set ourselves against him, to risk everything we have and everything we are—all so we might hypothetically keep another teenager from losing his or her heart?" He paused.

"We're horrible people," said Dee.

"Yes, we are," agreed James. "But somehow I think I can live with it."

TWENTY-EIGHT

Days passed and the weather went from fair to foul. Sunlight was chased away by clouds, and the light took on a grayish quality. Torrents of rain lashed at the windows, making it look as though the entire building was being put through a car wash. But no one paid the rain any real attention; the teacher went on talking about irregular polygons—half of the students were taking notes and the other half were passing them.

Dee was averaging out the two heights of her polygon when her phone buzzed in her pocket. She jumped; she usually kept the thing turned off—but Gremma had overslept and Dee had ended up rushing her morning routine. As subtly as she could, Dee reached into her pocket and withdrew her phone. She tucked it behind her geometry book and eyed the screen.

James: **have you heard from cora at all?**

Dee's lips pressed together in a frown. She glanced up at the teacher; his back was to the room, his attention on the whiteboard as he sketched out a new polygon. Hastily, she typed a response.

No. Why?

His reply came a moment later: **she's gone quiet for a week. making me nervous, tbh.**

A cool tendril of dread seemed to settle in her stomach. This wasn't anything out of the norm, she reasoned. Cora might have given up or become busy with other responsibilities. She had sisters, if Dee remembered right. There were plenty of reasons that Cora might have relinquished her vendetta against the Daemon.

But then Dee remembered the look on Cora's face: bedrock certainty, accompanied by an unhealthy amount of righteous fury.

No. Cora would not have given up.

Perhaps—

No.

Dee refused to even let herself think the words.

But they rolled around in her brain until she typed them out.

You don't think, she texted, **that Cora did something. Interfered somehow. And the Daemon got angry.**

James's response took a good minute to come and that was enough to make Dee jittery with nerves.

maybe.

Her lips formed a silent curse and she picked up her pencil and shoved her phone beneath a stack of graph paper. She couldn't think about this right now. Cora was strong-willed; she was independent; if she was going to do something stupid, it would take more than the likes of Dee or James to stop her.

Another thought occurred to her—one so horrible that Dee immediately reached for her phone again.

How angry do you think the Daemon would be if we interfered?

Another long pause; another frightful minute of her teacher droning on about x-coordinates. The sound of the rain on the windows almost drowned him out and he was having to speak more loudly.

U saw him after Cal died, came James's reply.

And abruptly, an old memory came back to her. A party in the Grover dorm, a handful of pretzels, and a very drunk girl with a prosthetic arm saying, *They won't kill people. Not can't, but won't. My demon, she said that it's too much trouble for what they get out of it.*

Not can't—won't.

Dee texted James one last time before jamming her phone back into her bag.

We should check on Cora tonight.

༄༅༄༅༄༅

Sneaking off campus was becoming frighteningly easy.

She told her dorm monitor she was off to the library. As a junior and a known quiet student, she was given more freedom than perhaps she should have been.

Dee hurried to where James was waiting in his Mom Car. The wind tore at her hair and she slid into the car with undisguised relief. "It's getting bad out here," said James, by way of greeting. "You sure you want to come along?"

Dee gave him a look. "You think I should stay at home while you go tracking down Cora?"

He was trying hard not to smile. "You look as though I've slipped from gallant to patronizing."

"Maybe you have."

"Or," he said, abruptly serious, "it's possible that I'm worried about what we're walking into, and I'd rather not see you get hurt."

Surprise made her pause. She couldn't remember the last time someone worried over her. Perhaps it was when she was young, much younger, but no true memory came to mind. It was...she wasn't sure how it made her feel, to be honest.

She regained herself. "So if you're worried, that means you're not being patronizing?" But she said the words with a smile, to let him know she wasn't offended.

"Oh, it's very likely I'm being patronizing," he agreed. "But I'd rather have you be offended than dead."

A sudden chill swept through her and it had little to do with her damp clothing. James had been doing this longer than she had—he knew the dangers more clearly. And if he was worried, then perhaps there was a reason for it.

But when she considered getting out of his car, going back into her dorm, and remaining quiet and waiting, her stomach turned over.

Whatever this was, she didn't want James walking into it alone.

James took them into a part of the city clustered with old apartment buildings and college dorms. Probably for PSU. James found a parking spot entirely by accident and hurriedly parked before anyone else could take it.

The two of them ran from the car into a nearby apartment building. It wasn't a nice one; there were broken grates and the distinct scent of mold permeated the air.

A girl answered the door when they knocked. It swung open and Dee caught a glimpse of the interior. It was clean and neat, and it smelled of green apple air freshener. A bright blue rug covered most of the hardwood floor.

The girl at the door couldn't have been more than thirteen. When she saw James, her eyes widened slightly. But then she looked at Dee, in her school uniform, and relaxed slightly. "Can I help you?" she asked, her tone suspicious.

"Hi," said Dee, taking the lead. "I'm a friend of Cora's. Is she around?"

The girl didn't open the door any farther. "What's your name?"

"I'm Dee, and this is James."

The girl's gaze alighted on James. "Oh. You're that dick artist," she said.

James blinked.

"It's what my sister calls you," said the girl. "She's not here, you know. She said she was going to a farmers market or something. I told her it was raining, but she said there was something she had to pick up there."

And then she shut the door.

"Dick artist," said Dee. Her voice actually trembled with suppressed laughter. James looked so thoroughly wrong-footed, as if his charm had never been deflected with such ease.

Dee burst out laughing; she had to press a hand to the wall to keep herself upright. Even James smiled.

"Well," he said, recovering himself. "I have been called worse things." But his humor melted away. "I know where Cora's gone."

Dee looked at him. "Where?"

James didn't smile. His gaze had slid out of focus. "It makes sense. I mean..." He seemed to come back to himself. "There are places, in every major city, where demons are known to frequent. The place you go to sell a limb. In New York City, there is a bar. In Rome, there was a church. In Vegas, there is a casino."

"And in Portland...?" Dee prompted.

James let out a heavy breath. "There is a farmers market."

Mephisto Market didn't advertise its presence.

The market was tucked away on the edge of the Willamette, removed from the bustle of the city. To get there, James had taken his car down a gravel road; more than one raccoon had scurried out of the path of the car, eyes reflecting green in the headlights. The car jerked and wrenched though water-filled potholes, and the curve of James's mouth drew tight, anxious. His Mom Car wasn't equipped for offroading and Dee wondered if they would even make it to the market, or if they would find themselves trying to call a tow truck.

The market was just barely visible. Tents and tarps had been set up on a flat space of gravel and dirt just before the river. Clumps of trees blocked out the lights of the city, and Dee had the sudden sense that they were in the middle of nowhere, that if something went wrong, there would be no help for them.

James unearthed an umbrella from the trunk and Dee drew her coat tightly around herself. They tried to fit themselves under the single umbrella, and ventured toward the cluster of tents.

Candles guttered in the wind and the tarps flapped loudly. Rain spattered along the muddy path; figures were wearing plastic ponchos and hoods.

"Why isn't this place closed down?" said Dee, barely able to make herself heard above the sound of the rain on the umbrella.

James grimaced. "Because the weather doesn't care if people are dying in car accidents or if people need jobs or help or even a nose job. The desperate don't stop being desperate just because it's raining."

It was true. And more than that, the rain seemed to have sluiced away any pretense—no one was here to flirt with danger or seduce a supernatural being with pretty limbs. The only people here were those with haunted eyes, who gripped at plastic ponchos with shivering fingers or clutched at umbrellas. They came because there were no other options.

Fairy tales with all the shine taken away from them were simply stories of desperation. Of hungry wolves devouring children and jealous stepsisters who hacked off their own toes to fit inside a glass slipper.

James and Dee shuffled beneath the umbrella like two particularly uncoordinated competitors in a three-legged race, and once they found themselves beneath the first tarp, the scent of moisture and heat and bodies was stiflingly close. Dee stumbled and was grateful when James pulled her against him, his arm tight around her waist.

Dee glanced through the multitudes of people for Cora—the one-armed grocer with the raspberries, the old woman with the tarot readings, and a young black man who moved with a slightly awkward step. Dee thought she glimpsed a flash of metal in the gap between his shoe and the hem of his jeans. A pretty girl with nut-brown hair was speaking quietly with the man, but when Dee saw it wasn't Cora, her gaze moved on.

"Maybe she isn't here," said James. He sounded uncertain, but hopeful.

"Maybe," replied Dee. She was still eyeing the passersby, peering through the plastic hoods and umbrellas. It was difficult finding anyone in this mess, never mind a petite teenage girl. But perhaps they were wrong—perhaps Cora was simply at another market, buying normal things. Perhaps the Daemon was in his bank, counting his hearts or whatever demons did in their spare time.

James jerked hard on her sleeve and said hoarsely, "He's here."

A slender, elegant figure strode through the crowds. He wore a heavy woolen pea coat over his suit, and for once, the umbrella in his hand looked utterly normal.

And then Dee saw the figure prowling behind him. Cora moved with significantly less poise. Her unzipped coat flapped in the wind, and as a gust lifted the fabric, Dee caught a glimpse of something silver tucked into Cora's back pocket. For a moment, she didn't recognize it—but then years of movie watching came back to her and she recognized the shape of the object.

"Cora's got a gun," said Dee. Her voice slid up a few octaves.

"What?" James's jaw clenched. His next words came out through his teeth. "How—where would she even get a gun?"

"She's eighteen, isn't she?"

James cursed quietly. "And the Daemon's found his target."

Sure enough, the Daemon walked up to a produce stand and the teenage girl Dee had seen earlier, the one with the nut-brown hair, gazed up at him, mouth slightly agape.

Dee took a step forward, trying to see better, but the crowds flooded in before her. She grimaced, dodged the sharp edge of someone's umbrella, but in the chaos she found herself pushed back. When the crowds parted again, she blinked.

There was no sign of the Daemon or the girl.

"Where'd they—" Dee began to say, but James was already moving.

"He'll need a moment of privacy, or this mob would... well, mob him," James said as he walked. "Where's Cora?"

A scan of the crowd. "Gone," said Dee. "This—this isn't good."

They fought their way to the edge of the tarps, where the market ended. Together, they stood on the cusp of darkness, and Dee felt her breath freezing in her lungs. This was the moment when the wise would turn back.

"James." She breathed his name and he turned to face her.

Her every instinct told her to run, that people were not good, that letting him in would only lead to more hurt.

She hated that part of herself, hated that little voice that told her that anyone who might want her was either flawed or insane.

But James was neither. He was kind and brave, and he had the fashion sense of a raccoon that had blundered into a discounted bin of used clothes. But it was just another part of him, and she found she liked that part of him as well.

Standing on the edge of that darkness, she felt the stirrings of reckless want. A wild sort of bravery beat within her, taking up the hollow space in her chest where a heart should have resided.

She might not be alive—but she wanted to live.

"Can I try something?" she asked. The words spoken aloud helped drown out her inner voice.

James looked at her. His face was serious when he answered, "Anything."

Her fingers fumbled for his shoulder, and she angled him toward her. He looked confusedly at her, but then Dee rose on the tips of her toes. She grabbed his jacket in her fist.

When she kissed him, his mouth tasted of rainwater, fresh and sharp, and the heat of his mouth was a startling contrast to the chill along her skin. He made a soft sound of surprise, but then a groan rose in his chest.

This was nothing like their first kiss—all hesitancy and fumbling attraction. It was raw and needy, a desperate desire for reassurance before stepping off a ledge into the unknown. His left hand, the one not holding the umbrella, found the small of her back and pulled her closer. He felt sturdy, warm, and solid. She tried to draw some of his wild courage into herself, and he responded in kind, his lips moving hungrily against hers. It was heady, this knowledge that he wanted her, that he had seen all of her broken edges and still thought her desirable.

When they parted, their breath fogged the air beneath the umbrella. James looked slightly dazed and a flush crept along his cheeks.

"I just wanted to try that," she said, "in case we both die horribly tonight."

He laughed, and it was a quiet, comfortable sound. "Well, if that isn't the most romantic thing I've ever heard."

But his hand found hers, and their fingers twined together as they stepped out of the circle of light.

TWENTY-NINE

The river was a green-gray smudge against the night, and Dee could just barely make out its edges. The tall, spindly trees were framed against the city lights, only visible for their own darkness. Rain and mud spattered her school uniform—and she knew it was ruined.

Her phone was cupped in both hands, beneath the shelter of the umbrella. She had her flashlight app on, and it cast a weak half circle of illumination before them. She and James shuffled in little quick steps, each trying to adjust their stride to match the other's. It made for slow, awkward going, and Dee was sure they were going to be too late.

But then the thin light caught on the glimmer of a rain jacket and Dee gasped.

It was the girl Dee noticed before—with brown hair the color of hazelnuts, tanned skin, and features perfectly in balance. She was nearly as beautiful as the Daemon. But her face was twisted with fear.

And then Dee saw why.

Cora stood, her arm raised. She was indeed carrying a handgun, and she aimed it like she knew what she was doing.

"I won't let you do it again," said Cora. She was very calm. "Never again, demon."

The Daemon did not recoil. "Are you threatening me?" he said, amused.

"I am bargaining," replied Cora with a grim smile. "There's a difference. Now, back away from the girl and I don't put two bullets in you." Then she added, to the girl, "You don't want this. Trust me, you don't want this. You think it's worth it—whatever it is, but it's not." Her voice turned beseeching. "I thought it was worth it, too, but I was wrong. Walk away."

Defiance flashed across the girl's face. Her full lips pulled back in a snarl. "Fuck off." She turned to the Daemon and said, the words coming out in a rush, "I agree to the terms of the covenant, Agathodaemon."

It was different seeing it from the other side. Much quicker than Dee remembered it—one moment, the Daemon stood before the teenage girl, and then his hand was inside her chest.

Everything happened at once.

Cora pulled the trigger—a noise like thunder cracked

the air and the Daemon jerked once, twice. Dee thought she might have cried out, but her ears were torn apart by the sound of the gunfire. Then the teenage girl was on the ground, still and silent, and the Daemon was staggering back, one of his pale hands touching his chest.

Blood spilled across the front of his suit. It mixed with the rainwater, and something about its color reminded Dee of pomegranate juice.

In his fist was a heart.

It is so small, Dee thought.

The Daemon staggered. Fell to one knee. Got up again.

Cora's finger tightened on the trigger.

And that was when James slammed into her. The gun went off again, but the shot went wide; bark was torn from a nearby tree and then James ripped the gun from her hand. "Are you insane?" he was saying. "You could've hit the girl—"

Cora pushed him off, teeth bared. "Get off of me!" She scrambled to her feet, spun around in a circle, looking for the weapon. It was on the ground, in a mud puddle. Cora lunged for it, but then the Daemon flexed his fingers.

The weapon vanished.

And reappeared in his hand.

For a moment, no one moved.

The Daemon closed his fist.

The gun shattered. Shards of metal and plastic fell to the ground.

"Do not try that again," he snarled, and for the first time, Dee was truly afraid of him. She watched as the torn flesh of his chest and throat began to knit together. "You think this is a game? You think I do this for my own pleasure? You try and stop me—and your kind will suffer as much as mine will."

He gave the group one last cold once-over, and then the air pressure changed. With the fresh heart in hand, he vanished.

"No," snarled Cora, and rushed to where he had been standing. She looked desperate for a moment, then she rushed back in the direction of the market.

James glanced between Cora and Dee, his expression torn. Then he appeared to make up his mind. "Cora, damn it! Do not—" He sprinted after her. The shouting died away, until all Dee could hear was the sound of the rain.

She forced herself to breathe. She felt quivery, shaken from the sound of the gunshot. It would draw people here. They needed to move.

Dee picked her way through the mud to the girl's side. She was still on the ground, her hand on her chest, as if feeling for something that wasn't there.

Dee squatted next to her. "What's your name?"

The girl looked up at her with steady eyes. "Riley."

"Right. Riley." Dee pushed a hand through her soaked and tangled curls. "We need to go somewhere. Out of this damn rain."

Riley rose to her feet. She was covered in mud, but she

didn't seem bothered by it. "I've been couch-surfing," she said. "But the owner of my current couch made it clear that if I ever did a deal with a demon... well. It's time to find a new couch."

Dee uttered a quiet curse. She'd just remembered something—something that this girl was going to need. She scanned the ground, turning in a circle. Then she caught sight of something red.

There was a knitted heart resting in a puddle. It was soggy with moisture and Dee carefully picked it up. She walked up to Riley and placed the heart in her open palm.

"You'll want this," Dee said.

THIRTY

*G*remma stood just outside Whiteaker dormitory. She lounged against the brick wall, her arms crossed. She wasn't smiling. "Well, well, well," she said. "I think I've heard this story before.

"It was a dark and stormy night. A girl does what she should—she stays inside and minds her own business. Only, she hears a wailing at the window, a ghostly cry. So, tell me. Does our intrepid hero venture outside to see exactly what kind of swamp creature would try to coax her into the terrors of the night? Or does she leave the creature on its own?"

Dee shivered. She was soaked through, her hair caked with mud and rainwater. They'd had to slog all the way back to the road from the market, where Dee had called a cab. The driver hadn't been happy to have two muddy girls clamber into his backseat, but he'd taken them to Brannigan without comment.

"I didn't wail at the window," Dee said through chattering teeth. "I texted you."

Gremma nodded at the girl standing a few feet behind Dee. "And who is this?"

"Please," said Dee. "It's an emergency. Can you distract the dorm monitor while I sneak her inside? She needs a place to stay tonight."

Gremma's pale, freckled arms were crossed over her chest. "Tell me what's going on," she said. "No bullshit this time."

Riley stepped forward. The rain dripped off the edge of her hood. "Listen, if this is going to cause trouble—"

"Not you," said Gremma, shooting Riley a quelling glance. "Dee."

Dee looked at Gremma, at her red hair bundled into a frizzy bun, at her pajama shorts and her slippers shaped like bears. The faded remnants of red lipstick edged her mouth, and she looked like some beautiful wild creature, her mouthed stained with old blood.

To hell with it, Dee thought.

"I'm working for a demon," said Dee. "My scholarship ran out, and I'm working for a demon in exchange for money."

Gremma went still. It reminded Dee of the times she watched Gremma cut into a dead frog—her body frozen, eyes narrowed and focused. Those eyes now slid over Dee, presumably checking for missing body parts.

"My heart," said Dee, and Gremma sucked a sharp breath between her teeth.

"And this girl," said Gremma, nodding at Riley, "and that art guy."

"We're all working together," said Dee, the words tumbling out of her. "It's temporary—a two-year contract. But it's screwed up and dangerous, and Cora thinks we're fighting angels, but I think we're fighting an eldritch abomination but I'm not sure, and Cal died, and Riley needs a place to stay."

Gremma shook her head. "And I thought you were a drug runner."

Dee laughed, and it felt like a release. "It'd probably be safer."

Gremma's mouth puckered up, as if in thought, and she nodded at Riley. "All right, then. I'll go to the dorm mom and tell her I need a tampon or something—you take her in the back."

"Thank you," said Dee, unable to hide how grateful she felt.

They went up the stairs, going barefoot so as not to leave muddy footprints. Dee veered into the bathrooms first and gestured for Riley to follow.

Riley hesitated.

"Come on," said Dee. "We both need a shower. Everyone'll

be doing homework or something. No one will even notice that you don't live here."

With a little doubtful sigh, Riley walked into the bathroom and began stripping off her muddied clothing.

Dee stepped into an adjacent stall and twisted the water on full, not bothering to get undressed first. Head bowed, she watched swirls of brown circle the drain. Then she began pulling at her sodden clothing.

It wasn't easy, getting undressed in an already-running shower. She tugged at her shirt. Working the buttons free took far longer than it should have, her fingers clumsy with cold and exhaustion.

As she worked, she heard a soft sound.

A tiny sob. Muffled, as if someone had pressed their hand to their mouth.

"Are you okay?" Dee asked, loudly, above the sound of the shower.

"I'm fine," Riley's voice snapped out.

Dee went back to working on her clothes.

Riley had a backpack with her and clean pajamas, and soon the two girls were sitting on the floor of room 209. Gremma was perched on her bed—a box of tampons next to her.

Dee explained things. About the demons, about her theory, about the knitted hearts being the only thing keeping them alive, about the voids, about the giant thing made of human body parts—

"Holy shit," said Gremma. "*That's* what they do with them? I thought they ate them or something."

—and how those homunculi were sent into the voids to destroy them. About the duffel bags full of river rocks and C-4. ("Okay," said Riley, "now that part could be fun. I like explosions.") About how the Daemon seemed to be an oddity among his kind, tearing the hearts from teenagers rather than building creatures without a heart. About Cal. And lastly, about Cora's desire to stop the demon.

Riley listened while Gremma insisted on feeling for Dee's wrist.

"You don't have a pulse," said Gremma.

"I told you," replied Dee. "No heart."

"That's... well," said Gremma. "Think about it. You're, like, frozen in time or something. But you're still breathing, why are you still breathing?" She pressed a hand to Dee's forehead, as if trying to take her temperature. "Maybe it's habit. Are you still eating? Peeing?"

"Pretty sure being heartless doesn't come with a fever," said Dee, scooting back. "And, yes. Although it's none of your business, I have been doing both." Her eyes fell to the tampon box. "I haven't had a period since then, though."

"Okay," said Gremma, "now that's a perk I want."

After Dee thought she had explained everything that Riley needed to know, she made her a bed out of blankets and pillows on the floor. "Thanks for letting me stay here tonight," said Riley. "I've got a few other friends I can ping tomorrow, see if they wouldn't mind me crashing."

Dee climbed into bed and pulled her own covers up, shivering slightly. Her phone buzzed.

She let out a breath of relief when she saw the familiar name.

James: **r u ok?**

Fine, she texted back. **You?**

i look like i crawled out of a bog. but cora looks worse.

Cora's okay?

Pissed off. I asked her about the gun and she said something about a concealed carry license she got when she turned 18. U know most people just buy cigarettes or try to sneak into a bar, but nooo. Cora just has to be original.

She could almost hear him say the words and she smiled. **Hey. Do you have room in your apartment for someone to crash for a while?**

A moment later, he replied: **sure.**

Dee rolled over, looked down at the nest of blankets and pillows. "Good news. I just secured you temporary lodging."

Dee went to the dining hall in the early hours, before anyone else would see her piling food onto a tray and sneaking it back into the dorms. On one plate were scrambled eggs with cheese, toast, and bacon. On the other was fruit, cottage cheese, and a bagel. Riley emerged from the blanket nest, her hair sticking up in every direction.

"You," said Riley, "are officially my newest favorite person."

They ate breakfast on the floor, crowded around the tray. Gremma sipped black coffee and devoured a cinnamon roll in three bites. Then she was up on her feet, declaring she needed a shower.

Only when they were alone did Dee feel more comfortable speaking about their shared predicament. "So," she said. "What'd you sell your heart for?"

Riley swallowed her mouthful of cottage cheese with care, as if using the time to consider her answer. "Isn't that sort of like asking how much someone makes at their job? Taboo and all?"

"If you don't want to tell me, that's fine." Dee shrugged. "I was just curious. It seems like the icebreaker question for the heartless troop. The only person who keeps it a secret is Cora—and I don't know why."

Riley ate another two mouthfuls. Then she shrugged. "Trans," she said simply. "No money. Parents who disapproved. Need I say more?"

Dee drew in a breath. "So you found a demon."

Riley let out a small breath. "I'm a teenager," she said. "I was on my parents' insurance policy—and they wouldn't have allowed it." Her gaze darkened. "If you're like that other girl—what was her name. Cora. If you're going to tell me what I did was wrong, you can fuck right off. Making a deal was my decision and—"

"Oh," said Dee, surprised. "No. I mean, I'm not judging you for making a deal. I mean, I did, too."

Riley's mouth twisted into a half smile. "And you asked for money for school?"

Dee smiled in return; also, not a happy smile. "Bad home life."

"Ah." Riley's face softened. "Well. Thank you for letting me crash in your dorm."

"It was nothing."

"It wasn't nothing," said Riley with quiet insistence. "You said you sold your heart to stay here? Couldn't you get kicked out for smuggling someone into the room?"

Dee looked down. "Well…"

"Thank you," repeated Riley. "And thank you for asking that heartless guy if I could crash for a few weeks. It'll be temporary, I swear. I've got a part-time gig as a barista and another friend who's also looking for a place. We were planning on finding something together."

"Don't thank me yet," said Dee. "Out of curiosity, how do you feel about paint fumes?"

Dee sat on one of the stained couches and watched as James put together a bedroom.

Well, sort of.

"Is that supposed to be a curtain?" asked Gremma. She strode through the apartment's open front door, flopped down beside Dee, and tossed her purse onto the coffee table.

Sure enough, James was on a ladder, attaching large swaths of cloth to the ceiling. "This place doesn't have a lot of walls," Dee replied. "He's decided the best they can do is curtain off that far corner, put in a mattress and storage, and Riley can sleep there for now."

James wobbled atop the ladder and Riley rushed to grab one of its legs.

"Wow," said Gremma. "It's like watching the world's crappiest home improvement show." She spotted the bottle of champagne sitting on the coffee table. There were four plastic red cups—Dee's was untouched.

"A toast," James had said, "to new housemates."

Gremma took Dee's cup without having to ask if she would drink it; Gremma knew her. She drained it in a few gulps. "So is this going to be weird?" she asked. "Your boyfriend living with another girl?"

Dee made a face. "I'm not sure which part of that statement I disagree most with. That you think James is my boyfriend,

or that you think if he were my boyfriend he would be so easily swayed by another girl, or that Riley would steal my boyfriend. Which he isn't," she added hastily.

Gremma gave her a flat look. "You kissed him. I saw you
in the car."

"That was on the cheek."

"I've seen how he looks at you."

"He's nice."

"He painted you." Gremma crossed her arms. "If that's not
interest, I don't know what is. And you want to jump him."

"What makes you say that?" said Dee.

Gremma looked away. "Because you trusted him with
your secrets long before you trusted me."

Dee opened her mouth, but only silence emerged. It—it
was true. She had trusted James first. And part of her wanted
to claim it was only solidarity, that both of them having no
heart drew them together. They faced life-or-death situations
together; that was sure to forge a bond.

But she hadn't felt that way about Cal or Cora. She'd liked
Cal well enough and she was wary of Cora—but James—
James was—

She looked at him. He was still on that ladder, arms lifted
above his head, trying to attach the curtain to the ceiling.
The gesture lifted his shirt, exposed a sliver of skin along his
stomach. She had one of those thoughts that simply comes to

a person with no warning—what might it be like to see him without the shirt?

Oh, hell.

She did want to jump him.

"I'm sorry," she said, turning her attention back to Gremma. "It's nothing personal. I never *not* trusted you."

Some of Gremma's hurt seemed to slide away. "No, I get it." She chewed on the edge of the plastic cup. "Some secrets you keep all tangled up in yourself, so tight that to pull them out is physically painful."

And that was it. Dee had bound so much of herself up in the appearance of normalcy, hoping the mask would some-day turn into the real thing.

Or maybe everyone felt this way—caught up in their own demons, trying to put on a good face for everyone else.

Riley came over, sat on the opposite couch. Even sweaty, with rumpled hair and no makeup, she was still beautiful. Between Riley and Gremma, Dee felt the tiniest bit frumpy.

"Have you heard from Cora?" called James. He was descending from the ladder, stepping back to survey his work.

"No," said Dee. "I figure...well. She's probably pissed at us."

"Would the demon really have hurt her?" Riley asked.

"Daemon," said Dee and James in unison.

"Call him the Daemon," said Dee.

Riley's nose crinkled. "Why?"

"Because Agathodaemon is a bit of a mouthful," said James, unrolling the mattress. "And the one time I tried to call him Aggie, he talked about ripping out my liver."

This comment had its intended effect—laughter rippled through the group, breaking the tension. James was smiling, content with his achievement. Dee knew that he was doing his best to fill the void Cora had left. He wasn't a leader; if anything, he was a class clown. But he had a way of defusing a situation and making people feel comfortable, and he would use it to his best advantage.

He was trying to take care of them.

He was a far better person than she'd first thought.

When he went to the fridge to retrieve more drinks, Dee followed him. "Thank you. For doing this, I mean."

He straightened, a bottle of water in each hand. He set the bottles on the counter, and their sides were already clouded with condensation. "For water?"

"For taking Riley in," she said. "For trying to make this better, when you didn't have to."

He blinked. As if that were a strange statement to make. "It's what anyone would do," he said with a half shrug.

No, it wasn't. She couldn't imagine her father doing such a thing. Dee had grown up with a desperate need to be self-sufficient, to never rely on anyone. Accepting help made her feel awkward.

She'd never felt that around James, though. Perhaps because he didn't make a big deal out of it; helping people was just what he did.

They stood in silence for a moment, and then he said, his voice quiet, "I'm worried about Cora."

She drew in a breath. She had been thinking about Cora, too. "You said she was okay."

"She *was* okay." James rubbed at the creases in his forehead. "Physically. Emotionally, well, she was pretty angry. I think—I think she was pretty dead set on keeping the Daemon from making any more of us. She feels responsible somehow. Like seniority gives her the automatic mom role."

"She's a good person," said Dee. "I think that's why she has more trouble with this than the rest of us. Someone should call her, see if she's doing all right."

James frowned. "Did you just call me a bad person?"

"I said 'us.' Remember, I count myself among those ranks."

James laughed quietly. "You're a good person, Dee."

"How do you know that?" She looked at him. "I could secretly be hiding a dark side."

His smile softened. "Because the first time we met, you thought I was homeless and you offered me money—despite the fact you came into that basement intending to ask a demon for money."

Oh. Well. She had never really thought about it like that.

"It was just going to be for a bus," she protested. "It wasn't like I offered you fifty grand or anything."

"Doesn't matter." There was a fondness she hadn't expected to see in his face. "You offered to help." His hand came up, fingers tracing her chin.

If she'd had a heart, it would have been hammering.

But she did not pull away—not when he leaned in, not when his breath mingled with hers, not when she felt the gentle touch of his lips.

"I chose this," she said, very quietly, and kissed him again.

THIRTY-ONE

Much to Dee's relief, there were a few weeks of quiet. A sense of normalcy settled over everything; the Daemon made no sudden appearances; there were no more mysterious explosions; Cora got back in touch with them and grudgingly accepted Riley as one of the heartless; Riley and James turned out to be surprisingly comfortable roommates; Dee no longer had to hide her double life from Gremma.

She learned that she liked kissing, the way James's lips could draw the breath out of her or soothe her into a state so relaxed she could have fallen asleep in his arms.

They went on dates. Real dates, with movie theaters and restaurants. He texted her in between classes and she tried to focus on calculus rather than the fact that he called her "adorible."

Even the misspelling seemed endearing.

It was nice to fall back into a familiar rhythm. To do homework and try to come up with trivial details to e-mail her mother. And when the weekends rolled around, James would often show up with two burlap sacks.

There was no point in getting river rocks; the Daemon wasn't pestering them to do it. But it was something to do, and besides—Dee enjoyed it.

If she were being honest with herself, she felt better when she was with James. She liked the way he seemed to settle into her—like plastering up the cracks in an old wall. He made her feel whole, like she wasn't some broken thing that needed fixing.

She learned that he always smelled of paint and fabric softener. His outfits may have looked as if they came from a dumpster, but he was meticulous about washing them. She learned that he liked holding hands, enjoyed his thumb stroking over her pulse point, as if it were a joke between them.

As spring crept toward summer, a heat wave rolled into Oregon. It was rare to see the clouds burned so cleanly from the sky. When they went to the river one day, she found herself kneeling in the shallow water, dribbling handfuls of it over her bare shoulders.

James ended up taking off his shirt and—

Dee did not stare.

Much.

All right, so maybe there was some staring.

Once they were done picking rocks, he insisted on being gallant and carrying both burlap sacks.

"I think our roommates are dating," said James, with as much solemnity as he could muster.

She snorted. "Oh, really? How'd you figure that out?"

His mouth hooked up into a grin. "I am a keen observer of the human condition. All artists must carefully examine human behavior and…"

Dee gazed at him.

"I walked in on them making out," he finished lamely.

Her laugh came out as a breathy exhalation.

"You can laugh," he said. "It's not like they were making out on your couch."

Dee crossed her arms. "Don't tell me you're bothered by it."

"Of course I'm bothered by it," said James. "It's *my* couch. I spent all of…a hundred dollars on it. If anyone was going to christen it with a naked butt, it should have been me."

Dee choked. "They were naked?"

"Not yet," said James. "Give it time."

"You really think so?"

James pointed at himself. "Keen observer of the human condition, remember? It'll happen."

They kissed against the hood of his car for some time. She never thought it could be this effortless. She never thought she'd find anyone she trusted enough to share such easy affection.

When they returned to his apartment, his door was unlocked. "You should lock your door," she said, pushing it shut behind her.

"I'm already working for the Daemon," said James airily. "Whatever decides to visit can't be scarier than him."

One of his paintings caught her eye. It looked like something from an old church, with figures and glowing halos, shining through with inner light.

"You're painting angels?" she said, unable to help herself.

"I'm calling it *Salvation*," said James. "Probably going to sell it to an old man who's obsessed with Rafael. He'll love it." He grinned at Dee. "Yeah, I know. It's pretty ironic."

"Where's Riley?" asked Dee, glancing around the apartment.

"She's enrolled at some community college. She says she's been taking classes ever since she left home. Basic courses, so she can transfer into a better school later."

"How old is she?" asked Dee, curious. There wasn't exactly a lot of time for personal questions that first night; Dee had been too busy getting grilled by Gremma.

"Seventeen," answered James. "But she said she left home a year before that. She got her GED while couch-surfing. But her last friend was...well, not too thrilled about the whole demon thing. That's why she needed a place to stay."

James took her hand and squeezed. "I get it. The whole not-wanting-to-stay-at-home thing. I mean, I didn't have birth parents who kicked me out—so on the one hand, I think I had it easier than you and Riley."

Her stomach twisted. "My parents didn't...well. I'm not sure they did kick me out. I almost wish they had," said Dee. "Like, maybe if they really did kick me out, then it would mean I wasn't overreacting. But maybe they're right, maybe it isn't as bad as I think it is—"

Fire blazed behind James's eyes. "You are not over-reacting," he said hotly. "Fuck that. And fuck them for making you feel that way." He gently tugged at her hand, until she sat beside him on the couch. His hip was pressed to hers, but all he did was weave their fingers together, his grip secure but not too tight. "That's how they sucker you back in. They make you think that it wasn't so bad, that they really love you, that it'll be different. But it never is, not unless they're willing to change." He looked at Dee. "You think they'll change?"

She answered without needing to think about it. "No. Not unless something drastic happens."

He nodded. "Then you're not overreacting. And you don't have to go back there, not if you don't want to."

A startled little laugh escaped her. "Are you offering me a place, too? Don't you think it'd be a little too…sitcom-y if I moved in with you and Riley?"

He returned her smile. "Do you have any other family? I mean, besides your parents?"

If he wanted the technical answer, that would be a yes. She had distant aunts and uncles—all her grandparents were dead, but there were cousins that she'd seen at family reunions. No one in the state, no one close. But they did exist.

Those distant relatives could have helped her. But they hadn't acted. For whatever reasons, they'd left her there— maybe it was easier to not get involved, maybe they had their own problems. Whatever the reasons, no help had come from them.

Gran would've helped.

"No," she said. "No other family."

James let the subject drop. He went back to his canvas, and for a while Dee watched as he painted. It was mesmerizing to watch as he cast colors across the canvas, every gesture sure and graceful. She could almost see why he would sell his heart for this—it was beautiful, the way he lost himself to the work. This was where he found his solace.

"You know," he remarked as he worked on the angel's wing, "it's kind of creepy when you stare at me like that."

"It's not creepy. It's...attentive."

"I can see you out of the corner of my eye." But he was smiling when he said it. "Just staring."

"Oh, hush," she said, and nudged him with her shoulder. He put down the paintbrush and turned to face her. His hands came up, lightly pressed between her shoulder blades.

"You are a distraction," he told her. "An adorable distraction, but a distraction."

She grinned and leaned in.

And then her phone buzzed loudly.

"Don't answer it," groaned James.

But Dee was already fishing it out of her pocket. "I can't not answer it. It bugs me when I know I have messages waiting."

James watched as she opened the text.

Cora: **We need to talk.**

Dee's stomach bottomed out. James went somber at once. "What does she want?"

Dee hurriedly typed a reply. **What's up?**

Her phone buzzed again. **This is the longest we've ever gone without being contacted by the Daemon. And he's not answering any of my messages.**

And then, a moment later, **I think he's abandoned us.**

Dee passed over her phone and let James read the message.

"No," said James. "He wouldn't just leave us. Not like this. Not like—"

His hand went to his chest.

Dee swallowed; all the happiness had gone out of her. "Has any troop ever attacked the Daemon before?" she asked.

James looked away and did not answer.

Another text came in: **We need to meet up. I have a plan.**

THIRTY-TWO

They met at the abandoned bank.

James unlocked the front doors and they took flashlights and lanterns and ventured into the decrepit building. Riley had never seen it before and she eyed the walls with curiosity rather than disgust. Cora picked her way through the rubble with delicate care, like a cat trying not to get its feet wet. Dee saw a rat scurrying along the floor, sniffing at a piece of wreckage.

At first, no one spoke. But they were all thinking the same thing. This was it—their Rumpelstiltskin clause. If they could figure out how to get their hearts back, fair and square, then the Daemon would be outwitted. They could leave this nightmare behind and keep their ill-gotten gains.

All that stood between them and their hearts was a heavy vault door.

"You think we could break in?" Dee asked.

"I'm not a criminal mastermind," said James, "contrary to what your roommate thought about me. I've never actually done anything illegal—well, except for that time I squatted in Italy, but I'm not sure that counts. You got any ideas, Cora?"

Cora crossed her arms. "Do I look like a criminal?"

And she had a point; Dee was pretty sure master criminals didn't wear frilly blouses and pencil skirts—or at least, the ones in Portland didn't.

"I might be able to do it."

Three heads turned in unison to look at Riley.

"What?" said James flatly.

Riley looked half-ashamed, half-proud when she said, "I may have attempted to build explosives before."

Dee felt her mouth drop open. James snorted and Cora took a step back.

"Just to see if I could," said Riley hastily. "I wasn't going to blow anything up. I just…I want to go into demolitions. That's my dream job. You know, taking down old buildings and stuff."

"You're the new Cal," Dee said, understanding. For the first time, she thought she might have glimpsed the Daemon's motives—why he picked this girl above all others at Mephisto Market.

Riley blinked. "I'm the new what?"

"Explosives expert," said James. He pressed both palms to the door. "But—I mean. Really? You think you could take down this door without blowing up what's inside the vault?"

Riley took a step back, surveying the vault door with a critical eye. "It depends on how large the vault is. I could go at the door with a thermal lance, but I'd need to know the dimensions of the vault. If the space is too small, I'd end up *cooking* everyone's hearts."

A collective shudder.

Riley added, "Also, it would take a while. Could you guarantee that the Daemon won't walk in on us trying to break in? Because I'm pretty sure he wouldn't take that well."

"We haven't seen him in weeks," said Cora, agitated. Her hands clenched and relaxed, clenched and relaxed. "I was hoping maybe he would be here, that we could get some answers out of him."

James rubbed at his chin, probably trying to look intellectual, but the day-old shadow took away from that image. Dee tamped down a smile.

"Out of idle curiosity, could you get a thermal lance?" he asked.

Riley's mouth turned down. "Um. No. Could you?"

"Maybe." James tilted his head, as if to get a better look at the door. "The art community here is pretty eclectic. I would bet that someone I know has one stashed away somewhere. Probably using it to cut steel or something."

"So we could do this," Cora said. Her eyes were wide, and there was hope in her face Dee had never seen before. "We could really pull this off—get our hearts back, never worry about the Daemon again."

"Well," said Riley, "that would be 'again' for all of you. I've never really had to deal with him."

"No more voids," said James, a little dreamily. "And I could just put my heart on a shelf somewhere, maybe paint it."

Dee snorted. "Or, you know, it could go back in your chest. Where it belongs."

James shrugged. "Maybe I like being heartless."

Of course he would, she thought. He liked being contrary like that.

She was about to answer, but the words caught in her throat.

It was the rat. The one she'd seen before. It had darted forward into the darkened hallway and vanished.

Dee blinked. Hard. Sure she was seeing things.

With a small pop, the rat reappeared, flung backward by some invisible force. It toppled over, squeaking wildly, then wobbled unsteadily away.

Dee took a step forward.

None of them had seen it. This corridor was too dark, their flashlights too focused on the shiny bright metal of the vault door.

The air shimmered like heat waves.

"Guys," said Dee, and her voice quavered, too high and thin for them to hear.

James was saying something about a sculptor he knew, Cora ribbing him about saying he knew everyone in the city, but the words blurred in her ears, drowned out by her own ragged breathing. It was like a dream where she spoke too quietly, couldn't be heard no matter how she screamed for help.

Her voice finally cracked out. "Void," she said. "There's a void."

Cora crossed her arms, brow wrinkling. "What? What do you—"

Riley looked similarly confused.

Only James reacted like Dee had; he moved onto the balls of his feet, looking down the dark corridor.

The void rippled, and for some reason all Dee could think of was plastic wrap, how she used to press her fingers to it as a kid, seeing how far she could push until the plastic warped and snapped.

Something was pushing through the mouth of the void.

A probing extremity pressed, and Dee saw the air warp around it, twisting and straining until—

She didn't hear it exactly. It was more like the thrum of a bass; she felt the sensation go through her bones: a *hum*, a *snap*.

Arms closed around Dee. She made a noise, high in her

throat. James. He held her, staggered backward, and she was suddenly so grateful to him. Absurdly, she felt safer in his arms but she shouldn't, because whatever that thing was, it meant none of them were safe.

She watched as the thing tore itself free—

It was not human. It was not animal, either. She could never have given it a name; its nature was unearthly, indescribably wrong.

It was shaped like something from beneath the ocean— long limbed, boneless, and it did not seem to have eyes. There was a clacking sound as it raised its...head? She saw again those illustrations in the Lovecraft books at the library, drawings of creatures rising from the depths, of monsters long forgotten from human memory.

Out of the corner of her eye, Dee saw Cora try to run. She skipped back two steps, eyes never leaving the creature, but her heel snagged on a piece of debris. She stumbled, a panicked whine caught in her throat, and she fell to one side. She looked up, terrified, likely thinking she had just doomed herself.

James held very still, his arms caged around Dee. He was tense, not breathing, and Dee felt much the same.

Riley stood in place, arms loose at her sides. She was gazing at the creature, squinting at it as if she needed a new glasses prescription.

We're going to die, thought Dee. The words came to her, almost calm in the midst of her terror. *We are going to die.*

And then the creature moved.

It darted for the vault. Its long limbs reached for the metal door, tearing it from its hinges and vanishing inside. The shriek of metal was deafening, and Dee found herself scrambling out of James's grasp.

Run. She needed to run, to escape. Every inch of her was screaming to get out of that bank, to get outdoors. That's what chased off monsters, right? Sunshine and people—if they could just get outside, they might be able to return to the real world and leave this nightmare behind.

And then she heard the crack of shattered glass.

"The hearts," gasped Cora. "It's after the hearts!"

James was paler than she had ever seen—his lips bloodless, his fingers trembling. The look he threw at Dee was full of terror. Then he ran into the vault, vanishing through the broken doors.

Dee's body seemed to have frozen, her joints locked and eyes trained on the vault's broken door.

And then she heard James cry out and a bolt of fury ran through her. Adrenaline sang through her blood and she was on fire with it, moving—running—toward the vault herself. She wasn't sure what she expected to find inside. Perhaps the lair of some fairy-tale creature, all silk rugs and castle interior, or maybe some sort of altar for sacrifices.

But what she saw was…well. It was a bank vault. Racks

of wire shelves ran along the walls and upon them were rows and rows of money. She saw dollars and euros and currencies she didn't recognize.

Resting upon the floor were crates of C-4. Burlap sacks full of river rocks were piled atop the crates. And beside those were a couple of laptops, a stack of umbrellas, and on the last shelf, the one farthest from the vault doors, were vases.

Elegant vases, the kind used by luxury florists, meant to hold roses and baby's breath and carnations. But tucked inside the swell of the vases, brilliant red and floating in some clear liquid...were hearts.

Dozens of them.

The monster was pulling them from the shelf, like a toddler smashing firecrackers upon the ground. James had picked up a broken piece of shelf and was beating the creature with it, a snarl of fury tearing through his teeth.

The creature shrugged off the blows with ease. Then it lashed out with one of its legs and caught James in the stomach, slamming him into a rack with a sickening crack.

For one long second, the world went still. Dee drew in the scene—the creature, the hearts, James on the floor.

Dee sprinted for the burlap sacks. She hefted one into both hands, rushed at the creature. Then she spun around once, twice, and brought the heavy bag of rocks down upon the creature's head with all her strength.

Or at least, what she thought might be its head.

The creature recoiled, chittering like some kind of insect. It staggered to one side, and Dee hit it again and again. Her senses were sharp with terror; she could feel the roughness of the burlap beneath her fingers, the sweat rolling down her back.

The creature struck out at her, swift as thought. Dee tried to dodge, but one of the legs struck her, caught her in the side of the knee. Her legs fell out from under her and the granite slammed into her back, driving the breath from her lungs.

Then it was on top of her—all legs and mouth and teeth and it was trying to tear her open, claws raking at her face, and it was all she could do to scream, to try to use her arms to cover her face.

"Dee!"

Something crashed into the creature and Dee felt the impact through her own body. The monster rolled off of her, graceful as it regained its footing.

Dee felt the sting of where its claws had drawn blood, and she tried to sit up, looking wildly around for the creature. James had picked up where she'd left off, using the bag of river rocks to bludgeon the creature.

Dee glanced around wildly, trying to find another weapon. She forced herself to try to think, to be the person who survived. Those people were smart, were canny, were—

Her eyes fell upon the umbrellas.

Every time she had seen the Daemon, he'd had an umbrella tucked beneath one arm. Even when the sky was clear, he carried one.

Certainty seized her and she snatched one up. She pressed the button and the umbrella sprang open, nearly blinding her. She flung her face back, but felt the whisper of metal as one of its arms slashed her cheek.

"Come on," she said, not sure who she was talking to—the umbrella, the Daemon, or herself. Her voice sounded ragged. "Come on!"

She clumsily twisted the umbrella, doubting her instincts, certain that this wasn't going to work, that the thing was going to kill them all.

The handle came free. The umbrella portion slid off, revealing a long, slender blade. A rapier.

Spinning around, she saw the creature had cornered James, plunging its legs at him, trying to impale him with one of its claws. Riley was behind it, beating uselessly at its back with her fists. Cora had entered the fray, too, using a fallen metal chair to try to injure one of its legs.

"Riley!" Dee screamed.

Riley turned.

Dee threw the sword. It skittered across the granite floor and Riley snatched it up. Her first slash was clumsy, ill-considered, and drew a line across the creature's flank.

It trilled, turning to face her.

And Riley drove the blade through the creature's head.

It spasmed and twitched horribly, looking like a squid speared by an agile fisherman. Then the colors along its skin began to die away, flickering into a sickened, dull gray. It slowly went limp, its many legs crumpling beneath it. Riley darted back, yanking the sword free. Her teeth were bared in a snarl and she held the blade at the ready.

But there was no need. The creature was dead.

Gazing at the creature's corpse, Dee began to shake. Her legs wobbled and she sank to the floor. Her palms pressed to the cold granite, her gaze blurred.

Cora hurried from the room; a moment later, Dee heard the distinct sounds of retching.

Riley was looking down at the sword in her hand as if she couldn't quite believe she was holding it.

Dee was dimly aware of all this—and then hands. Warm hands were on her shoulders, her arms, touching her as if to ensure that she was still whole.

"...Dee, talk to me. Are you okay? Dee?"

His voice came into focus, like a radio finally being tuned in to the right channel. Dee blinked several times. James knelt beside her. His tone was frantic, and she managed to find her words. "Fine. I—I'm fine."

But she wasn't.

"Your arms are all scratched up," he said. "We need to clean those out. I have first-aid supplies in my car. We should—"

She looked at him, truly looked at him. He had a bruise on his face, and he favored his left side, but he was alive. He was alive—they were both alive. Her fingers found his collar and she pressed her forehead to his. He breathed, one heaving gasp after another, and then they were kissing. Tangled, breathless kisses, one bleeding into the next. She needed to feel this, to remember that she was still alive, she was still here, he was still here. They'd survived and—and the thought of losing him had torn a hole open inside of her.

She'd never felt this before, this terrifying, head-spinning sense that she could lose someone she cared about.

When they drew apart, he was speaking softly, repeating the same words over and over again. "...Okay," he was murmuring, "you're okay—" His hand cradled her cheek. "We need to get out of here. That void—"

"Is closed," said Cora. She walked unsteadily back into the vault. "I checked. Whatever came through...well. It looks like the door shut behind it."

"We can't leave," said Riley. Her voice was tinny, higher than normal. "We can't just leave that thing here."

"Well, what are we supposed to do with it?" Cora said hoarsely.

It didn't sound like sarcasm—it was an honest question.

There was the corpse of something decidedly non-human splayed out before them. Dee looked to Cora. "Do you still know the Daemon's cell number?"

Cora nodded.

"Then call him," said Dee. "I think it's time we got some answers."

THIRTY-THREE

The Daemon arrived at the bank an hour later. None of them had left—and while Cora claimed it was because she wanted answers, Dee suspected that they were all simply too shocked to move. He stepped into the vault, eyed the carnage and the four teenagers.

Cora sat with her back to the wall. Riley stood, the sword still in her hand, like some kind of guard. Dee leaned against a crate, her arms stinging with rubbing alcohol and covered in small bandages. James sat beside her. None of them had gone near the vases with the hearts—only Cora had suggested it, but Riley pointed out that since none of the hearts were labeled, the endeavor would likely prove fruitless. The Daemon's attention slid over each of them in turn, and then he reached out and took the rapier from Riley. She relinquished it without a word. He pulled a handkerchief from his pocket and expertly ran it over the sword's length, wiping away any remnants of the creature.

"You did well," he said.

Silence.

Cora regained her voice first. "We—did well?"

He nodded.

But rather than defuse the tension, his cool voice seemed to ignite Cora's fury. "You son of a bitch," she snapped. "We were nearly killed by…by I don't know what the hell that was, but it nearly killed us—it smashed several of the hearts in the vault, and all you have to say is that *we did well*?"

"What would you have me say?" said the Daemon mildly. "'Congratulations, young humans. You did not die.' Would that suit you?"

"What was that thing?" This time it was Dee who spoke. She came forward and stood before the Daemon. He gazed at her, and something in his face changed. He looked at her with something like respect.

"It was not supposed to be here," he answered. "You remedied that. For which I must thank you."

"But what was it?"

The Daemon did not answer.

"Tell me what the thing was," she said evenly. Dee met the Daemon's eyes and did not look away.

Something had shifted between them. He looked at Dee, then at the creature's corpse, and she knew, she just knew that the fact they had slain it made them something *more* in the Daemon's eyes. They had proven themselves…well, not equal to him, but they weren't helpless, either.

The Daemon's eyes glittered. "You may call them what you like. People have had many names for them over the years. Personally, I have always preferred 'burrower.' Quite an apt description. They delve through space, carve little holes that ought not to exist. As for where it came from, it came from where I did," he said. "Stars die, worlds die with them. Some of us find new places to reside. My kind can stitch reality like so much thread, but those creatures are burrowers, immortal mouths and stomachs leaving holes behind. They are what we have been fending off for thousands of years, since we escaped to this place. They are devourers, and while you may not trust my kind, believe that we have the same interests as yours. It would serve neither humanity nor my people to see their like enter this world."

"You're not demons," said Riley. "You're *aliens*."

Cal was right, Dee thought. A pang went through her; she would have liked to tell him.

The Daemon tilted his head. "Whatever title you give us, it is of no consequence. What matters is that we are here, and we share the same desire as your species. To remain on this planet, to quietly exist. That is all we desire. Our world died thousands of years ago, but we searched and found this one to our liking. We are good neighbors to have, on the whole. We prefer to keep to ourselves, save for when our needs coincide with humanity's. And our needs do coincide—trust me on that. You may think an arm or a leg a difficult thing to give up, but it is a small price to pay. The burrowers are not like us. We may change reality if we wish it, but they do so... well. They would tear this world asunder if we let them. They care nothing for the inhabitants of this world; they will devour every living thing, if allowed." He tilted his head, in a distinctly not-human way. "That is why we take the measures we do."

"The hearts," said Dee. She remembered how that creature ignored the people in favor of the hearts in the vault, of how it tore into them. "They—they *eat* them?"

"Burrowers and their like feed off of emotion and memory," agreed the Daemon. "They themselves cannot feel—and the voids they create to enter this world are incompatible with human emotion. Your hearts register too strongly to those little gateways—you are recognized as alien and pushed out."

"This cannot happen all the time," said Riley. "If—if there were always aliens trying to break into this dimension, we would know."

The Daemon smiled approvingly. "That is correct. The burrowers only attempt to enter this world on occasion."

"Occasion?" repeated Cora.

"When stars die," he said, "the burrowers need a new place to live. They try to push through, every so often. These smaller voids, imagine them as foreshocks. They precede the larger quake. Soon, many thousands of creatures like this one will make a true attempt to push through—there will be several…larger voids. Placed throughout the world. Portland will be one of the places where a large void appears." His gaze drifted among them. "You will go into that void and close it."

"Just us?" asked James quietly.

"If you're asking if there will be more heartless, the answer is no." The Daemon spoke flatly. "There was a troop in Seattle…but no longer." He slid a cool look at the human hearts. "I should probably dispose of some of those, now that I think of it."

Cora choked.

"As for other servants," said the Daemon, "my colleagues are less than confident in your skills. Likely, they will send their own homunculi into the void. Ignore them—they are… less effective than you are. But the homunculi will fight back, and they will draw the attention of any stragglers, so that will be to your advantage."

"Why?" asked Riley. "Why are we more effective than homunculi?"

He seemed to consider the question. "I assume you heard about the explosion in Seattle? Well, that is what happens when a homunculus's unsteady hands cannot set off charges at the right moment.

"You are smaller, smarter, and the burrower will only take notice of you if you hurt it. I learned some time ago that ripping the heart from humans would allow them to enter a void."

"And how did you stumble upon that discovery?" said Cora tartly, but Dee ignored her.

"How long?" asked Dee. "How long until this mega-void appears?"

The Daemon's lips pursed. "A few weeks," he replied. "I cannot be more specific than that. In a few weeks, the world will be…thinner. Easier to push through. And then we will end the invasion before it can begin."

"And if we don't?" asked Riley flatly. "What if we tell you to fuck off?"

The Daemon smiled thinly. "You could, but I doubt you will."

"Why?"

The Daemon turned to walk away. He spoke over one perfectly tailored shoulder. "Because—should you fail, this city would not fare well. These creatures warp reality. They can change the environment or the land adversely."

"Meaning?" said Riley, sounding impatient. "What? We'd get some earthquakes or a lot of rain?"

The Daemon's mouth remained a thin line. "I believe the last place that endured such an incursion was Pompeii."

Silence. Someone drew a sharp breath, but Dee couldn't tell who.

"Like I said," continued the Daemon, "they can affect the environment in ways you would not want. After all, this city is near several active volcanoes, is it not?"

James looked angry. He edged forward, eyes hard and fists balled. "We didn't sign up for this," he said. "You didn't tell us anything—you took our hearts, promised us what we wished for, then led us blindly into war."

But Dee was not angry.

She had walked willingly into a fairy tale, into a world where she could trade her heart for her freedom. She may as well have donned a red cloak and strode into a darkened forest.

She had always known there would be wolves.

I chose this.

✺✺✺✺✺✺

Several days after the bank, Dee found Cora waiting for her outside of Whiteaker dorm. Cora sat on the steps, a visitor's badge clipped to her jeans. Of course she'd get a visitor's pass, Dee thought. It was the responsible thing to do.

Dee approached the other girl slowly. The way she might have walked up to a wounded animal. "Cora?"

Cora looked up at Dee, but not as if she truly saw her. "I hate this," she said hollowly. "I hate this so much."

And for the first time, Dee felt a twinge of sympathy for Cora. She took a few steps closer. "Why did you make a deal?"

There was no hiding, not anymore.

"I needed the Daemon to kill someone for me," said Cora.

Dee hesitated, then sat on the step beside her. She tried to compose her expression. She was doing a terrible job of it, she knew—she looked as appalled as she felt. "I—I thought demons didn't kill."

"Most won't," said Cora. The words seemed to float out of her, slow and steady, as if she were releasing a burden. "They don't want to tangle with the authorities. But the Agathodaemon—he's breaking all the rules. He's like, a renegade among the demons or something. He wants heartless teenagers, wants them badly enough to do things other demons wouldn't." She tilted her head up, and the light from the overhead lamp cast shadows over her pretty face.

"I wanted someone dead." She closed her eyes.

Dee wondered what could have driven Cora to do such a thing—she was always so set on everyone's survival, on keeping the team together.

"Did he do it?" asked Dee quietly.

Cora smiled—and it was a rueful little smile. "He has my heart, doesn't he?"

And then Dee truly saw Cora for the first time. Saw the girl who tried to keep everyone alive because she thought it was penance for a life she took. The girl who looked put together but was scrambling behind the facade.

"Making wishes like this never comes without a price," said Cora. "I thought the price was my heart, but it's more than that. I wanted everyone to live and I was the one to kill Cal." Her voice broke on the last few words. She sniffed, swallowed, gazed upward as if refusing to let the tears fall. "Nothing comes for free. We just don't know what it'll cost."

She took another breath, and when she released it, she looked calmer. She finally turned to face Dee, making no attempt to hide her own grief. "Listen. I'm telling you this because I'm not going to be there."

Dread unfurled within Dee's stomach. "Cora..."

"It'll be two years in a week," said Cora. "I'm getting my heart back. That's why I was so worried about the Daemon abandoning us. I wasn't sure I'd get my heart returned to me. But now he's back and...well." Her gaze dropped.

"You're not going to be there for the next void," said Dee.

"I'm not sorry. I mean, I'm sorry that it'll just be the three of you, but I'm not sorry about getting my heart back." Cora pushed herself to her feet. "I just wanted you to know. Why I tried to stop him. Why I didn't want anyone else to get hurt.

"Don't die," said Cora.

Dee wished she had something profound to say, to reassure Cora that Cal's death wasn't her fault, that accidents happened, that whomever she had wanted dead had probably deserved it.

But all that came out of her mouth was, "Good luck."

THIRTY-FOUR

There was comfort in having a deadline.

Dee looked at her calendar.

Then she made a list.

The thing was, knowing she might die made things simpler. It put life into perspective. Things that had seemed enormous became trivialities, and there were some things she wanted to do. Needed to do.

Dee woke early on a Saturday and stood next to Gremma's bed. Gremma rolled over, saw her roommate less than twelve inches from her nose and, to her credit, did not flinch or even gasp. She simply blinked once and said, "Paranormal emergency?"

"No," said Dee. "But I need your help."

She had thought about this. All night, she had tossed and turned, racked with shivers and nerves and so many doubts she thought she might choke on them. But she needed to do this.

And she wanted backup.

"Would you come home with me?" she said.

There was little traffic before eight in the morning on a Saturday. They got through a coffee drive-through in record time, and Dee sipped a hot chocolate. She felt jittery enough without too much caffeine in her system.

Gremma parked on the curb and looked at her. "You want me to stay outside?"

Dee had also thought this over. "No. Mind coming in?"

Surprise flashed across Gremma's face. "A-all right." She was so startled it took two tries to unclip her seat belt and follow Dee up the walkway, past the overgrown plants and up to the porch.

Dee did not bother knocking on her front door. Nor did she remove her shoes. She simply walked inside.

She heard voices in the dining room, but she ignored them. With Gremma at her heels, she hurried to the stairs and up to her bedroom. She pulled the empty backpack from her shoulder and placed it on the carpet, then glanced around herself.

There were a few things she wanted—old childhood books and knickknacks. A picture of herself and Gran. A snow globe with unicorns. Then she went to her desk and opened a drawer.

Tucked inside a folder were her passport and birth certificate. She slid both into her backpack.

"Social Security," said Gremma. It was the first time she had spoken and Dee looked up, startled.

"You'll need your Social Security card when you apply for jobs," explained Gremma. There was no surprise or judgment in her voice. Rather, she looked...satisfied somehow. As if all her wild theories were coming to fruition.

Dee found her Social Security card at the bottom of the drawer.

Gremma was the one to zip up the backpack and haul it over her shoulder. "Anything else?" she asked.

Dee shook her head. Together, they walked down the stairs—and right into Mr. Moreno.

He froze in astonishment; apparently, he had not heard them come in. Dee's stomach shriveled up, but she forced herself to meet his eyes.

"What are you—" he began to say, but Dee forged ahead with her plan. She pulled her cell phone out of her pocket and dropped it in his palm. A moment later, her house keys joined it.

"No more," she said. She meant to say the words firmly, but they came out thin.

Comprehension dawned across his face. A muscle jumped in his jaw and his fist clenched. "Deirdre—"

"Don't," said Dee. "Just—don't."

She knew all the things he would say.

Family does not abandon family; no one will ever want you besides us; if you leave you are a bad daughter; you are the worst daughter; you should—

Her mother came out of the kitchen, her thin fingers wound in an anxious knot. "Dee?"

Dee looked down. This was the hardest part. Jumping off a sinking ship to save oneself was one thing, but abandoning others in the jump...

It was self-preservation.

And she might feel horrible about it, it might give her nightmares and anxiety and she might spend years crying about it, but the thing was—she would have those years.

That was the beauty of saving her own life.

"I'm your father," Mr. Moreno started to stay, but again, she cut him off.

"You're an addict. You could have been my father. But you could never be both, not at the same time." She looked up at him, and suddenly her throat was too full. "If you ever want to change that…well. You know where I am."

She turned to her mother. "You too," she said simply. That was the only gift she could offer—simple words.

A quiver ran through Mr. Moreno's whole body. He shifted on his feet, reached for Dee. She stepped back.

He stepped forward. She could see the energy coiling in his muscles, the fury kindling to life behind his eyes.

Fear beat hard within her. She needed to leave, to escape, but he wouldn't let her run.

And that was when Gremma reached into her overly large purse and withdrew a fire ax. She hefted it over her shoulder. In her red leather jacket, she might have been Little Red Riding Hood—a Red who carried an ax and wore wolf pelts as accessories.

"All right," said Gremma. "We're leaving now." She beamed at Mr. Moreno, her pretty smile sharp as a blade.

Dee loved her roommate in that moment. For her fearlessness, for not asking questions, for being here.

Dee turned back to her parents.

And she said the words that both freed and shattered her in the same breath.

"Bye, Mom," said Dee. "Bye, Dad."

She walked out the front door and didn't look back.

She cried.

When Gremma went to the dining hall for lunch Dee retreated to the safety of her bed.

She curled up with her pillow and began to shake. It was inevitable; she felt the sorrow climb up her throat until it was impossible to hold in. It began with a small, tiny sob, and then the rest broke free. It was almost a release, this howl of grief that clawed inside of her. She had never truly given it voice before.

This was how babies were born—sobbing, gasping for air. Perhaps a rebirth was the same.

She cried herself out until her sobs were dry and her voice hoarse. Her eyes ached; her sinuses felt overfull. By the time Gremma returned to the room, Dee was sitting on her bed, staring at nothing in particular.

Gremma watched her. "You know, you learn a lot in human-science classes," she said. "Fear is one of the strongest human emotions. It serves an important biological function—mainly ensuring we as a species didn't get eaten alive by saber-toothed tigers. Fear keeps us alive, tells us when to run or escape, but fear has its downsides, too.

"I don't get scared," said Gremma. "I mean, I can get scared, but I really don't have to. My parents own a mansion in Seattle and after I came out, they were fine with it. I mean, I found in their browser history they'd googled 'How to be a supportive parent to a gay kid.'" She shook her head in fond amusement. "Some kids tried to bully me in middle school, but I pushed one out of a window. That's how I ended up at Brannigan." This time, there was a hint of smugness to her smile. "Point is, my life is pretty good. I don't get scared because I didn't grow up thinking there was much to be afraid of."

Dee gazed at her dully.

"The human body isn't designed to withstand that much fear on a daily basis," Gremma said. "That's why soldiers have PTSD. You go through constant terror for too long and it screws you up chemically."

She stepped forward, until she was by Dee's bed.

"I'm staying at the beach house for part of the summer— my parents think I'm finally old enough to stay there longer than a week on my own. You're coming with me."

Dee froze.

"I already asked my parents," continued Gremma. "They agreed. Actually, they were downright giddy—I think they think you'll be a good influence on me or something. No idea why. I mean, you're the one making demonic pacts. But you'll have a place to stay—" Her voice cut off as Dee slammed into her. "Omf."

Dee hugged her tight, let her panic-stiff fingers dig into Gremma's shoulder blades. Gremma was still for a moment, then her arms went around Dee. They stood there, and somehow the hug was not awkward or too long. It was a conversation in physical gestures: *Thank you* and *You're welcome* all tangled together.

Then, "You pushed a kid out a window?" Dee mumbled into Gremma's shirt.

Gremma let out a soft sigh, her voice almost regretful. "It was on the first story."

THIRTY-FIVE

A week passed.

And then another.

Dee felt each day slip by, each tick of the clock, and she felt herself grow tenser by the moment.

Cora would have her heart back by now. Which meant it was just Dee, Riley, and James going into that mega-void.

And then everything would be over. They would be safe.

She told herself that again and again.

She didn't really feel safe, though. She felt restless and uncertain and—

And she wanted to live. Even if she was going to die in the next few days or weeks or whatever, she wanted to live.

She let herself into James's apartment, taking the time to actually lock the door behind her. He was painting, of course. They were all dealing with the stress in different ways. James retreated into his work with a fevered intensity. She wondered what it would be like to have such a talent, to make something beautiful where there had been nothing before.

Fear fluttered in her chest—it almost felt like having a heartbeat again. She wasn't sure how to do this. She was dressed in a loose sweater and skinny jeans. But he had never cared about her clothes and—

And she wanted this. The want outweighed the fear.

"Hey," she said.

James looked up. Smiled. "Hey."

"Riley's not around?"

"I heard her saying something about visiting your dorm, actually," said James. He put his brush down and rose to his feet, stretching. There was a dirty rag on his workbench and he used it to wipe his hands clean.

Dee sat down on the couch and he eased down next to her. "Ah. So that's why Gremma was putting on extra lipstick when I left."

James laughed. "I told you. But at least I know my couch's

virtue is still safe." He patted the paint-stained cushions affectionately.

If that wasn't an opening, she didn't know what was.

Dee took a breath. "Actually. I came here—well. I mean. If you wanted to change that. The couch's virtue. I wouldn't be... opposed."

As seductions went, that line probably wouldn't go down in history.

Even so, he jerked in surprise. He gazed at Dee, as if he was sure he heard her wrong. "What?"

She kept her voice steady. "I distinctly remember you complaining about how if anyone was going to be naked on this couch, it should be you."

He looked at her. Swallowed.

"You want to—" he began to say, all hoarse.

"Yes," she said, too quickly.

Another swallow. "Have you ever...?"

"No," she said. "You?"

He gazed at her intently, as if he were afraid she might suddenly vanish. "Yes. But I'm clean. Tested and—well, it's been a while. Dee, we haven't known each other very long—"

"Months," she said. "That's longer than some people wait."

He hesitated. Just a little too long. Hurt flashed across her face and he saw it.

"Dee," he said. "Dee, I want to—but, Dee, you're going

through a lot of things right now, with your parents and the voids and the Daemon. I don't want you to want this because you're afraid or because you think you might not get another chance. Because you will have other chances."

"I want to," she said. "Not because I'm afraid—I mean, I am afraid. But I'd want to even if we weren't possibly going to die soon. I want to because...because I trust you. I trust you with this."

He knew what those words meant.

She had said as much after he told her he liked her for the first time.

I'm not sure I'm capable of loving anyone—not if I can't trust anyone.

His fingers shook slightly; his thumb brushed over her cheek. "If I do anything that you don't like or want to stop, please tell me." He kissed her, and it was sweet and gentle, and she pulled away for a moment.

"James," she said, but she was smiling when she said his name. "I'm not going to break."

They kissed again, and this time she could feel joy in it—a wild, breathless laughter in his mouth.

"Not on the couch," he said.

"All right, then," she said, and took him by the hand and walked to the bedroom.

It felt as if she were shedding her own skin in addition to her clothes—she was tingling with every soft touch. He pressed kiss after kiss to her throat, her shoulder, her collarbone. "You are beautiful," he told her. "So beautiful and strong and you've got the best sense of humor of anyone I've ever met—"

Her mouth found his and she silenced him, swallowing his words of praise. His fingers dug into her hip and she welcomed the sensation. When they broke apart, she said breathlessly, "You can leave off with the compliments, you know. I'm already in your bed." He had somehow lost his shirt on the way to the bedroom, and her fingertips dragged over his bare stomach, making the muscles jump.

He nipped at her neck. "What if I just feel like complimenting you?"

She laughed, her thumb sliding over the swell of his lower lip. "Gallantry?"

He shook his head. "Truth." His fingertips skimmed over her bare side, catching on the edge of her bra.

She had heard about people losing themselves in physical closeness. As if one might misplace their identity through a night of passion.

But Dee found herself in the heat of his mouth, the familiar touch of his fingertips against her bare skin. She felt more herself than she had ever been, happiness blooming beneath her skin, her chest full of joy.

"Condom?" he said, sounding strained.

Dee fumbled in her backpack; the school nurse had a box

of condoms in her office, even if the parents complained. He laughed, jubilant, pressed a kiss to her knuckles, said she was brilliant and prepared. His fingers laced through hers, and his gaze never wavered.

It was—well, it was a sharp inhalation, a bite of teeth on her lower lip, fullness, hands on her hips, a whispered curse, mingled breath, and tangled fingers.

She woke the next morning, an arm around her waist. Breath tickled along her skin as James breathed. His fingers rested lightly on her stomach. Perhaps he thought she was still asleep, for he pressed a kiss to the back of her neck.

"I love you." He murmured the words into her unruly hair.

I chose this, she thought, and smiled.

THIRTY-SIX

Dee was just getting off her shift of volunteer work at the hospital when she saw him.

The lean, beautiful figure standing on the sidewalk.

As she made her way toward the Daemon, the sound of her own breath became loud in her ears. The bustle of the hospital seemed to fall away around her, until it was as if they were the only two living beings there.

The lamplight caught on the Daemon's skin, making him look ethereally pale. Lovely and eternal. And yet, he came from the same place as that burrower, that creature of ill-formed legs and claws. She wondered what kind of world could birth two such different species.

She spoke first; somehow it made her feel as if she had some control over the situation.

"Tonight's the night?"

He nodded. There was almost a look of . . . that couldn't be sympathy on his face, could it? A chill went through her.

"Tonight," he agreed. "Come to the bank."

And then he simply vanished.

Well, she thought, at least he hadn't told her the world was ending via text message.

Dee wasn't sure how one dressed for a potential apocalypse.

"Doesn't matter, does it?" said Gremma. "If you fail, you'll be dead before the actual destruction happens."

"Thanks for that encouraging thought," said Dee.

It felt odd to be sitting in her dorm room, on her computer chair, lacing up a pair of running shoes. It was exceedingly routine, but she could taste the strangeness of the night on her tongue. Her skin felt as shivery as if someone had run a live current over it. Perhaps it was nerves, or perhaps her heartless body was attuned to this night, to the thinness of this world. To the closeness of another.

She closed her eyes for a moment, steadied herself

"You're going to be all right, right?" said Gremma. She sounded uncommonly worried. Her face twisted, annoyed she was forced to endure such an emotion.

Dee nodded. Her stomach felt as if she had swallowed shards of broken glass. She looked around her dorm room, acutely aware that this could be the last time she ever saw it—her bed with the worn blue comforter, her desk, their TV, Gremma's stuffed animals. She made herself say, "Listen. I—I've got a letter for my mother. In my desk. If—if something happens."

Just in case.

Gremma put her hands on her hips. "Oh god. Last requests. It's always the part of the movie I fast-forward through, usually because the character is dying in some factually inaccurate way."

"If I do die," replied Dee, "I'll try to do it accurately."

A choked little giggle escaped Gremma. Her hands fell to her sides. "Well, I've got something else encouraging for you, too." She knelt, reached beneath her bed, and dragged out a backpack. "Here."

Dee looked inside. Nearly dropped the backpack. She stared down into a space filled to the brim with small jam jars. Their metal lids were pierced through, cloth wicks dangling limply, ready to be set alight. "These…aren't stink bombs, are they?"

Gremma held out a lighter and Dee took it. "Riley had a recipe for Molotov cocktails and we decided to hold our own version of craft night."

Dee smiled.

She would not be helpless. A fierce joy seized her. She laughed, and some of her fear dropped away. She had something to fight for. She had something to fight with. And people to fight alongside.

This was how normal people survived their own fairy tales. They became their own kind of monster.

Gremma grinned. "Anything comes at you," she said, "burn the motherfucker down."

That evening, fog hung heavy through Portland.

The city lights were muted, headlights struggling to pierce the thick mist, and Dee watched as buildings and other cars slid by. She had decided to take the bus, to walk the last few blocks herself. Gremma would have driven her and James offered to pick her up, but she declined them both. This was what she wanted—the rattling engine of the bus, the smell of sweat and bodies, the squeak and hiss of the brakes, the gentle sway when it took a sharp turn.

It was strangely meditative, but that was not the true reason Dee got on the bus.

Dee got on the bus to see the other people taking it. She did not put in her earbuds, nor pretend to text on her phone. She simply watched the family of three, a mother and two young sons. Twins, perhaps. The single teenage boy with spiked hair and pierced eyebrows who gave Dee a polite nod when he passed her. The homeless man who spent most of the ride doing a crossword puzzle out of the *Oregonian*.

People. All people. All in danger, if the demons were to be believed.

Dee was no hero. She was afraid.

But looking at these people, she knew there was no running away. She watched them, wondered if their lives were as tentative as her own. And when her stop came, she rose to her feet, thanked the driver, and stepped off. The driver smiled at her—at the teenage girl with Molotov cocktails in her backpack.

The doors to the bank were not chained. They hung open and Dee took a moment, dragging a breath between her clenched teeth, and stepped inside.

James sat on the floor, fiddling with his phone. When he saw her, he scrambled to his feet and hastened to her side. "Hi," he said, and his smile was almost shy.

She thought she loved him. This boy with freckled feet and paint-smudged hands. This boy who played the world off as a joke, but took others' suffering seriously. This boy who looked at her and never saw a broken girl—just a girl.

She would say the words. Not tonight, not with the weight of everything hanging over them. But she would tell him.

And for the first time, she thought about what might happen after tonight.

She thought about this summer, and what it might bring.

About hot days spent in the loft apartment, of rooms cordoned off with curtains, of a half-constructed kitchen and couches that always smelled of paint. She thought of the freedom of being able to come and go as she pleased, of making her own life. She thought of days spent with James, of going to more art galleries, of watching his ascension into history. He would do it, she knew. He would climb his way into the ranks of the great artists, and she would be proud of him.

Her own future was less defined. Perhaps she would travel, use a fraction of the Daemon's money to go somewhere she'd never visited. Perhaps James would go with her—she thought of the two of them on some road trip, driving to who knew where with no schedule to bind them.

The thought was a happy one. "Hey," she said, smiling, and took his hand. Their fingers laced and he gave her hand a squeeze.

She half expected him to make some sort of joke about tonight, but he did not. He simply pressed a kiss against the crown of her head, and then turned to his left.

Riley was sitting by the vault. She was dressed in worn boots, black jeans, and a loose sweatshirt. Her thick eyeliner looked as if it belonged on a football player. She looked ready for war. "Save the lovey-dovey stuff for after we've blown up a void, okay?"

James smiled, but it was brittle.

"We'll be all right," said Dee, and bumped his shoulder with her own. He felt solid, comforting, and she took strength from that. "We've done this before. We'll have creepy-as-hell backup from the other demons, and thanks to you and Gremma, we have a few weapons."

Riley shrugged. "Hey, demolitions experts have to know how things burn. I may have…tested a few recipes."

"You and Gremma are well-matched," said Dee drily.

Riley gave her a carefree grin.

Then Dee heard the approach of the Agathodaemon. He strode around the corner in his usual suit, an umbrella tucked beneath his left arm. He surveyed the three of them, heaved a little sigh. His step was slow, and he eyed the teenagers the way a buyer might look over a prospective car.

"I should have made more of you," he said, a little regretfully. "Or brought in another troop."

"Why didn't you?" asked Riley bluntly. "Three of us. Seems a bit thin to me."

The Daemon sighed again. "Unfortunately, my methods are considered…dangerous by most of my kind. They frown on me making more than three or four of you in a single location. The one time I attempted to do so, the constructs were taken from me. You are not easily controlled, not when you still possess minds of your own. Random, chaotic, fragile."

"Then why do it at all?" said James in a low voice. He was more serious than Dee had ever heard.

The Daemon slid him a look. "Because you heartless are more effective than the homunculi, but you carry too many memories in your heart. The voids will seek to expel or tear apart anything that is real, that is vibrantly alive. Memories and emotions are incompatible with a void. Thus, the only creatures that may enter are like the burrowers—empty, hungry things. Or the homunculi—dead and controlled. And you—my hollow little constructs."

He said the words fondly, though, and perhaps that was the most frightening thing of all.

"And if we hadn't shown up," said Riley, "what would you have done?"

He glanced at her. "Well, for one thing, it would have taken longer to track you each down individually. And this wouldn't have been nearly as impressive."

Dee expected him to reach for her, to take hold of her arm the way he had when he transported her before. But he did no such thing.

He snapped his fingers.

The world *shifted*.

Blurred beneath their feet.

It was as if he had yanked the floor out from under them; when Dee stumbled and forced herself to balance again, she stood in an entirely new location. James's hand tightened around hers, and she blinked several times, tried to make sense of her surroundings.

They all stood outside of what looked like an abandoned mall.

Of course the world would end in a mall, she thought.

"Come," said the Daemon. His moment of levity was over; his features were drawn, pale, and his long fingers twitched toward his umbrella. He strode through a shattered window.

The three teenagers lingered on the threshold for a moment. "Whatever happens tonight, I'm glad I met the two of you," said Riley.

"Same," answered Dee softly.

James did not answer, but his thumb stroked the back of her hand.

Dee stepped into the remnants of the mall, a backpack full of Molotov cocktails slung over her shoulder. She glanced around, at the cracked linoleum, the shards of broken glass, and the walls bending in on themselves. The ceiling was half caved in, and the dim moonlight fought a losing battle against the shadows.

"No rats yet," she said, and Riley and James followed her inside. The acrid scent of burned plastic hung in the air, and Riley tried to breathe through the sleeve of her cotton shirt.

James glanced around and said, "I get the whole post-apocalyptic-fashion thing, but this is taking it a bit too far."

Riley coughed and turned it into a laugh. "You never know—the look might catch on."

Something scurried along the wall, darting through a crack in the granite. The rats were here after all. "Let's get this over with," Dee said.

Riley let out another shaky laugh. "Oh, this is the part where you give us a pep talk, right? 'We can do it.' 'If this is how the world is going to end, at least we won't feel anything, right?'" She shook her head, straight dark hair falling in her face. "Come on, then. Give us a pep talk."

Dee gave her a disparaging look. "First of all, I'm not Cora. I don't do pep talks. But I'll tell you this: We're going to win. Because we'll do whatever it takes. We're heartless."

James looked over the destruction, and there was a twist to his mouth when he said, "'This is the way the world ends. Not with a bang but a' bad pun.'"

"You wouldn't have it any other way," said Dee.

THIRTY-SEVEN

The Daemon led them through the decaying building.

They followed around several corners, until the space widened out into what must have been the mall's main center. Wallpaper peeled in long strips, and the fog had slipped between the broken cracks in the walls. It hung low to the ground, making this place look as though it had no floor—as if they strode atop clouds.

The Daemon rounded another corner, turned so that they faced what might have once been a food court.

Dee saw the figures.

They stood, silent sentinels, side by side, their faces staring straight ahead. As if they had been placed there by some enormous child, putting his toy soldiers in a row. They were just the same as Dee remembered—all desiccated flesh and yellowed bones, horrific jigsaw puzzles of human pieces. Each was different, a sculpture shaped by individual hands—some had too many fingers, others were built thick and heavy like tanks, while others were thinner and smaller, lean as skeletons.

This is what comes of wishes.

Two smaller figures sat on a table. They maintained the illusion of humanity, even if their otherworldly beauty gave them away.

One of the other demons was the female, the one whose homunculus had been lost to the void in the field. She was straight-backed, her shaven head gleaming in the moonlight. She looked over the three teenagers with an air of grudging indulgence. "Heart-Monger," she said, inclining her head to the Daemon.

"Cobbler," replied the Daemon.

The last demon, this one blond and male, slid the Daemon a cool look. "I see you brought your flimsy little constructs."

Riley snorted. "Flimsy my ass," she said. "We'll see who gets to the prize first and whose Franken-freaks end up in tiny pieces."

The demon looked vaguely scandalized.

"Your creature is talking to me," he said to the Daemon.

"Yes," replied the Daemon. "That's what happens when they have mouths."

The male demon snorted and turned away.

Dee was only half listening; her gaze swept over the large room, looking for the smudge of unreality. It was against the far wall, larger than any of the other voids they'd faced. The distorted ripples made it look as though the entire food court's floor was heated, but the air remained chill and damp.

"Hey," said James softly. "I don't know what we're going to face in there."

Dee turned to look at him. "No last speeches," she said firmly. "We've done this before. We're getting out of this." She pointed at herself with their linked fingers. "Survivor, remember?"

A smile flickered across his face.

"That is what I love most about you," he told her, and when he pulled her close, she shuddered with relief. For a moment, the mall ceased to exist, the demons weren't there, and the breathless danger was gone. There was only the scent of paint, the familiar closeness, the top of her head tucked beneath his chin, and the silence in his chest.

This was all that mattered.

"Come," said the Daemon. "It's time." He gestured to Riley. "You will stand half in, half out of the void. Without you, the void will collapse too quickly for the others to escape." He slid a look at the other demons. "They may not care about losing their servants, but I like to keep mine intact." He gazed at the three of them. "You are short-lived things, but you have served me well and I would not like to see you destroyed."

Dee supposed that was *his* idea of a pep talk.

Riley went first. Her chin was lifted high, her shoulders rigid. She pressed her fingers to the void's shimmering surface, then she stepped through, angled herself so that she was half in, half out.

One of the demons spoke an unfamiliar word.

The homunculi all moved in unison. Jerky, stiff steps. Their gaits were rigid, as if their joints and tendons were dried up, but the sheer size of their strides made up for it. One by one, they shambled into the enormous void, vanishing through it.

"They will fight, and that will distract the burrowers," said the Daemon quietly. "Here."

He held out a duffel bag.

Dee took one strap; James took the other. Her own backpack was still slung over her shoulder, its contents clinking. A lighter was in her right pocket. A knitted heart was in her left.

"Let's get this done," said James quietly. His hand found hers, squeezed.

They held on to each other as they stepped forward.

Dee squeezed her eyes shut as they passed through.

And opened them to chaos.

The wind tore the shout from her lips. James shoved Dee sideways and they stumbled, staggered out of the way as the shuddering body of a burrower slammed into the ground beside them.

It had been torn in half, twitching like some squashed beetle, all legs and jerky spasms. Utterly inhuman.

Dee and James lurched away from the creature, out of reach of those claw-tipped legs. Dee tried to catch her breath, but the air was thick and hot and heavy with the taste of burning metal.

This void resembled the interior of the mall—complete with the hollowed-out shells of the food court's booths and tables. The walls and floor were raw, too new to be real, but that was not what caught Dee's attention.

All the other voids had been terrifying, but it was because they were *voids*. Places of screaming wind and emptiness, where her own memories were dragged out of her, as if the void needed them in order to crystallize. But this—this void was not empty.

A battle took place before them.

There were alien creatures with too many legs, some resembling underwater animals, while others looked vaguely insectoid. They were enormous, straight out of a nightmare. And the homunculi—slow-moving but determined—were using their massive, ill-formed hands to slam the creatures out of their paths.

"Do we hang behind?" shouted Dee over the screaming of the wind. Beside these massive beings, she was small and insignificant. The void tugged at her mind, and she could feel the beginnings of a memory, a sickening twist—

She was young and too small and helpless—

And then James's hand was on her cheek. His fingers were cold. "Dee, stay with me."

She blinked several times. *Focus*, she thought. *Focus.*

Gazing into James's face, she saw the same struggle in his eyes. The push and pull of *then* versus *now*. He swallowed, shivered, and she wondered what memories the void tried make him relive.

Dee's hand raised to cover his. A moment of understanding passed between them, an acknowledgment. "We can't rely on the other demons," said James, speaking above the wind. He was scanning the area, and Dee could see the thoughts working behind his eyes. "We need to move farther in, get the explosives in place."

She nodded. "We should try to keep to the edges," she said. "Out of sight—"

A clawed leg emerged from one of the half-formed booths. James cried out, leaping backward, but then a burrower was scuttling toward them. It had no eyes—but a wide mouth, snapping at James's leg.

But whatever these creatures were, they were not prepared for Gremma's homemade Molotov cocktails.

Dee's shaking fingers took two tries to set the wick alight and then she threw. The glass shattered upon the burrower's armored hide. The flame caught and her eyes watered, blinded by the sudden glare of light.

Did such a thing as fire exist in this creature's world? Had it ever felt the heat of a flame, the searing agony of a burn?

Probably not, judging by its reaction.

The burrower screamed. It sounded like no creature she had ever heard, no animal cry. It was the screech of metal being rent apart.

Dee reached for the fallen duffel bag and sprinted off, James at her side. They scrambled away, left the creature to burn.

"That was badass," James shouted above the din.

They darted around a homunculus; it was staggering, one of its legs chewed off at the knee. It was trying to haul itself forward by the strength of its enormous arms, its mismatched eyes on a burrower.

The burrowers were devastatingly quick, all swiftness and grace, but the homunculi were slow, steady, and refused to give ground.

One of the homunculus's arms nearly clipped Dee. She felt the air rush past her, the whisper of almost-touch, and then James had her by the arm and yanked her to one side, a snarled curse caught between his teeth. A burrower fell upon the fallen homunculus, sinking its claws in again and again, like a scorpion stinging its prey.

There was no time to think. Dee's fingers gripped another jar, the lighter in her other hand. One of the burrowers seemed to sense their presence—it circled them at a distance, its legs skittering across the floor.

The burrower kept the tables between itself and the teenagers. Warier or smarter than those who had attacked before. She tried to keep her eyes on it at all times, frightened that the moment she looked away would be the moment it struck.

A crack split the air. Dee's head jerked around, and she saw three of the creatures on one of the homunculi—biting and clawing. The homunculus fell, and its enormous body slammed into the floor. Cracks spun out, as if this fragile half reality could not bear the weight of such a blow.

Panic seared through Dee; she had been watching the homunculi, and not the—

The burrower fell upon her and James with the force of a charging bull. The strap of the duffel bag slipped from her hand.

She felt it slam into her, and she fell, staggering as she hit one of the tables. Her head clipped the edge and stars burned through her eyes. She tried to kick, to writhe like she had been taught in all her self-defense classes—but the lesson on what to do if she was pinned became a lot more complicated when the attacker had eight legs.

She screamed, heard someone else screaming, too, and she struggled to get her arm up, to ward its claws away from her face. She was dimly aware of James trying to pummel the creature with his fists, but it seemed to be doing little good.

She kicked again and again, and she must have gotten lucky, because suddenly her shoe punched through something. A joint, perhaps, or a weakness in the burrower's armor. It paused, staggered, and that was all the time Dee needed. She threw the backpack beneath the creature, lit the cocktail in her hand, and threw it down into the backpack. She crawled backward, clumsy with haste.

The backpack lit—and the rest of the cocktails went up in one fiery burst.

The creature burned. Dee felt the heat of the flames on her face, but James's hands were on her shoulders, dragging her upright. She tried to catch her breath, but sand stung her lungs and her face was too hot, as if she'd been sunburned.

And then Dee saw it—the center of the void. It was where things seemed most solid, where the metal scent was harshest. Her eyes stung with grit and she tried to blink the world back into focus.

At that center, something tore through. Another burrower. It pushed through the center of the void, found its equilibrium, and joined the fray. And then another followed. This was where the burrowers came from—from wherever that center led.

Her stomach caved in on itself; there were not enough homunculi to counter all of them. Even with their inhuman strength and determination, they would be overrun.

They weren't going to make it out again. They might destroy this place, but there simply wouldn't be time to get past all these creatures. Twenty seconds wasn't nearly enough.

Something inside of her hardened.

Fine, then.

They would do this. They would save the world and all it would cost was two heartless teenagers.

"Come on," said James, and they rushed ahead.

It was rough going—a headlong sprint into the chaos. Dee barely managed to avoid being stepped on by a homunculus, and then James was sliced by one of the burrower's claws. A shallow cut opened up on his forearm before James kicked at the creature, and it scurried backward into the reach of a homunculus. The cobbled-together monster wrapped its fingers around it and squeezed. Dee looked away.

The center of the void was firmer beneath her feet, and suddenly the wind quieted. The eye of the storm, she thought. James set the duffel bag down, tore the zipper open. He fumbled for the remote, for the detonator and timer. Dee stood over, taking comfort in his nearness.

And then he went still.

His trembling fingers held something up and Dee drew in a sharp breath.

In his palm was a mess of shattered plastic and wires.

"What—what is that?" she said.

James looked up. "The timer."

It must have happened when that last burrower attacked them, when its leg struck the duffel bag.

Broken.

Dee's last hope slipped from her.

"It's broken," he said. "We can't—we can't—" The wind swallowed up his words. "There's no timer to set." His gaze settled on Dee and his face hardened. But even so, his fingers were trembling as he pulled the duffel bag open. "Manually," he said, his voice shaking. "We can set off the C-4 manually."

She knelt beside him and his arms went around her.

This—this would be all right.

Her hand pressed to the place where his heart should have been. "It's okay," she said. "I knew—I knew this might happen. I knew what being heartless might cost me." The words came in little fits and starts, but she said them. And she meant them.

He had been right, the first time they met. After she lost her heart, she had lived. Not simply existed, but *lived*. She couldn't regret that; she was only sad it had not lasted longer.

James pressed a kiss to her brow and it felt strange—not like any kiss they had shared. It was affectionate, rather than passionate. He reached inside the duffel bag and withdrew something else. It was not part of the explosives; it was not a river rock—it was wrapped in a clean shirt. He unwrapped it, and then Dee drew in a sharp breath.

The object was red and gleaming, like a fist-sized ruby.

It was a heart.

A heart brought into a void. No wonder those burrowers had zeroed in on them. Dee looked up at James, uncomprehending. She did not—she did not understand why he would have carried that with him. How had he even managed to carry it? She would have thought a heart needed the warmth and breath of a body.

"James...?" she said, his name a question.

But James was smiling, truly smiling, as if he were looking at his final masterpiece, the greatest artwork he had ever created.

He said, "You're not heartless, are you?"

And then he shoved the heart against her chest.

She had only a moment to gasp. The heart should have hit her clothes, her skin, but whatever power the Daemon used was still upon it. The heart passed through cotton and skin and bone as if they were not there.

It sank into her chest.

It hurt; it was like the snap of shoving a key into a lock, of fitting pieces together. She could not speak for the pain, could not think for the shock.

James kissed her. A press of heat, his mouth against hers, and it was too quick. Abruptly, it felt as if gravity had upended. Her fingers clawed at the air and she fell backward, wrenched away from James. She reached for him and caught only air.

Nothing living can enter the voids. Nothing with a heart.

She remembered the rats being spat out, hurled by some invisible force. The same force that gripped her. With a cry, she tried to hold on, tried to stay—

James was still smiling—and it made him look so beautiful her heart ached.

Her heart.

But it couldn't be her heart—her time wasn't up—

She understood. It wasn't her heart.

It was his.

The weight of it dragged at her, a heavy anchor hooked through her rib cage, and then she was crashing downhill, no, not downhill there was no downhill, but she was falling, falling sideways and tumbling and staggering, all elbows and knees, sand catching in her hair, her stomach turning over, and then the pop in her ears as if the air pressure had suddenly changed.

She was flung from the mouth of the void, and as she went, she had enough sense to grab at Riley and the two of them hit the ground together. They rolled, still caught by the momentum, and Dee desperately tried to right herself. She scrambled to hands and knees, faced the void—still glittering and half there, and maybe there was enough time.

She lunged to her feet, rushed toward the void.

James. She was not sure if she thought his name or spoke it aloud, but—

The void imploded.

The world was saved.

A girl got her heart back.

And lost it in the same moment.

THIRTY-EIGHT

The second time James Lancer lost his heart, it was in Portland.

His two-year contract was up. The Daemon came to his apartment, a heart in hand.

But James would not let him put it back in. He accepted the heart, shoved it in his backpack.

Because he had discovered his own Rumpelstiltskin clause.

He knew how to outwit a fairy tale. All it would cost was one heart, one life.

Which was really nothing at all, to him.

He took his heart into the void, and when the moment was right, he gave it to the girl to whom it already belonged.

As for the girl, Dee sat on the floor of the ruined mall, back to the wall, damp and numb, silent and hurting more than she could ever remember. She distantly felt Riley's hands on her, trying to rouse her. Riley was speaking all the while, senseless words that blurred together.

But Dee couldn't hear what Riley said. All she could hear was the pulse of a heartbeat loud in her ears.

THIRTY-NINE

Time passed in fits and starts.

Dee barely noticed; she moved through the world in a daze. The only part of her that felt real was the too-loud thumping in her chest. The rest of her body felt numb, as if she'd been held under cold water too long.

The weeks leading up to finals were a blur. She had a few recollections of that time—mostly of Riley determinedly quizzing her on history dates and English authors. "You saved my life," she had said, her mouth set in a grim line. "And I am not going to let you flunk out of your ritzy-ass boarding school." And then she shoved another textbook in Dee's hands and began making flash cards.

As luck would have it, she did not fail any of her finals.

She sleepwalked through essay answers and gave an oral presentation without a single memory of how it went, but apparently Riley had done her work well, because Dee found herself packing up at the end of the year with the knowledge that she hadn't flunked out.

She wasn't eating much. Anything she put in her mouth was about as appetizing as raw clay. Going to the dining hall felt like an enormous undertaking. Gremma tried to feed her.

The first morning, Gremma brought a bagel and cream cheese.

It didn't happen again.

Then Gremma began bringing her soft food—oatmeal and cubed melon pieces, as if grief were some sort of illness. She also took to carrying around little boxes of cereal in her bag, and passing them to Dee at intervals throughout the day.

Riley was still living at the loft apartment. She said she had received paperwork saying that the lease had been put in her name several weeks ago—and it had been paid for two years.

Dee couldn't be sure, because phone conversations were fuzzy like that, but she thought Riley might have been crying when she said it.

James, thought Dee, and a fresh wave of misery swept through her. He had done his work well, ensuring that Riley would have a place to stay for as long as she needed it. And of course it was just like him to do it without telling anyone—the underhanded bastard.

She snorted out a laugh that dissolved into a sob.

There was no funeral.

According to the Internet, James simply vanished. There was no body to be found anyway. It had been exploded.

Imploded, came Cal's wry voice. Another ghost living in her brain.

Luckily for Dee, no one had known James well enough to identify his friends. No police came knocking at anyone's door, and there was no great fuss over his disappearance. Most people thought he'd gone the way of a tortured artist and thrown himself off a bridge.

She barely remembered the chaos of moving out of the dorm, of placing her belongings in boxes and taping them shut. But then she was handing over her dorm key, signing out her name, and striding to the Camaro.

She settled in the backseat, numb and silent, as Gremma revved the engine. "Newport," she said, "here we come."

The Newport beach house was situated...well, along the beach. It was two stories, decorated with what Gremma referred to as "vacation house tacky chic." There were too many seashells and a miniature buoy in the bathroom, and it was designed so all the windows could be opened. A porch led out to the beach; there was a wooden picnic table, several chairs, and a fire pit.

Dee could see how easily this place might become Gremma's party den—the roof was just sloped enough to sit on comfortably, and there was a fully stocked liquor cabinet in the basement.

Dee took the smaller, upstairs bedroom while Gremma and Riley claimed the master. There was a moment of awkwardness when Dee walked up the stairs; she felt clumsy, out of place, a hanger-on to their romantic summer getaway.

Slowly, though, Dee began to come back to herself. She helped make meals, walked with Riley and Gremma to the local arcade, watched as Gremma played first-person shooter games and tried to win a giant stuffed bear. They made meals together, cobbled together stir-fries and even tried making homemade pizza once.

Gremma's parents called and informed them they would be visiting at some point. "To check up on me," said Gremma. "But whatever. They're cool, we're cool. And besides, they'll want to meet the girlfriend."

Riley had flushed, but looked unmistakably pleased.

If Dee were being honest with herself, it was painful being with the two of them. Riley and Gremma were affectionate, comfortable around each other, and Dee's chest ached every time she saw them kiss or hold hands.

The days dragged on, until one morning when Gremma was making scrambled eggs.

A loud knocking came at the front door.

"If it's the neighbor boys asking to borrow a cup of vodka, tell them we're out," called Gremma.

There were other vacationers, of course. Notably, a house of college boys who seemed to show up every time Gremma wore a bikini to the beach.

Dee pulled the front door open and blinked.

It wasn't a college boy.

It was a middle-aged man. Dressed in a suit.

Not a demon. There were lines around his eyes and gray in his hair. Definitely human.

Her heart began to pound. Lawyer, she thought. Undercover cop. Someone hired by her parents, someone to drag her home. But, no. She would not go, she wouldn't—

"I'm looking for a Deirdre Moreno," said the man.

Dee felt herself begin to tremble. "Who's asking?"

The man smiled, not unkindly. "I'm a private investigator. I was hired a few months ago to deliver something to you— on this date, actually. I was supposed to find you and make sure you got this."

He looked down and nudged a box with his foot. She hadn't noticed it before, so focused was she on his suit and official demeanor. "Why?" she asked. "And by who?"

The man shrugged. "I'm just the messenger." And then he was walking away, toward a car parked on the curb. Dee lingered in the doorway, eyeing the box with suspicion until Riley appeared behind her.

"Postman?" she asked.

"Private investigator," replied Dee. "And a mysterious package."

Riley tilted her head. Then she reached down and rattled the box. "Well, it's not a bomb."

"You can tell that from the noise?" Dee snorted.

Riley grinned up at her. "Actually, I could tell because it didn't just explode." Then she hefted the box into her arms and carried it into the dining room. "Yo, Gremma! Some man just delivered a mysterious package to Dee!"

"Cool." Gremma came out of the kitchen, still wearing an apron that read KISS THE COOK.

"We should—" Dee began to say, but Gremma already had a very large kitchen knife in one hand. Once the box was open, Gremma dug into it and came out with a folder; Riley grunted and pulled out a boxed set of books; Dee found a slim manila envelope. She opened it and her fingers closed on the edge of a sheet of paper. It was expensive, thick, the kind used by artists, and her stomach fluttered. She knew this paper, had seen it in his hands many times.

She pulled a painting from the envelope.

It wasn't large—perhaps the size of a normal, printed sheet of paper. But the style was different than she had ever seen. It was in watercolor, a medium Dee had never seen James use. It was lighter, more ephemeral, the brushstrokes were messier.

It looked clumsier than James's other paintings, but it was still beautiful.

The painting was of a girl. A girl with frizzy dark hair and brown skin. She was wearing a shirt with a private school pin, and she gazed out from the painting with steady, serious eyes.

Beneath the painting were two lines of cramped, familiar handwriting.

"Girl in Hospital Basement"

And beneath that, *This is how I would have painted you if I hadn't sold my heart.*

Dee carefully set the painting down on the table and looked to Riley. Her throat was aching, too full, and she barely managed to say, "What are you holding?"

Riley was looking down at her own discovery in confusion. "A complete set of the Harry Potter books," she said. "No idea why, though. I mean, who hasn't read these?"

A laugh escaped Dee. She closed her eyes for a moment, drew herself together.

There was a knitted heart resting at the bottom of the box. It was worn, one edge knotted together. Dee forced herself to touch it, to stroke the soft yarn.

"What'd you find, Gremma?" asked Dee, if only to distract herself.

Gremma had a dark, semitransparent plastic sheet in her

hand. She was holding it up to the light. "It's a CT scan," she said, squinting at it.

Well, that wasn't what Dee had expected. She walked around the table, trying to get a better look. "Why would there be a CT scan?"

Gremma's eyes flicked over the sheet. "Listen, I'm not an expert, but I think... well. It's a brain tumor," she said.

Dee felt the breath freeze in her lungs.

Gremma frowned. "I've seen stuff like this before in some of my medical textbooks." She tilted the scan. "Notes on the bottom say it's malignant." Her mouth scrunched up in thought. "Based on my limited medical knowledge, I'd say this person would only have four to six months left."

Dee looked down at the scan. *Lancer, James.*

Her gaze fell to the small painting, the one of herself. James had gotten two things out of the demon's deal: art skill and a body frozen in the moment that his heart was taken.

She felt the words as they left her mouth. "Two years, actually."

FORTY

There was a demon knitting outside of the beach house.

He was beautiful, because fairy-tale creatures always were. Red yarn tangled around his long fingers, and his features were sharp and pale beneath the moonlight. Dee approached him without fear—a Red Riding Hood who had faced the wolf.

He sat upon the sandy bluff, knitting steadily. Still dressed in a suit, he looked laughably out of place. Dee strode across the sand, her feet bare, past the seaweed and the skeletons of driftwood.

Dee sat beside the demon. He kept knitting.

"You knew," she said. "That James was dying."

He did not look at her, nor did he bother with any denials. "Yes. He tried to change his deal shortly after he met you. Asked if he could give back his art talent if I removed a tumor. But once deals are made, they cannot be unmade."

Her hand drifted to her own chest; he saw the gesture.

"And you have slipped free of your own deal," he told her. "You are no longer heartless, despite not truly owning your own heart." A soft sigh. "You have escaped our bargain—as your kind would call it—fair and square. What shall I do with your heart? It is not as if you truly need it anymore."

The Rumpelstiltskin clause, she thought, with a stab of pain. James had outwitted the demon, and it was she who would reap the benefits.

"Give my heart to Riley—free her from her contract now," she said impulsively.

He looked at her.

"This troop is finished," she said. "Either give my heart to Riley or else give it back to me and I'll do it myself. Of course, I'll probably end up putting it in upside down or something."

The Agathodaemon tilted his head slightly, as if in acknowledgment. "Pull the wrong string," he said, eyes going to his knitting needles, "and everything unravels."

She didn't think he spoke of knitting.

Dee watched the play of moonlight on the waves, listened to the metallic clink of his knitting needles, and the sound of the heartbeat in her chest.

"Is it over?" she asked. "Are the voids gone? No chance of alien invasion?"

He looked down at the half-finished heart. "For the moment."

"Why do you call yourself a demon?" asked Dee. Her voice was toneless, uncaring. "You're not. Not really."

He took a moment to reply. "Demon," he said, slowly, the way people stepped onto thin ice—like he wasn't sure of his footing. "Daemon. It had a different meaning when I first came to this world. Helpful spirit, one of the supernatural."

Cal would've known that. Dee closed her eyes for a moment, trying to block out a pang of regret.

"What you do kills people," she said, echoing Cora's words.

The Agathodaemon lifted his gaze to the ocean waves. "Soldiers die in the name of the greater good every day. What makes you any different." He spoke too flatly for the sentence to be a question.

"I'm not different," she said. "But soldiers *volunteer.*" She shook her head. "You're doing this wrong."

The Agathodaemon looked at her in silent question.

"Taking limbs," said Dee. "Ripping out hearts. It's all very clumsy, the way you've gone about it."

He narrowed his eyes. "And how exactly would you deem was an appropriate way to keep this world safe?"

She met his gaze unflinchingly. "Tell everyone."

He scoffed.

But she did not. "If people knew that you weren't truly demons, that you're not even of this world—well. If they knew we had similar interests, that we both want to live here, then you could tell people of the threat. If there are more voids, tell people that they should be closed, that our world is at stake." She shivered. "Don't trick people into this. If they knew the stakes, they'd volunteer."

"You," said the Agathodaemon, "you truly believe humans would risk their lives for both their kind and ours? You think they could be so...compassionate?"

Dee thought about Cora, a gun in hand, ready to take on a demon to protect a girl she'd never met. Of Cal smiling and cheerful and brave. She thought of Riley, stepping into the remnants of a broken building because she would not let her friends venture in alone. Of Gremma, who smiled and snarked, but, when Dee needed her, was always there.

And she thought of James.

James, who had worn a mask of smiles and cheer. Who discovered he was going to die and welcomed it, because in his mind, that was his only chance to live. Who thought he was little more than scribbles and paintings, and was sure that was all he'd ever amount to.

He was wrong, she thought.

He was more than the artist, more than the boy who wore hobo-hipster clothes and loved bagels. He had been kind, and gentle in a way she'd never known before. But he would never be more than a memory, because he'd given up on himself long before he met her.

She loved him.

She'd never told him that.

Pain twisted in Dee's chest. She would carry part of him with her forever.

Another form of immortality.

And lastly, Dee thought of fairy tales. Of how knights in shining armor could be girls with Molotov cocktails, of how people could fight off monsters, whether those monsters were human or something different altogether.

She had survived both—the monsters and the humans alike.

A smile curved at the corners of her mouth.

"Yes," she said. "I believe that."

ACKNOWLEDGMENTS

This is a book very close to my heart. As are the people who helped me write it.

Thank you to Mary Elizabeth Summer for reading this book proposal in an hour and cheering me on the whole way. s.e. smith for listening to me ramble about "that heart book" for nearly two years. Brittney Vandervelden, my own biology-major roommate—although, to my knowledge, she has never vivisected a teddy bear. The OneFour crowd for always being on this journey with me.

A heartfelt thanks to my champion of an agent, Josh Adams, and everyone at Adams Literary—Tracey and Sam. Thank you for always being in my corner.

My sincerest gratitude goes out to the people at Little,

Brown. My tireless editor, Pam Gruber, deserves all the credit for taking a rough manuscript and making it the book I dreamed it could be. Marisa Finkelstein, Regina Castillo, and Chandra Wohleber for their wonderful editing. Marcie Lawrence and Maricor/Maricar for the beautiful design. David Klimowicz for all the production work. Saraciea Fennell, Emilie Polster, Jennifer McClelland-Smith, Jane Lee, Victoria Stapleton, and Jenny Choy for sharing my books with the world. And of course, another big thanks to Alvina Ling, Megan Tingley, and Carol Scatorchio.

To my family at Gallery Bookshop, Christie, Sally, Terry, Jeanette, Katy, Alena, Mary, Joan, Johanna, Jane, Rachel, Sichelle, and Zoe. You rule.

To all the indie booksellers who have faved, hand-sold, or simply listened to me ramble about my books. You are all amazing—and also a lot of fun at conferences.

And the biggest of big shout-outs to my mother, who has always supported me. (Don't worry, Mom. I promise my next book will be funnier.) And to the other family members who have encouraged me over the years. You know who you are, and you are awesome.

And, lastly, a big thanks to my readers. Because it always comes back to you.

I <3 you all.

Turn the page for a sneak peek at
a bewitching new fantasy from
Emily Lloyd-Jones

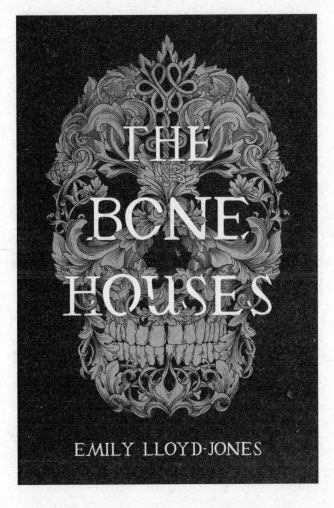

AVAILABLE SEPTEMBER 2019

THE GRAVEDIGGER'S CHILDREN *were troublemakers.*

They chased chickens through the neighbors' yards, brandishing sticks like swords, claiming that the fowl were monsters in disguise. They went to the fields and returned with berry-stained lips, crunching seeds between their teeth. They tumbled through the house, slamming into walls and breaking one of the wooden love spoons their father had carved. And once they'd tied a small wagon to a pig and raced through the village, screaming with mingled fear and joy. It was widely thought that the eldest, the only daughter at that time, was filled with mischief, and her younger brother trailed in her wake.

They would settle down, said Enid, the innkeeper. Children raised so close to Annwvyn were bound to have a spark of wildness in them. Their parents were both considered decent folk. The children would follow.

And if they didn't, said Hywel, the girl would make a fine recruit for the cantref's armies.

Their father dug graves and when he came home at night, his fingernails were stained with dirt and his boots were muddy. When there were no deaths in the village, he would vanish into the woods, reemerging with plump mushrooms, wood sorrel, and all sorts of berries. They were never rich, but their table was laden with good food. Their mother kept account of their bookkeeping, talked with the mourners, and planted fresh gorse along the edges of their graveyard as a protection against magic.

For all their freedoms, the children had one rule: They were not to follow their father into the forest. They would trail after him until the shadows of the trees fell over the rocky ground—and then the father would lift his hand, fingers splayed: "farewell" and "no farther," conveyed in a single gesture.

The children obeyed—at first.

"What are you doing?" asked the brother, when the girl stepped beneath the tree boughs.

"I want to see the forest."

The brother tugged at her arm, but she shook him off. "You can't," he said. "We aren't allowed."

But the girl ignored him.

The forest was beautiful—lush with ferns and thick with moss. At first, all was well. She picked wildflowers and wove them into her tangled hair. She tried to catch small fish from a stream. She laughed and played until evening fell.

With the creeping darkness, things came awake.

A figure stood nearby, watching her. For one moment, she thought it was her father. The man was tall and broad-shouldered, but too thin around the waist and wrists.

And when the man walked closer, she realized it was not a man at all.

It could not be. Not with a face of raw bone, with bared teeth and hollow eye sockets. She had seen bodies before, but they were always gently wrapped in clean cloths and then lowered into the ground. They were peaceful. This thing moved slowly under the weight of armor, and a sword jutted from a belt. And it stank.

The girl had a vague idea of picking up a fallen branch to defend herself, but she was frozen with fear.

The dead creature came so close that she could see the fine pockmarks and cracks in its bones, and the places where its teeth had fallen out. It knelt before her, its empty gaze fixed on her face. It pulled her close.

And then it inhaled. Sucked a rattling breath through its teeth, as if it were trying to taste the very air.

She quaked with terror. Every gasp was raw with it.

The dead thing drew back, tilting its head in a silent question. Then it rose to its feet and looked beyond her. Heartbeat hammering, the girl glanced over her shoulder.

Her father stood a few strides away. In one hand, he held a basket of forest greens, and in the other he wielded an axe. The threat was unspoken but heard nonetheless.

The dead thing retreated, and the girl shook so hard she could not speak. The father knelt beside her, checking her for injuries. "I told you not to follow."

Tears welled in her eyes.

"Death is not to be feared," he said. "But nor can it be forsaken. One must be mindful."

"What was that?" she asked. "Was it truly death?"

The father placed his hand on her shoulder. "A bone house," he replied. "They linger beyond death. It is why the villagers do not disturb the forest."

"But you come here," she said.

"Yes," he replied. "Those of us who deal in the trade of death are familiar with it. I don't fear them—and as long as you know how to navigate the forest, nor should you."

She looked at the trees—their tangled branches wreathed in fog, the chill of the night settling all around them. And she was not afraid—rather, something like excitement unfurled within her.

"Teach me?" she asked.

Her father smiled. He took her hand. "I'll show you. But hold on, and do not let go."

For two years, he showed her how to find paths through the trees, where rabbits made their warrens, how to tell between the sweet berries and the poisonous ones. And always, he carried his axe with him. On the days when they did not go to the forest, he brought her to the graveyard. She learned how to break up rocky topsoil, how to wrap a body, and how to pay last respects to the dead.

Winters came harsh and cold, and their provisions of food dwindled. Soup was watered down, and the memory of plump blackberries and buttered greens kept the children awake at night. The village became smaller; farmers packed up their families and went elsewhere, leaving empty homes and barren fields. And fewer people required the services of a gravedigger.

The mother became pregnant a third time, and when the father was offered a job as a scout, he accepted. The local cantref lord wished to investigate a collapsed mine, and the only way to get there was through the forest. And so he asked the man who did not fear the woods.

The daughter begged to go with him, but the father refused. When she protested, he gave her half of a wooden love spoon. He had carved several for their mother during their courtship—and this one had been broken when the sister and brother were tussling in the kitchen. The whorls of dark wood were smooth against her fingers, and she traced the overlapping hearts and flowers. "Here," he said, cupping his larger hands around hers, pressing the spoon gently. "You take this half, and I'll take the other. So long as you have it, you'll know I'll find you."

She clutched it to her chest and nodded. The father kissed his children and his pregnant wife, and he went into the forest.

He never returned.

By night, the daughter slept with her half of the spoon beneath her pillow, and by day, she carried it in her pocket. He will come back, she said, when anyone asked.

Some days, the daughter went back to the woods. She stood in the forest, beneath the shadow of the mountains and waited. She waited to see another dead man.

The forest did not scare her; rather, she wanted to be like it: ageless and impervious, cruel and beautiful.

Death could not touch it.

CHAPTER 1

THE EVENING AIR smelled pleasantly of a fresh grave.

Ryn breathed it in—the sweetness of overturned sod, mists rising from the green grass, and the woodsmoke drifting from the village. The spade felt comfortable in her hands, slotted in amidst familiar calluses. She hacked at the damp earth, dislodging rocks and thin roots. She'd marked the outline of the grave with twine and nails, and now it was just a matter of cutting through greenery and topsoil.

Her spade glanced off the edge of a rock, ringing high in her ears. She grimaced, grasped at the rock with her bare hands, and yanked it free. A worm came with it, squirming with the discomfort of a creature unused to sunlight. She picked it up between thumb and forefinger, and then she tossed it over her shoulder.

Someone made a noise behind her.

Ryn looked up.

Her brother stood over her, the worm caught in his ink-stained fingers.

"Sorry," said Ryn. "I didn't hear you coming."

Gareth gave her a flat stare, walked a few steps to her left, and dropped the worm into the grass. "It never occurred to you to put the worm back, did it?"

"Usually if something crawls out of a grave, I take an axe to it," said Ryn. "That worm should be grateful."

His frown cut fresh lines around his mouth. Despite being the younger of the two, he carried the weariness of an old man. "You needn't bother with the digging, Ryn."

A snort escaped her. "Because you're going to do it?"

Gareth's clothes were impeccable. Not a smudge of dirt upon his tunic, nor a stray blade of grass on his boots.

"Because," he said, and his voice was heavier, "Master Turner came by this morning and informed us that our services will not be needed for Mistress Turner. They've decided to burn the body."

For a heartbeat, she remained in place—caught between her task and the knowledge that it was no longer necessary. Her hands yearned to return to the digging.

She rocked back on her heels and began rubbing her dirty hands on her leggings. Gareth made a pained noise at the streaks of grime, but she didn't pay him any mind. "Well, that's unfortunate."

"That grave was our last hope." Gareth took a step back. "We were counting on Turner's ball-penny to get us through the winter." A breath rattled through his clenched teeth. "Come on. Ceridwen will be finished making supper by now."

Ryn rose to her full height. She was as tall as her brother, something that had always made her smile and him frown. Tall and lanky as a sapling, her mam had once said. And as graceful as a drunken colt, her father had added fondly. "I saw a bone house this morning," she said. "Caught a glimpse of it. I went for my axe, but the sun was up before I returned. It must have fallen in the tall grass, because I couldn't find it." She shrugged. "I'll wait for nightfall. Let it find me."

"A bone house?" A crease appeared between Gareth's heavy brows.

"Yes," she said. "I know, I know. You're going to tell me that bone houses don't leave the forest. That I'll probably just scare a vagrant half to death."

Gareth frowned. "No," he said. "I—I believe you. It's just that's the second one." He had their mother's eyes—the brown of healthy earth. And he had a way of looking through a person that made Ryn want to hold her secrets tightly to her chest. "They never used to leave the forest," he said.

It had the ring of an accusation and Ryn crossed her arms. "I haven't gone into the forest." The words were sharp. "Well, only the outskirts." Part of her wanted to remind him that the reason they still had food in their larder was because of her willingness to flirt with the edges of the forest.

"All right," he said. "Take care of the bone house. But when Ceri cries because I'm not good at telling her bedtime stories, that's on you."

"Just read her your accounts ledger," said Ryn. "That'll put her right to sleep." She softened the words with a grin and a clap on the arm.

Gareth winced, his eyes on where she had dirtied his shirt. "Just don't get yourself killed, all right?" He began to walk away, but he called over his shoulder: "And if you do die, that's still no excuse to be late for breakfast."

Colbren's graveyard was set outside the village proper. When Ryn was young, she'd asked her father why they buried the dead so far from the living. She still remembered his broad fingers carding through her hair, a smile on his mouth as he answered. "Death's something of a frightening thing to most people. They like a bit of distance between them and eternity. And besides, the dead deserve a spot of privacy."

The graveyard had been built before the Otherking fled the isles. As such, the old protections remained: Gorse grew at the edges of the graveyard, thick with yellow flowers. The thorny shrubs hid iron rods that had been driven into the ground. Gorse and iron. It would not stop a human from entering the graveyard, but it would stop *other* things.

The light faded from the sky, falling behind mist-shrouded mountains.

Ryn saw the familiar form of a man walking along the road leading from the village. His shoulders were bent by years of hard labor, and he carried a rusty sword. The damp, overgrown grass brushed at her fingertips as she approached him. "That looks a bit heavy for you, Mr. Hywel."

Old Hywel snorted. "Been carrying heavier things than this since before your parents were born, Ryn. Leave well enough alone." He spoke with a gruff fondness.

"Why does a miller need a sword?" she asked.

He grunted, and there was a shrewd edge to his words. "You know why."

She grimaced. "They haven't been at your chickens, have they?"

"No, no." Hywel huffed. "My chickens can fend for themselves." He slid her a look. "Your brother went past here a few minutes ago," he said. "Looked a bit out of sorts, if you don't mind me saying."

"If Gareth weren't worrying about something, he wouldn't be my brother."

Hywel nodded. "Any word from your uncle?"

It was a question folded into another question, a worry that neither of them would say aloud.

Ryn shook her head. "We haven't heard from Uncle. But you know how travel is from here to the city."

The loose skin around Hywel's mouth sagged in disapproval. "Never been, myself. Don't trust those city types."

There were those in Colbren who had never left the village. They might as well have grown up from the rocky soil like trees; they seemed to draw their lifeblood from the land, and they would not be uprooted.

"How is your sister?" Hywel asked.

"Likely baking something that would shame the finest cooks." When she'd left the house that morning, Ceri had already been up to her elbows in flour.

Hywel smiled, showing a missing tooth. "Those rowanberry preserves she made...there wouldn't happen to be any of those left, would there?"

There were, in fact. Ryn thought of the berries spread over sweet grilled cakes, and her stomach cramped with hunger.

"Our roof has a leak," she said. "Would be a shame to see all my sister's fine baking go to waste the next time it rains."

Hywel's grin widened. "Ah, that's how it is. You're a sharp one, Ryn. All right—two jars of preserves for the roof repairs and you've got yourself a deal."

She nodded, not precisely pleased so much as satisfied. Trading food for favors had become something rather common of late. She let out a breath and pressed her fingers to her temple. She could feel a headache building, stress forming a knot behind her jaw.

"You should be getting back," said Hywel, breaking into Ryn's thoughts.

Ryn inclined her head toward the fields of tall grasses. "I saw one of them. I need to take care of it before I return home."

Hywel gave her a despairing sort of look. "Listen, girl. How about we *both* head back to the village, stop by the Red Mare. I can spare an hour before returning to the mill. A drink on me."

"No." A hesitation, then, "Thank you. You shouldn't walk home in the dark, not tonight."

"Your family needs you," he said, more gently than she expected.

She stood a little straighter. The sun was all but set, casting a golden glow across the fields. Shadows crept in along the trees, and a cool breeze whispered through Ryn's loose shirt.

She thought of the grave mounds. Of the sleeping bones warm and safe beneath the earth.

"I know," she said. Hywel shook his head, but he didn't protest. He gave her one last nod before walking away from the village, toward the nearby creek and mill. The sword dragged, a little too heavy for the old man.

The village would be preparing for nightfall. Latches on all the doors locked. Gareth would blow out the candles, and the scent of burnt tallow would linger in the kitchen. Ceri would be getting ready for bed.

Ryn reached into her pack. She'd brought a bundle of hard bread and cheese and, lastly, her axe. She liked eating out here, amid the wilds and the graves. She felt more comfortable here than she did in the village. When she returned home, the weight of her life would settle upon her once again. There would be unpaid rent, food stores that should be filled for winter, an anxious brother, and a future that needed sorting out. The other young women of Colbren were finding spouses, joining the cantref armies, or taking up a socially acceptable trade. When she tried to imagine doing the same, she could not. She was a half-wild creature that loved a graveyard, the first taste of misty night air, and the heft of a shovel.

She knew how things died.

And in her darkest moments, she feared she did not know how to live.

So she sat at the edge of the graveyard and watched as the sun vanished behind the trees. A silvery half-light fell across the fields, and Ryn's heartbeat quickened. It was not truly dark, but it was dark enough for magic.

The sound of shuffling feet made her stand up. It was not the gait of an animal—but of a two-legged creature, one who could not walk properly.

Ryn rose and gripped her axe in one hand.

"Come on," she murmured. "I know you're out there."

And she did know. She'd seen the figure in the wee hours of the morning: a half-broken thing that had vanished into the tall grasses.

She heard the approach. It was slow—a staggering gait.

Thump. Shuffle. Thump.

The creature rose with the night.

It looked like something out of the tales that her father used to tell—a spindly creature of rotted flesh and tattered clothing. It was having trouble walking and every other step made the figure stagger.

Shuffle. Thump.

It had been a woman: A long dress trailed behind it, dragging in the dirt. Ryn didn't recognize her, but she must have died recently. Perhaps a traveler. A turned ankle could kill a person in the wilds, if they were alone.

"Good evening," said Ryn.

The creature went still. Its neck gave a sickening pop as it turned to look at her. Ryn wasn't sure how it could see—the eyes were always the first bits to go.

The bone house did not speak. They never did.

But still, Ryn felt obligated to say something.

"Sorry about this," said Ryn. And then she swung the axe at the dead woman's knees.

The first time, she'd gone for the head. Turned out, the dead were like chickens. They didn't need heads to blunder about. Knees were a much more practical target.

The blade bit into bone.

The woman staggered, reaching out for Ryn. Ryn ducked back, but the woman's brittle fingers caught her on the shoulder. She felt the rake of nails, the fingers stiffened in death. Ryn tore the axe free, and there was another nauseating wrenching sound, like tissues being rent apart. The dead woman fell to the ground. It rolled over, dug its bony fingers into the earth, and began to crawl toward Colbren.

"Would you please stop that?" Ryn brought the axe down a second time, and then a third. Finally, the creature went still.

Ryn pulled on a pair of leather gloves and set about searching the body. No coin purse, no valuables. She exhaled sharply, trying to hold back a sinking disappointment. She wasn't a grave robber—and she didn't take coin from the dead she was paid to bury. But these creatures that haunted the forest were fair game. After all, the cursed dead cared little for money. Only the living had need of it.

And Ryn did have need.

She'd gather up what was left of the woman, place the parts in a burlap sack, and bring them into the village for burning. Only the forge burned hot enough for bone.

It was the only peace she could offer the woman.

Ryn clenched her teeth as she hauled the burlap sack to the graveyard. She tied it shut, just to make sure no parts escaped. Her muscles burned with exertion. Despite the chill of the night, a sweat had soaked through her shirt.

The sack gave a twitch. "Stop that," said Ryn.

Another twitch.

Ryn crouched, settling on the ground beside the sack. She gave it an awkward sort of pat, the way she might try to calm her little sister. "If you'd stayed in the forest, you would have been fine. Want to tell me why death suddenly has an urge to wander?"

The sack went still.

Ryn pulled her gloves off and ate a few mouthfuls of bara brith. The dark bread was sweet and studded with dried fruit. The food eased the hollow feeling in her stomach. She looked at the sack and had the sudden urge to offer it a piece of bread. She tilted her head back and closed her eyes.

This was the problem with being a gravedigger in Colbren.

Nothing stayed buried forever.

© Tammie Gilchrist

Emily Lloyd-Jones

grew up on a vineyard in rural Oregon, where she played in evergreen forests and learned to fear sheep. After graduating from Western Oregon University with an English degree, she enrolled in the publishing program at Rosemont College just outside Philadelphia. She currently resides in Northern California with a temperamental cat and an ever-increasing book collection. She is the author of *Illusive, Deceptive, The Hearts We Sold*, and the historical fantasy horror novel *The Bone Houses*.

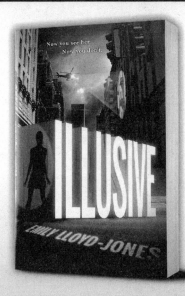

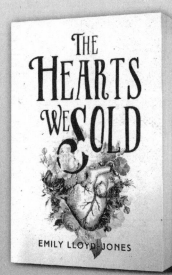
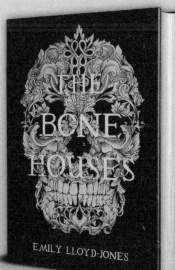